THE CHATEAU

CHATEAU #1

PENELOPE SKY

HARTWICK PUBLISHING

Hartwick Publishing

The Chateau

"How did I escape? With difficulty. How did I plan this moment? With pleasure."

-Alexandre Dumas

The Count of Monte Cristo

CONTENTS

Prologue 1

1. The Eiffel Tower 9

2. French Alps 25

3. Kill the Weeds 35

4. Show Your Face 49

5. Eaten by Wolves 67

6. Red Snow 87

7. The Count of Monte Cristo 105

8. Magnus 117

9. Trendsetter 137

10. Friends in Low Places 153

11. If You Must Die, Die Bravely 167

12. Hero to One, Villain to All 183

13. Silence of the Bells 197

14. Thief 211

15. The Storm 231

16. Crack of the Whip 267

17. The Demand 283

18. The Chateau 315

19. Rose 339

20. Paris 361

21. The Boss 383

22. Live Well. Be Happy. 409

23. Survivor's Guilt 415

24. With Knives and Fire 429

Afterword 443

PROLOGUE

POURING RAIN MADE THE ROADS SLICK WITH darkness, reflecting the sliver of moon that emerged for just a glimpse between the passing clouds. The asphalt of the street and the wet concrete of the sidewalk were indiscernible from each other because everything looked black and white in a storm like this. An iron lamppost stood at the corner, the only beacon to the Parisian neighborhood.

Face hidden under the raised hood of his jacket, a young man took the steps to the front door of his home. His jacket was sprayed with rainwater, the drops bouncing off the material like smooth pebbles, and he unlocked the door before stepping into the dark apartment.

There were no lights.

No signs of life.

The clock on the wall showed the time.

Two a.m.

He stripped off his soaked jacket and hung it on the coatrack, family portraits on the wall, a mother, a father, and four children, all dressed in sweater vests and dresses, highlighting the numerous family vacations that had been taken throughout the years, no thought to expense.

A muffled gunshot erupted in the house.

He stilled at the sound, the water from his shoes soaking into the rug on which he stood. Eyes darted back and forth as he looked into the darkness, trying to distinguish the threat he couldn't see. Every member of his family was fast asleep at this hour.

Turning around and darting back out of the house was the smartest decision for a young man, but he remained rooted to the spot, as if he weren't sure if he heard the murderous sound at all.

He grabbed a knife and took the stairs.

Thump. Thump. Thump.

At the top of the stairs, he heard it again.

A silenced gunshot.

With a heartbeat thudding loud in his ears, a terror nearly paralyzing his heart, he crept down the hallway, knowing he had no chance against a gunman when he was only armed with a knife.

But his family was on the line.

The master bedroom door was ajar, the bed visible from his place in the hallway. The lump of a body was noticeable in the sheets.

He crept into the room and grabbed his mother by the shoulder. "Mother." He gave her a gentle shake, looking back at the door to watch for the assailant that was creeping in his home. "Mother." He shook her again, his restrained voice under a cloak of a whisper.

When he shook her again, he noticed the dots of blood on her pillow.

Two—the size of bullets.

That was when he noticed her open eyes, the ghost of life in her gaze, the sudden feeling of death.

He jumped back, stepping away from the bed as if he might be sick. Tears welled in his eyes, but the current threat in his home restricted the sobs to the backs of his eyes and not his throat.

When he crept back into the hallway, he gripped his knife a little tighter, with more resolution than before. The next bedroom belonged to his younger sister, and when he spotted her motionless in the bed, he knew she'd met the same fate.

He didn't even bother to walk inside.

Footsteps sounded farther down the hallway, a man's footsteps audible to his sensitive ears.

He held his breath as he listened.

The door creaked slightly as the man entered the bedroom of his older brother.

He couldn't keep his breath even, couldn't keep his heart steady. He gripped the handle of the knife so hard his hand ached.

Then another gunshot sounded.

And he knew his brother's fate.

The bedroom door to his younger brother's room was ajar. There was no time to waste, no time to linger. Based on the man's movements down the hallway, this was the last bedroom on his list. His younger brother could still be alive.

He moved into the bedroom and found his younger brother lying on his back.

But he was breathing.

He set the knife on the nightstand and gripped him by both arms before he gave the boy a harsh shake. "Wake up." He placed his hand over his mouth so he wouldn't scream in protest.

But he didn't wake.

His eyes moved to the cup of water on the night-stand, the murky color of the liquid, as if something had been dissolved for every member of the family to drink. His own bedroom was last, so perhaps that murderer assumed he was in bed like everyone else.

His arms scooped under his brother's limp body and curled him to his chest. He groaned as he used all his strength to lift his brother's weight as he rose to his feet. There was nothing he could do for anyone else, so he carried his brother into the hallway, casting a glance in the direction of his assailant. The coast was clear, and he made for the stairs.

"What...?" His brother stirred from sleep, moving slightly, his voice muffled from the haze of the sleeping pills.

"Come on, wake up." He shook him as he took the stairs one at a time, quietly reaching the foyer.

A footstep creaked against the floorboard at the top of the stairs.

He should run, but he stopped to turn to see if the sound was his imagination—or something worse.

At the top of the stairs stood his father, tall and lean, glasses sitting on the bridge of his nose. And in his slender fingers was a gun, a silencer attached over the barrel. With narrowed eyes and a promise of retribution, he looked down at his two boys as they tried to flee.

Paralyzed, the boy stood there, holding his brother in his straining arms.

A standoff of silence emerged, a battle of silent hostility. The family home was the scene of a murder, every family holiday and birthday erased by the blood staining every pillow.

He raised his gun—and pointed it at his son. "Don't you run."

But he did anyway. He sprinted to the door, almost losing his grip on his brother, and made it out the front door to the steps. But he tripped, dropping his brother in the process. "Wake up!" He tried to scoop him into his arms, but the pouring rain and darkness made it impossible to get a grip.

The impact shattered the spell, and his younger brother sat up. "What's going on—"

"Run! Come on! Run!" He grabbed him by the hand and pulled him down the sidewalk.

Gunshots rang into the night, aimed right at their backs.

Both boys sprinted down the sidewalk, heaving with the exertion, running away from something that neither understood. With only the clothes on their backs, they escaped without a single coin in their pockets, without the experience to survive the cold and harsh world that had just welcomed them with open arms.

1

THE EIFFEL TOWER

Raven

I sat at the desk facing the window on the second story, my notebook opened to the page that held the notes I'd quickly jotted down. My stack of books was beside me, all the classics, *Les Misérables*, *The Count of Monte Cristo*, *The Hunchback of Notre Dame*. It was a beautiful evening at sunset, the skyline a subtle pink color, a clear sky in the depth of winter. Far in the distance, I could see the most recognizable example of French architecture—the Eiffel Tower.

My eyes dropped down to the street below, the sidewalk filled with Parisians in their winter coats, walking home from work or on the town for an early dinner in a city with the best assortments of breads and cheeses in the world, not to mention wine. I grabbed my mug and lifted it to my lips, taking a drink of coffee full of cinnamon and nutmeg, along with a hint of pumpkin.

That was when I noticed a man down below, on the sidewalk and against the iron lamppost, standing behind a blue Fiat. A cigarette was between his fingers, and he brought it to his lips for a deep drag, his eyes focused on the front door of my apartment.

At least, it seemed like that was what he was looking at.

A thick beard covered his jaw and his neck, and the dark color matched the curls on the top of his head. He had brown eyes of the same color, nearly black. In a brown trench coat, he looked like a man who worked at a local newspaper, someone who had stepped out of the office to enjoy a cigarette break.

But his gaze unnerved me.

Melanie's footsteps were audible behind me. "Alright, I'm heading out." She passed by my door without stopping, her feet loud on the wooden stairs because she was taking them two at a time, running late like usual.

"Bye," I called after her, my eyes still on the man who had his eyes trained in my direction.

The front door shut behind her, announcing her departure.

He brought the cigarette to his lips and took another drag, his eyes shifting as his gaze followed my sister's progress up the sidewalk—as if he'd been waiting for her.

I rose from my chair, fear erupting in my heart like an explosion. My younger sister was the beautiful one, the one who got free drinks everywhere she went, who could have any guy she wanted—because every guy wanted her.

And I'd kill any guy who would do her harm.

But his interest faded, and he dropped his cigarette on the ground, stepped on it with his shoe, and headed up the sidewalk in the opposite direction from my sister.

Was I just paranoid?

Or did something just happen?

"YOUR SISTER IS FUN." Samantha sat across from me with her glass of rosé. The wine bar was lit up while the streets of Paris were dimmed outside the large windows, showing everyone enjoying the city during the busiest time of the year. It was known as the city of love, and there were definitely a lot of couples taking in the sights during winter break. "How long is she staying with you?"

"Until mid-January. But I'm afraid she might not leave because she's having so much fun." I looked past her to my sister on the other side of the bar, sitting at a table with a glass of wine in her hand. Two guys sat across from her because she'd joined them thirty minutes ago, taking advantage of the cheese platter and fresh baguette sitting in front of them. Magnetic, she attracted everyone's attention around her, not even intentionally. She was like a black hole, her pull so strong even light couldn't escape. She always managed to be the center of attention, and most of the time, it didn't bother me, but there were times when it became too much. I loved my sister more than life, but I was happy to see her go back home to New York.

Samantha chuckled. "Paris is a special place. Couldn't blame her."

Neither could I.

"Have you told her yet?"

My eyes stared at her across the room, watching her laugh uproariously at something one of the guys said, looking even more beautiful when she laughed like that. The rest of the tables were full of young people like us, students enjoying their Christmas break, first dates, and tenth dates. It wasn't a tourist spot, so it was special, a wine bar full of all the other delicacies I couldn't get enough of like assorted cheese, chocolate croissants, pâté, a variety of freshly baked breads, and escargot. I came for the wine, but I always stayed for hours because of the food. "No."

"How do you think she'll take it?"

"She'll be furious. And she'll probably move here to join me." I'd relocated to Paris because I'd joined a study abroad program that allowed me to stay for a semester, but I loved it so much that I'd decided to be a student full time, to study classic French literature, to work as a barista in a café to pay my bills, to learn some French, completely adopt the lifestyle because it felt like home almost instantly.

Melanie was under the impression that I would return home once my education was finished.

But I had other plans.

I felt obligated to return because I was all she had—and she was all I had. But I'd been taking care of my sister our entire lives, and it was time for me to do something for myself, to have my own independence apart from her.

But she would be livid with my decision.

"Would you hate that?" Samantha asked.

"No, as long as she doesn't expect to live with me." My sister was a few years younger than me, but she'd never grabbed on to independence the way I did. Why would she, when she always had someone to take care of her? If it wasn't me, it was a guy who had fallen under her spell. Why would she buy a drink at a bar when someone would pay her tab? I accepted who she was, exactly in the package she came in. I just didn't want to be her caretaker anymore, and I feared if she moved here, that was exactly what would happen.

"So..." She swirled her glass of rosé, her short dark hair in frizzy curls. "Anything going to happen with you and Gabriel?"

I preferred French men to American men because they were more passionate than the men I was used to. They were great lovers, but they were also more independent, knew exactly how to care for themselves, and were proud, eager to stand on their own feet. They could be a little standoffish at times, but underneath that dark exterior was deep complexity. "I was thinking about..." My thoughts became distracted when I saw one of the guys Melanie was talking to rise from the table and approach the counter to speak to the waitress behind the counter.

His beard was gone, and his hair had been cut—but it was him.

I recognized those eyes, those distinctive facial features.

He took the tab from the woman, put the bills on it, and then turned back to the table. Words were exchanged with Melanie and the other guy in the group, and they rose from the table to leave.

Fuck that.

I left Samantha with no explanation and went after them, catching up just as they made it outside. "Melanie."

She turned to me, her cheeks flushed from the wine that made her belly warm, from the good conversation that she thought was genuine and not a trap.

"Raven, we're going to a party. You want to come along?"

There was a car parked at the curb, and one of the guys already had the back door open. The man I recognized spoke to him quietly, exchanging words in French.

"You aren't going. Let's go back inside." I grabbed her by the wrist and tugged her inside.

She twisted out of the grasp. "What the hell are you doing?"

I lowered my voice. "I saw one of these guys outside our apartment yesterday. He stood right across the street and watched you leave."

Melanie laughed like it was funny. "Girl, you need to chill. Your mind is playing tricks on you."

"It's not," I snapped. "I know what I saw, and it's too much of a coincidence."

"Raven, it's fine." She patted me on the arm. "We're just going to a party. I'll see you later, alright?"

The guy I recognized whispered to her, "Come on, beautiful. We'll show you a Paris you've never seen."

She blew me a kiss before she walked away.

I was so sick of this shit, so sick of being the logical and reasonable one, of being the one to look after her because she was so unintelligent and clueless about her surroundings. I grabbed her by the wrist again. "I don't like these guys, Melanie. Let's just go back inside—"

"Stop telling me what to do." She pulled away again. "I'm a big girl who doesn't need you to take care of me anymore."

That hit too close to home, and I lost my temper. "Obviously, I still do need to take care of you because these guys have got psycho written all over them, and you're too stupid to see that. I'm sick of this shit, Melanie. I'm sick of you making stupid decision after stupid decision. I'm telling you, I saw that mother-fucker outside our apartment, and he's gonna put you in an oil barrel or something. There're a million guys out there. You'll find someone new tomorrow."

Her eyes were heavy from the alcohol in her blood, but they were still aware enough to react, to show how much those words stung. "Then maybe they will put me in an oil barrel and I won't be your problem anymore." She walked to the guys waiting at the car.

"Alright." The other guy clapped his hands and rubbed his palms together. "Let's get this party started."

I clenched my jaw and sucked the back of my lips, furious enough to move mountains but helpless to do anything but watch. While my sister had a lot of good qualities, she also had a lot of bad ones, like constantly getting herself into trouble. And you know who cleaned up those messes?

Me. Always me.

I resented her for constantly putting me in positions I didn't want to be in, constantly setting me back in life with mistake after mistake. My life was easy in Paris, and I realized I never wanted to go home; I was ready to finally start a new life for myself. But she was my sister...and that love, that bond, that sense of protectiveness, would never leave me.

So, I did the only thing I could...and went after her.

She was already in the back seat when I walked up.

"You want to join us too, beautiful?" He opened the back door again. He gave me a wink that wasn't the least bit charming.

"You're going to come?" Melanie asked in surprise. "My sister is finally gonna pull that stick out of her ass." She scooted over and patted the seat beside her. "Girl, let's go."

I took the seat beside her, watching the two guys, hoping that my paranoia was just a hypersensitive intellect. The doors shut, and the guys got into the two front seats.

I watched them both like a hawk.

"What should we listen to?" the driver asked as he turned on the radio. "How about some American shit?" He changed the channels until he found an upbeat pop song from a female artist. "Now, that's good shit." He started to dance in his seat. The other guy did too.

"Hell yeah!" Melanie threw up her hands and started to dance, getting into it like she was in a club and had all the room in the world to throw her arms left and right, smacking me in the shoulder without even realizing it.

There were a million fun things to do in Paris. Getting in a car with these two weirdos wasn't one of them. She could have any man she wanted with beauty like that, but she settled for any man who asked her out. It was baffling.

The guy in the passenger seat turned to look at me. "Come on, have some fun. We'll show you a good time."

"Where are we going?" I barked.

"Chill, chill." He faced forward again. "Let's drive by the Eiffel Tower."

"Yes!" Melanie shrieked in excitement, still dancing to the music, even though she'd been to the site before—because I'd taken her.

The guys pulled onto the street and drove through traffic, passing all the coffee shops, restaurants, and the other nightlife that we could be visiting. The radio continued to play music, and the guys talked to Melanie.

As time went on, they seemed harmless. They asked Melanie about her life in New York, tried to get information out of me because I wasn't receptive, and then we pulled up to the Eiffel Tower.

"There it is," the guy in the passenger seat said. "On your left—in all her glory."

I turned to look at the base of the tower, the long pathway with the fountains down the center, full of pedestrians walking with warm cups of coffee in their hands, enjoying the white Christmas lights wrapped up in the trees on either side. It was something I looked at all the time, a pathway I'd taken on afternoon walks with friends. It was beautiful every time I looked at it, and even now in my disgruntled mood, I still thought it was magnificent.

And then a sharp pain erupted from my leg.

I looked down to the needle piercing through my jeans into my thigh.

My sister had one too.

"You motherfucker." I lunged forward and grabbed the guy by the throat, slamming my hand into his face to beat him fucking senseless.

Melanie had a harsher reaction to the drug because she immediately slumped back against the seat, her eyes glazing over. "Oh my god... What's happening?"

The guy pushed me off. "Damn, this bitch is strong."

"That's perfect," the driver said. "She's better than the weaker one."

I lunged at him again, but he punched me in the face.

Melanie continued to slip away. "Oh my god...oh my god." She gripped the handle of the door and just sat there, as if she were hallucinating.

I grabbed the door and tried to open it, feeling my mind begin to slip away, the strength in my extremities fading. The door was locked, so I couldn't get it open. So, I slammed my arm into the window over and over, trying to break through it.

"Jesus, did you give her enough?" The driver swerved slightly when I kicked the back of his seat.

"Yes," the passenger yelled. "I don't know what the fuck this bitch is doing."

I tried to hit the window again, but I couldn't. My strength left me, and I slumped in the seat, unable to do anything other than look out the window and watch the lights pass as we continued our drive. People on the sidewalk had no idea of the duress in the car, enjoying their beautiful night in this glorious city.

"It's kicking in," the passenger said. "We're fine."

I tried to fight my eyes' urge to close, but I was losing the battle. My eyelids closed, and my body suddenly relaxed in the seat. The last thing I heard was the voice of my sister as she whispered to me.

"I'm so sorry..."

2

FRENCH ALPS

VIBRATIONS SHOOK MY BODY, A BUMP MAKING MY frame rise slightly from the surface before it thudded back down once more. I was vaguely aware of the cold, of the way my lungs hurt with every breath I took because the air was so dry. Sunlight was on my face, but it didn't mask the chill that froze every single extremity of my body.

As I came into consciousness, I was vaguely aware of the last time I was awake. My eyes had opened to a dark room, two moth-eaten mattresses on the floor. My sister was on the other mattress, still passed out from the drugs. When the men realized I was awake, their approaching legs came into view. I wasn't strong enough to fight the needle they injected into my arm. I was pulled under again.

But now I knew I was in a different place.

I tried to move my body, and that was when I realized my wrists were bound together. My legs moved next, and they were in the same predicament, my ankles tied together with rope so thick that I would never be able to rip through it.

Then my eyes opened.

I looked at the wood underneath my cheek, the little holes in the material showing the snowy ground underneath. We must have hit a bump, because it made the vehicle sway and roll my body slightly forward. The sound of the wheels against the earth was loud on my ears, and then I heard the distinct neigh of a horse.

I was in a wagon.

Why the fuck was I in a wagon?

I rolled to my back so I could look up at the sky. It was a sunny day, not a single cloud in the sky, and the air was so dry it was like sandpaper on my lungs. Tree branches extended from trunks into my vision, wooden slices without leaves.

I raised my chin to look across the wagon.

Melanie was there, fast asleep with her face against the wooden cart that carried us. She was bound at her hands and feet too, the small breaths coming from her nose visible as vapor.

"Melanie?" I whispered.

Her mouth was open, and she drooled onto the wooden plank.

I rolled to her spot and hit her with my shoulder. "Melanie? Wake up." When I'd stirred initially, I'd awoken to a reality that seemed dreamlike. Taking in my surroundings with a dose of skepticism, I didn't feel much panic. But now that reality had sunk into my flesh, I realized my fate was still in jeopardy.

After I hit her a couple more times, her eyes fluttered, and a pained moan came from her throat. "What? What happened?" She was more affected by the drug than I was, so she struggled to grapple with reality.

I metabolized stuff much quicker because I was furious rather than scared.

But also scared...

"We're in a wagon."

"A wagon?" she whispered. "Going where?"

"I don't fucking know, but we aren't going to find out. Turn around so I can get these ropes off."

She groaned as she turned over, and then we both bounced off the wood when the wheel hit a rock in the road.

I scooted down and used my teeth to work the rope, to wet it enough to turn slippery and get it over her wrists, but the knots were tight, the rope was thick and scratchy, and I wouldn't get her free even if I did this for a month straight. "I can't get it."

"Let me try."

It was totally hopeless. If I couldn't do it, then she definitely couldn't, but I didn't argue and turned over.

After a couple tugs, she gave up. "It's too tight."

I lay there, wearing different clothes than I had before, beige pants and a thick matching jacket. But the clothing wasn't enough to keep us warm when we were exposed to the air like this. The sunshine wasn't enough either. I didn't focus on the fact that someone had changed me when I was unconscious. I didn't even ponder what else had happened in that time frame, a span that was undetermined. Was it days? A week? Or just a few hours? There was no way to tell.

I assumed we were being trafficked, but that didn't explain the wagon. Unless we'd been bought by some weirdo who preferred to spend his life living out a western fantasy.

My sister's quiet voice came from behind me. "What now?"

I stared at the opposite end of the wagon, absorbing the vibrations of the transportation, feeling that sense of calm in the face of danger because there was no chance of survival. There was just peaceful acceptance, cutting the line of grief and moving right to the front.

I rolled to my back and sat up, raising myself high enough to see what was in front of me. The person driving the cart sat on a solid wooden seat, so his body was hidden from view. If I wanted to attack him, I'd have to crawl over the structure, and being completely bound like this would make that impossible.

I turned around to look at the way we'd come.

It was a weathered path with deep tracks through the thin layer of snow. Trees were on either side, thinned out because the leaves had fallen in the fall and the snow had covered it shortly afterward. I stared in each direction, but I didn't see anything for miles... and miles.

I faced forward again, and in the distance was the only marker to tell me where we were.

The French Alps.

That meant we were close to the Spanish border, northwest of Italy, if there was this much snow. The remote location and the odd choice of transportation told me there would be no tourists on our way, no police officials, that wherever we were going probably wasn't even on a map.

It was stupid to check because I already knew the outcome, but I wiggled my body and rolled around in the hope of finding something in my pockets.

"What are you doing?" Melanie whispered.

"Checking for something in the pockets." I wiggled and moved and found nothing. There was nothing in the back of the wagon either, not even a rock to cut the rope with. All we could do was wait for whatever was supposed to happen to us.

Samantha was smart, so she'd probably witnessed the conversation outside, and when she didn't hear from me in a day or two, she would call the police and tell them what she saw. The cameras would probably pick up the license plate of the men who took us, and if they still had the vehicle, that could be a lead.

But I suspected this wasn't their first kidnapping, and they no doubt swapped out the license plates or ditched the car altogether. They were probably the scouts that hunted the women and handed them off to the buyers.

The saliva in my mouth was acidic with bitterness, full of resentment. I'd moved across the Atlantic Ocean to start my own life, and the second Melanie visited me, I was stuck in another one of her idiotic messes. I could have stayed on the sidewalk and watched her drive off with the strange men, knowing she deserved whatever happened to her because she refused to listen to my warning—despite all the times I'd gotten her out of trouble.

But I knew that was just the anger talking.

If I'd really never seen my little sister again, it would have haunted me every single day, hollowed out my existence, and made every single breath painful. I would resent her then too...for making me live without her.

"What do you think's going to happen?" Melanie couldn't hide the tremble of her voice, the way her breathing picked up as her imagination gave her answers she didn't want.

"We were trafficked and bought by a man who lives out in the middle of nowhere...or I have no idea."

"Do you have a plan?" She always turned to me for answers, always asked for my help before even trying to find a solution herself. Even apart, she was dependent on me, texting me and asking for help with problems she needed to learn to figure out how to solve on her own. She always asked for money and wiped out what little I had in savings. I never told her how broke I was and just wired the money, knowing she needed it more than I did, even though I was the one who worked for it.

"Do I look like I have a plan?" Until I got these ropes off my wrists and ankles, I couldn't fight for our freedom. And even if I could, I suspected they would continually drug us into submission, and once the dosage lost its potency, they would crank it up...until our hearts gave out.

She turned quiet.

I didn't do what I always did and tell her everything would be alright. I didn't make false promises so she could sleep at night. I didn't fill her life with pink wallpaper and fake stories of triumph.

The best way to protect her now was to not protect her.

When this wagon stopped, we would be in the presence of evil, with someone who lacked empathy, compassion, and even worse, humanity. Our bodies would be used until they ran out of gas, and then we would be buried somewhere in this forest to later be scavenged by wolves and other woodland animals after the snow melted and revealed our bodies underneath. The cold would preserve our bodies, so the flesh could be ripped from our cheeks by a pair of strong jaws. Piece by piece, we would be stripped down to bones. We had no family, so no one would cross oceans to find us. If someone did uncover our remains, it would be decades later, and the only way to determine our identity would be through dental records. But what would be the point...when none lived to care?

How did you protect someone from that?

"Raven."

I continued to face the other way, staring at the passing landscape through a small hole in the wood. "Don't. Just don't..." I already knew what she was going to say, and her remorse had no effect on me. I didn't want to hear it, not when I couldn't forgive her.

I couldn't forgive her... Not this time.

3

KILL THE WEEDS

I HEARD VOICES.

Lots of voices.

Men. Women.

It sounded like we were approaching an establishment, but what kind of establishment would exist out here in the middle of nowhere? A place that couldn't be accessed by car? I focused my hearing to gain as much information as possible before we were thrown into the fray.

A man's deep voice sounded from up ahead. "What do you have for me?"

"Two. Both fresh."

Fresh? Who described someone as fresh?

The wagon came to a stop. One of the horses released a loud breath, as if he was tired from the long trek through the cold. Our bodies rolled slightly once the forward momentum ceased.

Melanie's breathing went haywire.

"Save your energy," I whispered. The unknown was the most frightening thing to all living beings, and I really had no idea what to expect, what my purpose was in this isolated place, but my heart rate was low, my focus primed, my instincts for survival high.

A man emerged into my sight and unlocked the hinge of the wagon, so it opened like the bed of a truck. The man didn't have a face because it was hidden in a bulky hood, animal fur lining the edge of the heavy fabric, giving it weight so it remained slumped down over his face. The material was gray like London fog, and it was part of a cloak, a kind of garment I thought only existed in stories. His outstretched arms showed the thick leather material of his jacket underneath, the gray stitching matching the color of his cloak. The edges of his sleeves were cuffed with the same animal fur as his hood, and black leather gloves covered his hands. He looked well-dressed and warm.

I would have demanded answers and tried to kick him in the face, but I was stunned by what I saw. It was as if I'd stepped into a nightmare about a cult living deep in the forest of the French Alps.

Except it wasn't a nightmare.

This shit was real.

He grabbed the ropes that bound my ankles and dragged my body toward him.

I snapped out of my stare, and when I was pulled to the edge, I raised my knees and slammed my feet hard into his chest. "Don't fucking touch me."

He fell back at the hit, as if he didn't expect me to fight back, as if the other girls they brought here didn't fight back.

He righted himself and stared at me for a moment, looking at me under the shadow of his hood. His face was invisible because his cloak gave his face all the anonymity in the world.

It definitely raised the stakes, because I couldn't see his reaction, couldn't gauge what he might do next.

I breathed hard, ready for him to make his move, yanking at the bindings that tied my wrists together, so desperate to fight but so helpless to do a damn thing.

He came back to me and grabbed me by the ankles again. To my surprise, he cut the ropes holding them together.

I stilled, unsure what was happening.

The knife moved to my wrists next, and he sliced through the restraints.

What the fuck was happening?

He grabbed me by the arm and yanked me from the wagon before he shoved me back, making me trip and land on a patch of snow on top of the cold, hard ground. He sheathed his knife somewhere in his pocket, dressed in all black, his pants the same material as his long-sleeved shirt, waterproof fabric, the kind of stuff skiers wore on the mountain.

I got to my feet, breathing hard, my hands raised and prepared for a fight even though I didn't know how to throw a punch. Blood pounded in my ears, and I didn't dare take my eyes off the man who stared me down from the darkness of his hood. There were buildings and people in the background, but it was just a blur because he took all my focus.

He stepped closer to me, his boots crunching over the hard snow, vapor blowing from the hood like cigarette smoke. He raised his hand and pointed behind me. "A hundred miles." His voice was deep and steady, full of restrained annoyance. He shifted his arm clockwise and pointed to his right. "A hundred miles." He raised his arm, and his thumb indicated the mountains behind him. "Alps." Then he pointed the other way. "Hundred miles. You want to run, go for it."

He could be lying, but I suspected he wasn't. I wasn't familiar with the French countryside, but I knew there were lots of uninhabited areas outside the major cities. And while there were villages spread out through the landscape, it would still be hard to find them. I glanced at the stables where a few horses stood, covered and warm. I could do it—if I had a horse.

He shook his head slightly, like he knew what I was thinking. "On foot."

"Give me my sister." I'd rather take my chances in the cold than do whatever he had planned.

He stepped toward me again. "No."

The harder I breathed, the more vapor escaped my lips, the moisture from my sinuses drifting away into the wind. "I'm not leaving without her."

"Then you aren't leaving at all." He turned back to the wagon and dragged my sister to the edge.

I sprinted at him, knowing where he'd put that knife in his jacket.

As if he'd been expecting it, he turned and grabbed me by the throat, his thick gloves getting a strong grip on my dry skin before he slammed me down into the ground. Then he turned me over and pushed my face into the pile of snow, shoving my face deep until the snow started to fall in, surrounding me with the icy powder. Instantly, I struggled to breathe because my heart rate was fast. It was like being slowly suffocated, the air becoming less available with every inhale.

After a moment, he released me. He shoved me to my back and stood over me, the hood falling even farther over his face. "Save your strength—at least, if you want to live." His grip loosened, and he stood upright to grab my sister. He pulled out his knife and did the same to her before shoving her into the snow beside me.

Another man, dressed identically, approached, his boots audible against the powder. "What have we got?"

"A strong one and a weak one." He turned back around and pointed at me. "Put her on the line. The other can be a stuffer."

On the line? Stuffer?

"Names?" He approached me and extended his hand to me.

I glared at him in defiance.

Melanie was too scared to fight. She submitted immediately. "Melanie."

The second man grabbed her by the arm and yanked her up. "Let's go."

The first one continued to stare at me. "The only escape from this place is death. So, I suggest you make the best of it."

I spat on his extended hand, landing right in the center of his palm.

He raised his palm and looked at the spit before he dropped his arm to the side. "You'll take longer to break than the others. But you'll break...like they all do."

It was a lot to take in.

It was a settlement of cabins outside the tree line, the Alps the backdrop. It wasn't fenced in like a prison, probably because there really was nowhere to run. I'd been living in metropolitan areas my entire life, so surviving in such harsh conditions with no wilderness experience was just stupid—at least without YouTube. There was a chance to make it to a village if I had a horse, but from what I gathered, they were in stables under lock and key.

The man who'd tried to suffocate me in the snow held me by the arm and guided me forward, my sister in front with the other man. I didn't attempt to fight him because I really was helpless. His clothing hid his frame from sight, but the strength he showed told me that he was strong as hell. And even if I overpowered him...then what?

We came to an opening between the buildings, a long line of picnic tables shoved together, making tables that were fifty feet long. There were rows of them—and women sitting at all of them.

The scene reminded me of elves in Santa's workshop, working fast to get all the toys ready for Christmas Eve. But instead of presents, there were tubes of white powder that were carefully being weighed on small scales before being shoved into small plastic bags.

It didn't take me long to figure out what it was.

Cocaine.

But then I noticed something else...something much worse.

A woman hung from a wooden pole, a noose around her neck, her body hanging down as she slightly swayed left to right from the breeze. Blood stained her t-shirt around her stomach like she'd been stabbed. The snow beneath her was a faint pink color...like she'd been dead for days.

Oh my god.

Some of the girls lifted their gazes from their work, watching us walk by. They were mostly young women, but some were older, as if they'd been taken as young women and had been there for a decade...or maybe longer.

The man escorting me projected his deep voice. "Slacking off?"

Their gazes immediately dropped back to their work.

It was a labor camp. I shouldn't be grateful that I wasn't being trafficked to be raped, but I was.

The guy took my sister a different way, to a different set of cabins.

"Wait, we stay together." I tried to twist out of his grasp. "Where is she going?"

He tugged me hard and kept me on the path.

"I asked you a question."

"And I heard you."

"We stay together."

"I'm sorry," he said with a bored voice. "Did you think this was the Marriott?"

"You're a fucking monster." I tried to fight his hold again, desperate to get back to my sister, to protect her from whatever horrible things were about to happen. My life didn't seem important compared to hers, and I immediately turned into a sacrificial lamb meant to die for the greater good. "Please."

"You'll see her later." He didn't struggle to contain my movements, his size superior to mine, his experience with previous prisoners giving him the upper hand. He'd probably done this a million times, dragged an innocent woman to her grave.

"What's a stuffer?"

"What you just saw back there." He guided me farther past the clearing and into the rows of small cabins.

"So, that's what you want us for? To make drugs for you?"

"Drugs are already made. We need you to weigh them, stuff them, and prepare them for distribution."

"What does on the line mean?"

"I love the enthusiasm," he said sarcastically.

I twisted out of his grasp again because I wanted to get that knife and slit his throat. "There's more of us than you. We'll get you motherfuckers."

He kept his eyes forward, escorting me through the snow to one of the cabins. "Good luck with that."

"You just keep us here forever?"

He shrugged. "Not quite." He turned me to the right, escorting me up the steps to the door of a cabin. He opened the door and pushed me inside the small room, with just a twin-sized bed and a bathroom.

I took a quick look around and didn't find any weapons to use for an attack. There were a couple outfits folded on the bed, and the bathroom had a small tub and shower with no curtain. Just a bathtub up against the wall. I turned back to him. "I want to stay with my sister."

He shut the door behind him and took a seat in the single wooden chair against the wall. His knees widened and he leaned back, appearing relaxed like this was just another day in paradise. "We keep a garden here. We nurture the flowers, the best always getting the most water, soil, sunlight. Those that don't, start to wilt. When they become weak enough, they fade away...and turn into weeds."

I stared at him with my hands by my sides, unsure where to look because the darkness of his cloak made it impossible to distinguish anything about him. Sometimes there was a faint glimmer of his jawline, which was hard and covered with a shadow of dark hair. But I never got a look at anything else, like his eyes or nose. "What the fuck are you saying?"

He leaned forward and rubbed his gloved hands together. "We reward the obedient and the hard-working with essentials—warm clothing, food, water... And those who make our lives difficult don't get such luxuries. You're young, so you can probably get by with little sustenance, but over a long period of time, it'll age you...and make you weak. Before you know it, you'll be a weed. And we kill the weeds."

Fuck.

He rose to his feet. "Take a warm bath. Otherwise, you'll get hypothermia. You're already pale." He turned to the door and opened it once more. He looked back at me before he walked out. "Your work begins tomorrow. I suggest you rest...because it's going to be a long day."

4

SHOW YOUR FACE

LOCKED ALONE IN THE CABIN WITH NOTHING TO do, I really started to feel my fate.

I was a prisoner.

I checked every cranny of that cabin, and there was no way out. It didn't have a window, so I couldn't break through the glass and jump out. Surrounded by four solid walls, with a mattress that sat directly on the floor, there wasn't a single tool at my disposal. I tried to pull the faucet out of the wall to use that to hit someone upside the head, but it was impossible to accomplish without a wrench.

My biggest fear was my sister's treatment, but I suspected she was experiencing exactly what I was. Other than being locked up against our will and forced into servitude, there was no immediate danger. They didn't seem to hurt you unless they were forced to, and they seemed more interested in productivity than holding us down and taking us against our wills.

Most people were consumed with wallowing in self-pity, in venting their frustrations rather than acting on them, but I was a problem-solver, and I tried to think of a way to solve this problem.

The biggest hurdle to my captivity was the weather conditions. Snow was everywhere, there was no village in sight, and I would die from the cold before I could get far on foot...unless I found a village.

But did it snow here all year-round?

We were miles away from the base of the Alps, probably because there were chalets and ski lifts up the mountains there. So, I assumed it only snowed here from December to March. That meant I had three months of this before the weather improved.

Could I make it on foot in the spring?

Without food, water, or a map...probably not.

Were there maps somewhere at the camp? If I could find one, I had a chance.

But would they keep physical maps when they had phones? Did they carry phones? Would they even get reception here? How did they communicate with the outside world?

Whether I escaped in winter or spring, my odds were still slim, without any idea where I was going. Maybe if I were a French native, I would have a better understanding of the geography and have a greater chance of reaching a safe destination.

But I also had no chance without a horse, because they would hunt me down quickly if I were on foot.

When I thought everything through, it was depressing, because I realized I really had no chance of getting away, let alone with my sister. I could escape on my own and then alert the authorities to the location of the camp.

But I'd have to successfully escape first...and survive.

I spent that evening soaking in the tub, feeling the warmth infect my limbs and cure the developing frostbite. I didn't realize how cold I was until I was surrounded by warmth, until I felt the numbness. It took ten minutes for me to finally feel the temperature of the water, to feel my muscles relax in response.

Later, a knock sounded on my door.

I was in bed, wearing the clothes that had been provided for me, my hair still a little damp because there wasn't a hair dryer in the room.

The door unlocked, and a gloved hand appeared as the door was opened.

Then a woman set a tray of food on the chair against the wall. Her head stayed down, and she didn't look at me before she walked out. The man shut the door, locked it, and then they continued on.

I grabbed the tray and ate in bed, realizing how hungry I was once the smell hit my nose. The last time I ate was in that wine bar, when I'd smeared the assorted cheeses on the fresh slices of bread, topped with some dried cranberries and nuts. That'd been...I don't even know when.

I ate everything and drank the glasses of water left for me before I returned the tray to the chair. Then I got under the covers and lay in the dark, comfortable for the first time since my capture. The sheets were clean and warm, my stomach was full, and there was a sense of peace in my helplessness.

It could be worse.

At least that's what I told myself.

———————

THE DOOR FLUNG OPEN, bringing the morning light into the dark cabin. "Up." The coldness immediately rushed in, the dry air that made it difficult to breathe through the night without burning the nostrils.

I sat up immediately, jolted out of my dreamless slumber.

The light flicked on. "I said, get up." He threw a pair of snow boots on the floor for me to wear.

"I heard you the first time." I moved my legs over the edge of the bed and blinked my eyes a few times as I woke myself up. I'd slept hard that night, despite being drugged for so long, probably because my body was exhausted from the adrenaline of the day before.

"Doesn't look like it to me."

I picked up the boots off the floor and pulled them on, tightening the laces and securing them on the outside of my pants. The clothes they'd given me were made of a similar material to their own, waterproof because I'd be working outside all day. "I don't get breakfast first?"

He was still and silent.

I assumed he was staring at me. "Show your face."

He ignored what I said and walked out of the cabin. "Let's go."

I followed behind him and stepped into the morning light. It was another sunny day, and the powder that had fallen days ago was slowly melting into slush in several places. It was so cold that it hurt every time I took a breath, probably because I wasn't used to the conditions. I walked to university from my apartment, but it was a short walk, and then I spent the rest of my time indoors, usually with a warm cup of coffee in my hand.

I saw other women leaving their cabins and walking in the same direction as I was. When we passed another cabin, I saw several girls file out of the same doorway, at least a dozen of them. That seemed to be the case more often than not, that several girls bunked together at once. "Why do I have my own cabin?"

He kept walking.

"Hello?"

"You ask questions like you're entitled to answers."
He walked slightly in front of me, like he wasn't
afraid of turning his back to me, like there was
nothing I could do to defeat him. He had broad
shoulders that hinted at his strength underneath the
layers of dark clothing. He was tall, much taller than
I was, and when he moved his shoulder, the fabric
hugged the individual muscles of his arm.

I might have had a chance against him if I knew a
few moves, but since I didn't, I really had no shot at
overpowering him. He'd have me pinned down and
bloody so quickly. Also, taking him down wouldn't
get me any closer to escape. Pickpocketing something
worthwhile was probably a better use of my time.

I noticed he didn't carry a gun. That knife seemed to
be the only weapon he possessed.

I looked around and saw more women file out of the
buildings and head to work, like it was a normal day
in this hell. How did the men keep all these women
in line with no guns? How did they get so many to
submit when they were outnumbered ten to one?

Maybe I needed to orchestrate an uprising.

When we approached the clearing, most of the tables
were already full of women working. Other men

dressed identically stood around the edges, to keep an eye on the women. They were all wearing black garments with gray cloaks, their faces hidden.

Why did they hide their faces?

The guy walked me to the table full of brown boxes. "Open the box." He ripped through the tape and folded back the edges to reveal the white powder. "Replace the empty boxes along the table. It's that easy."

I glanced at the women, who were already filling small plastic bags with carefully measured amounts. "And I'm just supposed to do this all day, every day?"

"You catch on quick." He turned to walk away.

"Why do you hide your face?"

He halted in his tracks, taking a second before he turned around and regarded me once more. "Remember what I said about the weeds?"

I crossed my arms over my chest, still cold despite the heavy jacket they'd provided me.

"Don't be a weed." He walked away, moving to the edge of the clearing to speak to one of the men. Then he entered one of the cabins and disappeared from sight.

I turned back to the tables and searched for my sister. It took me a while to find her, but once I settled on her face, her eyes down on her work, I was relieved to see that she didn't have any bruises, that she looked physically the same. She was measuring the cocaine and putting the contents inside the small plastic bag.

I wanted to walk over there, but I suspected I would be reprimanded for leaving my station. But when would I ever get the chance to talk to her again?

One of the men at the end of the line addressed me. "Get to work." He moved down the line of tables until he picked up an empty box. He threw it on the ground then walked away, as if he expected me to come pick it up.

Now I understood why they didn't carry guns. Because when he turned around and walked away, his waist was level to the girls, so it would be easy for one of them to pull the gun from the holster at his waist and shoot him.

At least, that's what I would do.

I grabbed one of the boxes and hesitated, realizing it was at least forty pounds. I could carry it; I just hadn't anticipated the weight. I understood why they'd asked me to do this while Melanie measured the cocaine. She couldn't pick up these boxes once, let alone over and over.

Once I got it steady in my arms, I walked down the table until I found the vacant spot where the new box was supposed to go. I set it down with a thud, breathing hard from the exertion.

The girl across from the box kept her eyes down. "Welcome to the club…"

"Yeah…thanks. I'm Raven."

She kept her eyes down. "Get going, Raven. They don't want us to talk."

I glanced at the man who had just told me off and saw him staring at me again. I took the silent cue and turned away to grab the box left on the ground. I carried it back to the table, putting it in the pile with the other empty boxes.

A woman was there, dirty-blond hair pulled out of her face. She stood and studied her table, waiting for the next forty-pound box of cocaine to be depleted so it could be replaced. With her arms crossed and her gaze straight ahead, she spoke. "Some advice… The better you work, the more they leave you alone."

I stood at the other side of the table and copied her movements, trying to make it seem like I was waiting for the opportunity to replace the next box.

"If you replace a box before it's empty and pour the rest of the contents on top, they'll like you more, because you aren't disrupting the workflow of the girls."

I didn't care about the tip. "I'm Raven." I needed to make friends, to learn as much about this place as possible, to figure out a way to get Melanie and me out of here...someday. "You?"

She kept her arms crossed over her chest, the vapor rising from her nostrils with every breath. "Bethany."

I looked at the surrounding cabins, along with the large pine trees that stood tall around us. It was mostly an empty clearing, but nature was spaced throughout, the branches covered with blankets of snow like Christmas trees. The Alps were in the near distance, reflecting the sunlight off their potent whiteness. If I weren't stuck in a labor camp in the cold, I might actually think it was beautiful. "There's more of us than them. We can take them down."

She shook her head slightly. "I know you're new, and I get it. I used to be that way too. But it's been done... with no success."

I hadn't had much hope to begin with, but I lost a little more at her words. "What happened?"

"They killed a lot of us." She nodded slightly to the hanging woman at the edge of the clearing. "Like that."

I couldn't look. I'd already looked once, and I never wanted to look again.

"After you've seen your friends die like that...you don't want to try again."

I stared at the women as they all worked with their heads down, packaging the bags of cocaine with different amounts, doing the labor these men were too lazy to do themselves. When I'd moved to Paris, I was embarking on a new adventure, falling into the romantic haze of this beautiful country. But all of that disappeared as I was plunged into a living night-mare. "How long have you been here?" I kept my eyes ahead even though I wanted to look at her, to look into the face of an ally instead of the hooded cloak of an enemy.

"Five years."

I couldn't keep the breath in my lungs because it felt like someone had punched me in the stomach. "Fuck..."

She shook her head. "There're others who have been here longer, so don't feel too bad for me."

I felt bad for everyone, whether they'd been here for a day, a year, or a decade. "There's got to be something—"

"Shut your goddamn mouth." The man's voice projected across the clearing, making the women hesitate for just an instant before they worked faster. He stepped forward and walked down the line, heading right toward us.

Since they were all dressed the same, their identities were always a mystery, and that caused confusion, because it was unclear where they were looking at any given time. They could be turned the other way but still have their eyes trained on you—and you had no idea.

My heart started to pound harder as he came near. Tall like the man who'd escorted me here, he seemed equally strong, like he could crush my throat with the grip of his fingers. I went from a peaceful life to being afraid at a second's notice, my brain unable to dissociate from reality because terror was constantly present.

He moved past me and headed to Bethany. A black hand reached out and grabbed her by the throat, choking her right away. "What's so important that you needed to share?" He towered over her, squeezed her hard, pulling the life right out of her.

All she could do was choke and gasp.

I couldn't watch. I couldn't listen either. I couldn't handle any of it. "It's not her fault. I was the one talking." In survival mode, it was stupid to stick out your neck, to take a hit meant for somebody else, but my humanity was too great—at least, right now, it was. Bethany gave me information when she didn't have to, and now she was being punished for it.

His hood turned my way before his fingers released her throat.

She fell to her knees, coughing and gasping.

He slowly walked to me, his steps making the earth shake. He came closer to me, making me step back because there was nowhere for him to go unless he hit his chest against mine. He didn't grab me by the throat. He towered over me, vapor appearing from his hood in long trails, like he was huffing and puffing like an angry bull.

I held his gaze, held my ground, but I was terrified... terrified in a way I'd never been before. The energy around this man was much different from the first man who had escorted me to and from the cabin.

He pulled his arm back then punched me so hard in the face that I collapsed backward, landing hard on the ground, my vision turning black for a moment like I'd just received a concussion. My back struck the cold earth, and I stared at the sky through the branches, bewildered but aware at the same time. Then his face appeared in my vision, and because of the angle, I could see the black beard at his chin, the only visible characteristic. "That's just a warning."

I SAT AT THE TABLE, my eyes down, the pain throbbing in my temple.

A tray of food was placed in front of me. It was an apple, a couple slices of bread, and a few strips of ham. It was meager compared to the dinner I'd had in my cabin last night, which was a full meal of greens, meat, and grains.

But I was in so much pain that it really didn't matter anyway, because I had no appetite.

Bethany took a seat across from me, sitting at the very end of the line like I was. The tray presented to her was the same.

But the girls next to me had a full meal, meat lasagna with salad and bread.

Bethany kept her head down and ate quietly.

I ripped a few pieces of bread from the loaf and placed them in my mouth.

One of the men passed, keeping an eye on us, and then continued on his walk.

Bethany whispered to me. "You get less food and water if you disobey them."

"I'm not very hungry right now, so...that worked out." The thudding in my skull was so bad that I wasn't sure how I'd get through this without painkillers.

"You need to keep your strength up as much as possible. You have to do your job well." She spoke right before the food hit her mouth, carefully disguising her lips so her whispers would go unnoticed.

"You shouldn't talk to me. I don't want you to get in trouble."

"I can tell you don't know how things work around here, and you need to know."

I picked up the apple and took a bite, and just digging my teeth into the apple was painful for my head. Maybe a hot shower would increase circulation and get rid of this headache naturally. "I don't give a shit about doing my job well." I didn't care about their drugs, the millions they were making off our hard labor. Fucking disgusting.

"You should. Because every week, they pick the worst worker for the Red Snow. If you don't eat enough and feel like shit, you don't work as well, and over time you get weaker and weaker...and then it can be you."

I took another bite of my apple and turned quiet as another man passed, his footsteps loud because he was close to the edge of the table. When he was out of my peripheral vision, I addressed what she said. "Red Snow?"

She nodded behind her. "The woman hanging."

I stared at my apple, thinking about the pink drops on the snow.

"They hang them, and while they choke, stab them to death."

I had to set down my apple because now I really couldn't eat.

"And they make us watch..."

My fingertips moved up to my lips because I thought I would be sick. "They do that every week?"

"Yes," she whispered.

"But they'll run out of workers that way—"

"They say they're pulling weeds, getting rid of the weak and keeping the strong. There are always new girls being delivered, so it's survival of the strongest, basically, the least difficult. It makes the group more and more submissive as a herd."

It was fucking disgusting—but also brilliant.

"And good behavior is rewarded with extras. You know, books, medication, treats..."

"Like a fucking prisoner."

"Yeah...that's exactly what it is."

5

EATEN BY WOLVES

I SAT IN THE BATHTUB, MY NECK RESTING against the porcelain rim as I kept my eyes closed. The hot water made the migraine subside slightly, but not by much. I was sitting there, just existing in agony.

The door unlocked before it opened.

My arms immediately crossed over my chest, hiding my tits from view.

A woman set the tray on the chair, another meager meal while the well-behaved workers got something much more filling. She kept her eyes down and darted out again.

I closed my eyes, not eager for food because I still felt like shit.

The door didn't close, and then heavy boots entered.

My eyes opened again. "Do you mind?" I pulled my knees to my chest and kept my arms crossed over them.

"Not at all." He approached the bathtub, standing over me in the same attire he'd worn this morning and yesterday. I could tell it was the same guy because he had a distinctive voice, one that was threatening but also sarcastic. "What did I tell you?"

"Sorry?"

"I heard you had a rough day."

I held my silence, refusing to give any acknowledgment of my pain. I didn't even care that much that I was naked under the water, because the pain made me disregard my vanity. There was no mirror in my cabin, so I had no idea what I looked like, if one side of my face was completely black and blue.

"I've got some good shit—if you stop being a pain in the ass."

"Pain in the ass?" I whispered. It was best not to yell. Otherwise, the pulse in my temple would increase, but he provoked me, and my self-righteousness got the best of me. "I'm a pain in the ass because I deserve better than this? Because every woman here deserves better than this bullshit? Fuck off." I turned my neck to look elsewhere, to focus on something besides the tall man who stood over me, his hood placing his head in perpetual shadow.

He remained for a few seconds, the direction of his gaze impossible to see. There was no vapor inside the cabin, so I couldn't even distinguish his breathing. It was impossible to read a man with no face, no breath, and no voice.

Then he turned around and walked out of the cabin, locking the door behind him.

Every man in that camp deserved to die because of their crimes against humanity, forcing us into servitude after snatching us off the streets. They threw us into a frozen prison, controlled us with food and the threat of a brutal death. I hated every single one of them, especially the man who had just walked out of there.

But I also knew he was different from the man who had struck me. He wasn't nearly as hostile or violent. He didn't pound my face with his fist every time I talked back. I tried to remind myself that it could be worse, that the guard assigned to my cabin could be one of the monsters from the clearing.

WHEN I WOKE up the following morning, the headache was gone.

But I still felt like shit.

The door unlocked, and he stepped inside. "Up."

I groaned as I rolled out of bed, pulling on my boots and securing them over my pants before I stood up… and felt every muscle in my body ache at the movements. I swayed for a second, feeling the soreness everywhere. Carrying those heavy boxes all day really forced my body to work.

"I suggest you stretch before bed. Now, hurry up."

I grabbed my thick jacket and put it on, zipping up the front to trap my body heat before I went outside into the cold. I walked out the front door while hardly looking at him.

It was the same day as yesterday, the same clear sky, the same suffocating quiet of the outdoors. In the distance, a large bird circled the skies, probably finding a dead carcass in the snow.

My eyes scanned the cabins, wondering which ones housed the men who ran this camp. Did they sleep separately or together? Who was the leader of this camp? Where did they store supplies? To travel a hundred miles in any direction to civilization, they needed a reserve of supplies. "Do you live here?"

"You think I commute?"

I walked beside him, seeing the other women stepping out of their cabins with their guards to be escorted to the clearing to begin work. "I'm just trying—"

"I know what you're trying to do." Clouds of vapor erupted from his hood. "Let me save you some time. Not a single prisoner has escaped this camp. The ones who have tried to run were hunted down then hung. One woman made it farther than the others, but when we found her, she'd been eaten by wolves. Don't try it."

"So, I'm just supposed to live here for the rest of my life?"

"No. You're supposed to live here until someone stronger replaces you. We're the largest coke distributors in Europe. We need to work fast, every single day, to make sure these shipments get out."

That meant wagons must carry the drugs out of here often...back in the direction from which I came. "You couldn't hire people to do our job?"

"When we're just going to kill them? No." Another cloud of vapor came from his hood.

Every morning, I awoke from my dreams to the same nightmare—over and over. "Why do I have my own cabin when the rest of the girls bunk together?"

"We keep the difficult ones in isolation."

"Why?"

"You can figure it out."

They didn't want us to talk to one another, but they couldn't prevent that from happening at night in the cabins. If I were able to converse with the others, I would stage a coup. My sister was probably with a group of women because they'd known she was submissive the second we arrived. But I certainly wasn't. "So...you just live here? Like, forever?"

"You ask a lot of questions."

"I've got nothing else to do."

He continued to walk, his strides nearly twice as long as mine. "It's a new day. I suggest you take the opportunity to turn things around. Keep your head down, do what you're told, and you might have a nice time here."

"A *nice* time?" I asked incredulously. "Are you psychotic?"

"Not the first time I've been asked that..."

It didn't matter that every woman before me had been unsuccessful. I was too young to live out the best years of my life in this frozen hell. My sister was too young to let her beauty dry out in the winter wind.

"Good behavior is rewarded. Loyalty is worshiped."

"I don't want a goddamn book or extra meat for dinner," I snapped.

"There're better things besides books and food, but with an attitude like that, you'll never find out." He stopped when he reached the clearing. He turned to face me and extended his arm, indicating the table where I would slave away until lunchtime. "Good luck." He turned and walked away, passing the other guys who surrounded the clearing. He entered the same cabin as last time.

More girls entered the clearing and got to work.

I grabbed the boxes and put them on the table, the muscles of my back aching because I was sore from the day before. Within a couple of weeks, I'd be ripped, which was a good thing. I needed to be strong to get out of here.

It was difficult to distinguish between the men who watched us, but I was certain I recognized the man who'd hit me, based on his height compared to the others, the way he carried his body. I thought it was odd that my guard woke me up in the morning and locked me up at night, but I didn't see him at any other time throughout the day. The hierarchy of this place was impossible to gauge.

I moved to the table to grab a box.

Bethany was there, breaking through the tape to get the flaps folded back. "You look like shit."

"Yeah?" I did the same to my box. "I feel like it too."

"I brought you some pills." She pulled out the plastic and folded it down over the edges so it would be easier for the girls to scoop.

I kept my eyes on my work, but I was touched by the offer. "I'm feeling better, so I don't need it. But thank you." I didn't want to take her supplies when she worked for it by kissing up to these assholes.

"Keep it for another time. Trust me, you'll need it."

"Beth, I don't want to take your stash."

"It's not mine. I got it from a friend."

I continued to prepare my box, deeply affected by the kindness that still existed in this empty place.

"We've got one another's backs here." Bethany lifted the box and prepared to turn away. "At least, most of us do."

———

DURING LUNCH, she discreetly slipped me the white pill and continued to eat.

I dropped it into my pocket while keeping my eyes down. I'd desperately needed this last night, and when my guard offered, I was too stubborn to accept help from him—because it was conditional. If I was obedient like a good dog, then I would get a treat. I was too proud for that, at least right now. "Thanks."

She ate without acknowledging what I said.

My lunch was the same thing everyone else was having, a reminder of what I could have if I just stayed quiet and did my job. Yesterday, the food didn't matter to me, but having shit food for two meals in a row really made me hungry for something more substantial, like the chicken, rice, veggies, fruit, and bread they served. It definitely wasn't prison food. They made the meals something to look forward to, positive reinforcement.

If I were going to get out of there, I really had to eat well. I needed all the nutrition to keep a strong physique so I could survive out there in the wild, to keep going until I found humanity and called for help.

But I needed to get as much information as possible first.

And I needed to get my sister too.

That was going to be the difficult part.

The only good thing about my captivity was the fact that I could be there for Melanie. I never would have found her again after her kidnapping. I never would have suspected something like this, and the police wouldn't either. Otherwise, these guys would have been caught by now. I would have assumed she was being trafficked, based on her looks, and we would have gone in the wrong direction for years.

And that would have haunted me.

"I'm getting out of here...somehow." I kept my eyes on my food, the warm food that was quickly turning cold because we ate out in the elements, melted snow in patches around us.

"Don't advertise that."

"Why?"

"Some of the women are snitches."

"What?" I whispered. "Why?"

"Because they're rewarded," she said under her breath, shoveling food into her mouth to cover her moving lips. "Some of the girls here are practically guards. Some are brainwashed, some are sleeping with the guards, some are given a reward that ensures their loyalty...it's complicated."

"How could you possibly sleep with—"

She kicked me under the table.

A guard passed, surveying our table before he moved on.

I was so absorbed in the conversation I'd stopped paying attention. "How could anyone sleep with one of these guys?"

"Because they're treated even better."

"I'd rather die."

"You're new, so you're fresh, but the longer you're here...the staler you'll become. Your priorities will change. One of the girls here has her own cabin, a TV, games, a microwave with all the bags of popcorn she wants. And rumor has it... one woman even earned her freedom."

"Really?" I whispered.

"It was before my time, so I didn't witness it. But some of the girls insist it's true."

"Why would they just let someone go?"

She shook her head. "No idea."

"Was she sleeping with one of the guys?"

"Dunno."

I thought this place would be cut-and-dried, but I was wrong. Organizing an uprising would be complicated, especially when some of the women were more loyal to the guards than the women working at their sides every single day. "I want to talk to my sister, but they keep us apart."

"On purpose."

"Are there opportunities to talk to the others?"

"Maybe during one of the drops."

"Drops?" I asked.

"A plane will fly overhead and drop the coke."

My eyes narrowed. "Seriously?"

She nodded. "Most are flying from South America. It drops it from the sky, so there's no trace of it. That's why these guys haven't been caught in decades."

They'd been operating that long?

"They have us go out and put all the boxes in the wagons to be returned to camp."

"How far out is this?"

She lifted her gaze and looked at me. "Don't even think about it. The guys are on horses, and we're on foot. You've got no chance."

"Do they carry guns?"

"Bows and arrows."

"What?" I asked in surprise. "They don't have cars or guns?"

"I suspect they have guns, but I've never seen them."

"But why use a bow and arrow?"

She shrugged. "No idea. But I imagine it's to stay quiet. As for the cars, the journey to get here is too difficult to make in a car, even in a four-wheel drive. The path is too narrow at times for a car to make it through."

My eyes narrowed. "If they're trying to be quiet, that means someone nearby could hear it...right?"

She lifted her gaze and looked at me. "Raven, that's just my guess. I really don't know—and I wouldn't gamble your life on it."

WHENEVER I WAS in my cabin, there was nothing to do but wait until morning. There were no books for entertainment, so I spent most of my time soaking in the tub, just to get warm and try to relax.

The only entertainment I had was my thoughts— which made me feel worse.

I'd only been in the camp for about a week, and unless the weather was different, it felt like the same day over and over again. We went to those tables and bagged the coke. It seemed like the women at different tables were bagging different amounts, as if they already had a clientele that wanted specific amounts on a subscription basis. My job was to stand and watch, deliver a new box, and stand and watch again.

My mind used to be entertained by classic fiction, dissecting iconic literary heroes, thinking about their actions and the repercussions those had across time, their fictitious lines reverberating into the present. Those long papers I used to write late into the night. I loathed them and now it sounded like a vacation. I missed my laptop, the mug of coffee beside me, the view outside my window of the most beautiful city in the world.

All of that was taken from me.

The little things we took for granted.

Now I was just...existing.

I sat up in bed and waited for my dinner to be delivered, not even having a window to look through. I stared at my feet most of the time, wiggling my toes and watching them move through the socks.

The door unlocked, and the women set the food on the chair. She darted out again.

The guard entered, the same man who always came to visit me. With his face hidden inside that hood, his identity was obscured, but I recognized his movements, the breadth of his shoulders, the way he carried himself. He always entered my cabin like he owned the place. "You like Italian?"

With my arms crossed over my chest, I just glared.

He picked up the tray and set it on the bed beside me. "You're getting good food, so you must be behaving yourself." He stood over me, looking down at me.

I turned away, severing the eye contact I couldn't actually make.

He moved to the chair and took a seat.

Social isolation was suffocating, but no amount of distance would make me want to converse with a guard. It was probably part of their brainwashing technique, to make you grow attached to the man who locked your door every night since you had no one else. "I prefer to eat without company."

"Same." The chair looked too small for him based on the way he covered it entirely. He leaned back, his boots planted against the floor, and he crossed his muscular arms over his chest, his hood covering most of his face, but some of his chin was visible because of the light.

"Then you can go."

He didn't move.

I pulled the tray to me and ate, because I didn't want it to get cold before I enjoyed it. Food was one of the few things I had to look forward to, and their meals were actually pretty good. They purposely made us nutritional meals so we could work harder and pack their coke. I bit into a piece of garlic bread and kept my eyes down on my plate.

"You did good this week."

Since all I wanted to do was snap back, I didn't say anything.

"I thought it would take longer, honestly."

I held my tongue and continued to eat. Being defiant wouldn't get me anywhere, would only bring me closer to death, and even fighting my guard wouldn't do me any favors. My focus should be on escaping, getting information to do that, and then solidifying a plan—and getting to my sister. "You said good behavior is rewarded."

"It is." A deep voice came from the hood, his chin moving slightly as he spoke. There a shadow across his jaw, over his chin before it disappeared under the hood. His skin was fair, the limited amount I could see. "You want a book? Coke?"

Did women actually ask for that? A book would be nice, something to distract my thoughts while I was stuck in this cabin waiting for the sun to rise the next morning. We worked until dark, so there were several hours before bed that needed to be wasted. "I want my sister." I abandoned my dinner and looked at him, even though I'd never be able to see those eyes, to see the reactions I relied on when conversing with another person.

He was still, so quiet it seemed like he didn't hear a word I said.

"I want us to be in the same cabin." I wanted to assuage her fears, to promise her that I would get her out of here, that there was so much left to live for... and we had to keep going. I knew her so well, and I imagined she was crying herself to sleep at night, overwhelmed with the guilt that she carried on those small shoulders.

He shook his head. "Simple behaviors earn simple rewards. If that's something you really want, it's going to take a lot more than obedience."

"Then what's it going to take?"

He wasn't wearing gloves like he did during the day, so his large hands were visible, covered in veins, the skin slightly cracked because the winter air dried out his skin. He rubbed his thumb into his palm. "Build up to it. Start small."

I didn't want to start small. "The only thing I want is my sister. I don't care about a book or music."

His hood shifted up slightly, like he'd stopped looking at his hands. "I know what you're doing. I strongly advise that you don't."

"I just want—"

"You can't escape. You're going to get yourself killed. Your sister too. I know your life doesn't mean much to you, but can you live after seeing your sister hang, her dripping blood turning the snow red?"

The image came into my mind and immediately made me sick.

"You can make a life here. It's not the life you wanted, but you can appreciate the little things that bring you some joy. You work all day, just like normal people, and then you go home to a warm bed with books by your bed and crumbs in your sheets from the items that you earned."

This brainwashing attempt no doubt worked on other people, but it wouldn't work on me. They poisoned minds into accepting their conditions, into accepting the loss of freedom, to make them believe they should strive for approval, to work harder to earn the life that shouldn't be dictated by someone else in the first place. "This bullshit might work on the others, but it won't work on me. I know I deserve freedom, I know I deserve more, and these late-night talks and veiled kindness won't change what I know in my heart to be true. Years could pass, and it wouldn't change anything. But I don't expect to be here that long...so it doesn't matter."

He was still as he stared, his reaction impossible to decipher without a face. He could have threatened me into submission, come to the bed and made my face bloody because of my outburst, but there was no retribution.

Maybe it was just a ruse to make me feel comfortable with him, or maybe he really had no ill will toward me. Maybe he was different from the others. Or maybe he wasn't. "I have to protect my sister...and I will."

6

RED SNOW

HE CAME FOR ME THE FOLLOWING MORNING, but he didn't rush me to get dressed. He let the door creak wide open so the light could reach up the floorboards into the small cabin, but he stayed outside, waiting for me on the porch.

I pulled up on my boots and jacket and walked out.

He stood at the bottom of the stairs, looking in the direction of the clearing, two wisps of smoke coming from his hood.

I walked with him.

He was slightly in front of me, never walking directly beside me, like he needed to lead me in the right direction, when I'd taken this walk enough times to know the way. "Today is the Red Snow."

I stopped in my tracks, my foot stopping in a puddle of melting snow. It'd been sunny for the past week, so the warmth of the rays had eaten away at the piles of powder. I suspected more snow was on the way, that it would pile high with the next storm.

He must have realized I'd stopped walking because he turned around to look at me. "It's not you."

I'd been on my best behavior since I'd been punched in the face, because I had bigger objectives than getting beaten. The meals were good and the lack of confrontation comforting. I worked hard because I wanted them to forget about my existence altogether. Bethany and I had short conversations at lunch, and I learned as much information as possible about this horrific reality. "You know who it is?"

He nodded.

It didn't matter who the victim was, whether she was a snitch, whether she would stab me in the back at the first opportunity; she was a person who deserved to be outside this camp. The knowledge made me breathe so hard that my lungs burned with the cold and my eyes watered, only to dry out instantly because the air took the moist film away. "How can you live with yourself?"

"I have nothing to do with it."

I marched toward him. "But you can stop it."

"I can't stop anything, even if I wanted to. It was necessary, because without an incentive to work, no one did their jobs well. Now, they all work like their lives depend on it—which is what we want."

My temper flared, and without thinking, I shoved him hard in the chest.

He took a step back, anticipating my attack, and he grabbed me by both wrists and stopped the momentum, pushing me back slightly over a puddle in the dirt. His hands squeezed me tightly, digging through the material of the jacket and right into my flesh.

I didn't care about getting a terrible lunch and dinner, about getting struck in the face. This was wrong, and while my actions wouldn't stop what was about to happen, I had to do something, had to let all this pain out in some way. My eyes watered again, disturbed when I hadn't even seen it happen yet with my own eyes.

He pushed my wrists to my sides before he released me. After a long stare, he turned around and walked forward again, exposing his back to me like he wasn't concerned that I would slam my fist right into his back.

I watched him walk away, tears in my eyes, shocked that his fingers hadn't gripped my throat and choked me.

After a few more steps, he stopped and turned back to me slightly. "The first time is the worst. But you'll feel numb for the others."

———

THEY WAITED until the end of the workday.

I noticed my lunch was the same as everyone else's, as if my guard hadn't reported my bad behavior. But I couldn't appreciate the gesture because I was sick to my stomach, terrified of what was coming.

When the sun was nearly gone, torches along the perimeter were lit, like it was a ceremony. The flames blanketed everyone's faces in the dark. Most of the women looked indifferent, like they really were used to this, like they would go back to their cabins as if nothing had happened. Others looked afraid—like they might be the next victim.

Then a man came into the clearing—a man I'd never seen before.

He was taller than the others, had to be six foot five, and while he was dressed like the other guards, a hood didn't hide his face.

But he was more terrifying—because he had a metal plate over his face covering everything below his eyes. There were slits in the metal so he could breathe, but when his harsh eyes were the only things on display, it was somehow more menacing than no face at all. He walked down the rows of tables, his heavy footfalls echoing against the soil like he was stepping across the hardwood floor of a quiet house.

Every woman was absolutely still, eyes down, as if any contact would make him choose them.

Bethany sat across from me, her eyes on the table too, like she didn't want to watch the enormous man walk up and down the tables, selecting his next victim, even though my guard had told me they already knew who it was. Maybe because I knew that information, it made me less afraid to watch him, to see the most horrifying event of my entire life.

He kept moving, his eyes looking at every woman he passed, all of their chins down while the shakes made them shiver—and not from the cold.

My sister had been working like everyone else, so I doubted she was the victim, not when she was fresh...as they described us. I watched him move down my row, anxious for it to be over because he'd terrorized us for minutes now, acting like he could feel the palpable fear rising from each and every one of us.

Like he got off on it.

He moved farther down the row, his eyes moving left to right, glancing between the two tables.

I stared, watching him move, seeing the bulky muscles through his clothing, seeing a man who weighed more than an ox.

Bethany lifted her gaze and looked at me, her eyes wide as if she couldn't believe I was openly staring at him. His back was to her, so she gave me a slight kick under the table, telling me to drop my gaze.

But I couldn't.

He suddenly stopped, his head tilted, his wide and unblinking eyes focused on me. The stare lasted for hours, at least it felt that way, when it was only seconds. The women behind him turned to look at me, to watch him stare at me. He held his look, his eyes slowly widening into a maddening stare, as if he was waiting for me to back down first.

My entire body started to shake in terror, and I dropped my gaze.

Then he moved again, walking to a table farther away from us.

Bethany was shaking too, as if she feared she might be the next victim.

I lifted my gaze to watch him now that he was on the other side of the clearing.

He stopped behind a woman who was older than me, maybe in her forties.

She kept her chin down, but she started to shake uncontrollably as if she already knew her number had been called. Tears glistened in her eyes before she shut them tight, the moisture dripping from her lids and down her cheeks.

He grabbed her by the back of the neck and dragged her from the bench.

She screamed and screamed, her shouts of terror echoing across the clearing, burning hotter than the flames on the torches.

I dropped my gaze because I couldn't watch this, couldn't experience this, couldn't handle what was about to happen. I closed my eyes and heaved in pain, tuning out the sounds, disassociating completely.

And just waited for it to be over.

I DIDN'T SLEEP that night.

I watched the sunrise through the crack under the door. My cabin was insulated because it had no windows, but I could hear the wind rustle the trees, hear the distant howl of the elements. It wouldn't be a sunny and clear day like the last week.

It would be so fucking cold.

Footsteps sounded on the patio, and then the door unlocked.

I was already dressed, my boots on over my pants, my heavy jacket on in bed so it would warm up before I went outside into the cold. My hair was pulled back out of my eyes in a ponytail. I hadn't even combed it because they gave me nothing. It was probably one of the things women asked for in exchange for obedience, because some of the women had nice hair, even wore makeup.

My guard stood there in the open doorway, watching me sitting on the bed.

I sighed before I got to my feet, exhausted and cold. I turned to the door and didn't look at him at all before I stepped outside into the frigid wind, the trees blowing along with the harsh howls. My arms immediately crossed over my chest. "Are we working inside today?" The coke would blow away, and they wouldn't want to lose an ounce of their precious product that they were willing to kill for.

"No. We've got a pickup." He took the lead, going a different direction than last time.

I followed behind him, watching some of the women walking along the usual path to the clearing, but a few women went in my direction. "A pickup?"

"You'll see." He walked to the edge of camp, where there were a few wagons and guards on horses. Bows were on their backs along with quivers of arrows. Bethany was there, giving me a glance before quickly looking away so as to not draw attention to our friendship. The guard turned around again, facing me with his back to the others, coming close to me so more of his features were visible under his hood. "Don't run. They'll shoot you on sight." He stepped away and disappeared. He never seemed to participate in anything in the camp. His only job was to retrieve me in the mornings and in the evenings. He must have another position at the camp, but whatever that was was a mystery.

The girls huddled together, waiting for the last few girls to join us.

Bethany came closer to me, her hair blowing in the icy wind. "You okay?"

It was such a stupid question that I didn't know what to say. All I did was shake my head.

"You get used to it...at some point."

I would never get used to that. "I'm going to kill him."

She watched me with her bright blue eyes, her gaze shifting back and forth as she read the sincerity in my expression.

"I will." If I could never escape, then I would at least put him in the ground with me. He would pay for what he did to those women, for the years of corpses he'd created, the women he would continue to butcher until I shoved a knife in his gut.

Another woman joined us, one with jet-black hair and brown eyes. Her arms were tight over her body, and the vapor consistently rose from her nostrils. "You're the new girl?"

"Unfortunately." I didn't bother with a handshake. I'd only been here a week, but I'd already disregarded basic courtesies because they didn't apply in this hell.

"Cindy." The skin on her face was cracked in places, especially on the bridge of her nose, because her skin was so dry in this wintry weather. Her complexion seemed destined for warm and exotic places with lots of heat and humidity.

"She's the one who gave me the pill," Bethany explained.

"Oh...thank you." Now, I had a second friend, and that made me feel a little less alone.

Cindy nodded.

The guard escorted a few more girls to the group, and then we started to walk forward, leaving the safety of the tree line and heading into the open landscape before us. It was acres of snow, like a meadow replaced it in the spring. The wind pressed against us, making our jackets flap open like the canopy of a parachute. Two wagons were in the lead, while two other men rode on strong steeds, walking in line with us to keep us in their sights.

My guard told me not to run because it was pointless. In the wide open, there was nowhere for me to hide, no forest to escape into.

I'd never been so cold in my life. "Where are we going?" It was much easier to talk out here, with the wind blowing snow past us, making visibility poor, our voices trailing behind us and out of earshot.

"Pick up the next shipment." Bethany walked beside me, Cindy on her other side.

"Of coke?" I noticed the group was made up of women who were young and strong, mostly those who were on the line in the clearing, picking up heavy forty-pound boxes over and over.

"Yeah."

"That means we're meeting a crew out here?"

"No."

"Then where are the drugs coming from?" What was I missing?

Just then, the sound of a plane was audible, approaching us somewhere through the clouds. It couldn't be seen in the storm because a flake of snow would land in your eye if you looked up too long, but the powerful engines were unmistakable.

Three hundred yards ahead of us, crates fell from the sky and crashed into the mounds of powered snow that had built up over the night. The farther out we went, the deeper into snow our legs sank, making it harder to move forward, making us sweat despite the frigid temperatures.

These guys truly operated in complete stealth...so no one was coming to rescue us.

No one knew about this place.

No one.

It was so disheartening, I nearly collapsed in the snow and gave up.

And I might have given up—if I didn't have someone to protect.

If I gave up, Melanie would never be free.

So, I kept going.

It took a long time to cross the distance, to get the horses to pull the wagons over the snowy terrain, to fight against the wind. The more into the open we trudged, the more vulnerable we became to the wind that slapped across our faces and burned our skin. My lips were so dry they started to crack in real time. My eyes watered from the sting of the wind, only to dry up a second later. The cycle repeated over and over, getting more and more difficult the closer we came to our destination.

Then we finally stopped.

"Get to it." One of the guards barked at us to grab everything in the snow and place it on the wagons.

"Just watch me," Bethany said.

We moved into the snow and scavenged for the coke.

Most of the girls moved to lift the heavy crate from the ground, to pick it up and carry it to the wagon.

But one of the crates broke open, and the plastic bags wrapped in padding scattered everywhere, making holes in the blanket of snow. That was what Bethany went for, so I did the same. I was knee-deep in snow, picking up the bags as I went, holding them against my chest as I followed the bags like breadcrumbs farther out in the snow.

And then I heard it.

The sound of a bell.

I stilled at the sound, my ears numb from the cold.

Then I heard it again.

"Oh my god..."

Bethany moved to a bag nearby. "Keep moving. They'll hit you if you're still too long—"

"Did you hear that?"

She stilled. "Hear what?"

"The bell. I heard a fucking bell...like a church bell." I dropped all the bags into the snow and looked into the distant tree line, the tall pines that stood miles away at the start of a forest. My heart was beating so hard, the adrenaline was rushing, hope fluttered in my heart...replacing the emptiness I'd experienced just a moment ago.

I knew I fucking heard it.

It was faint.

Quiet.

Like it was really, really far away.

But it was there...a fucking lifeline.

"Beth, did you hear it—"

"Move." She glanced over her shoulder and kept working.

I quickly grabbed the bags and went back to work, knowing they were watching me, and I did my best to act like nothing had happened. I picked up the bags and held them against my chest as I approached the nearest wagon, feeling all of them stare at me. I added them to the cart then turned around to grab something else.

But I tripped in the snow, falling face first.

One of the guys on the horse laughed. "You can tell she's new."

My hands pushed through the snow to find the ground to lift myself back up, but I found an object against my hand, a piece of the crate that had come apart and fallen into the snow. I didn't pause to look at it and discreetly slipped it into my pocket as I got to my feet.

Maybe it was something useful.

But I didn't even care that much, because that bell continued to ring in my mind, a distant echo. It started to build louder and louder, ringing in my mind like a bell from a church in Paris, right in front of me, making me feel like I was far away from here.

7

THE COUNT OF MONTE CRISTO

WHEN I WOKE UP THE NEXT MORNING, IT WAS A clear day once again.

The storm had passed, the cabins didn't rattle, and it wasn't nearly as icy—but cold all the same.

My guard woke me up like clockwork.

My boots were tightened, my jacket was zipped up, and then I stepped out onto the porch.

He hadn't spoken to me about anything other than work in days. When he delivered my dinner, he left immediately. When he fetched me in the morning, he didn't give any orders because I was always ready to go. "You're shoveling today."

"What?"

"Shoveling the snow at the camp." He took the stairs then stepped into high drifts of snow. "Happens after every storm."

At least it was a deviation from the same mindless work. And it was a break from the clearing, where that woman's body still hung. "What's your name?"

He walked ahead of me, handling the accumulation of snow better than I did because he was nearly a foot taller. His legs were more muscular than mine, so he cut through the snow like he had blades on his boots. "Why? I don't know yours."

The church bell in the distance gave me hope of escape, so now I needed to get all my ducks in a row. The more information, the better. "Raven." There was no incentive to be difficult at this point.

He walked ahead.

"This is where you tell me yours."

"I don't remember agreeing to that."

I trailed behind him, moving through the snow that reached my knees. I had to swing my arms far to get through the powder, my legs burning because they were still sore from the trek into the wild yesterday.

Then I tripped and fell right into a pile, my face hitting the slush on impact.

Now I'd be frozen all damn day.

I pushed out of the pile, losing my grip and sliding through the frictionless wetness.

A gloved hand appeared.

I stared at it and almost didn't take it.

I was cold, achy, and exhausted. I placed my hand in his and felt his strength pull me to my feet, my tired body lifting effortlessly.

He turned away and continued to walk.

"Thank you."

"It takes time to get used to."

I moved behind and followed him until we reached the front of the camp where the main building was located. It faced the open landscape, the sea of whiteness until the next line of trees in the far distance. Women were already there, wielding heavy shovels as they dug into the snow and disposed of it near the trees. "Do you guys stay in that bigger cabin?"

He shook his head. "You're still on that, huh?" He was fully aware of my desire to escape, but he never tattled on me, never punished me for it. He seemed more amused than anything else.

"Just curious..."

He stopped near the porch, where a group of guards sat in their comfy chairs and drank from mugs with steam rising to their faces, probably hot coffee. "Grab a shovel and get to it."

"Am I doing this all day?"

"You're doing this for several days." He turned around and disappeared—like always. The guy was an enigma, because he seemed separate from the rest of the men even though he wore the same clothing. It was unclear if his station was lower or higher than everyone else.

I grabbed a shovel and moved into the crowd.

That was when I spotted Melanie.

She stuck the shovel into the snow, pushing down on the handle to scoop it up, and then picked it up and carried it to the pile.

I was so happy to see her that my elation chased away the cold—just for a moment.

I moved to where she'd been working, near the corner of one of the cabins.

She came back to me, her eyes full of surprise when she saw my face close up. Before this, all the eye contact we had took place across the clearing, far away from each other. Emotion filled her eyes, the guilt written all over her face.

I was just thankful to see her.

I wanted to rush to her and hug her, to hold my sister in my arms again, to tell her I would solve this problem like all the others. But the guards watched on, and if I did anything out of the ordinary, they would separate us.

I carried the shovel to her area and dug it into the snow, using my foot to push down. "Do it like this. It's easier than pushing with your arms."

She was still beside me, like she was too upset to do anything, too overrun with emotion.

"Melanie, come on."

She breathed a deep sigh, the vapor coming from her nostrils in a long trail like smoke from a cigar. Then she pushed her shovel into the snow and copied my movements.

"Pick it up like this. Otherwise, you're going to hurt your back." I showed her how to scoop it up with the least amount of work. Then we both carried our snow to the tree line to add it to the pile.

Her back was turned to the guards, so she started to break, her emotions bursting through her skin like water through cracked glass. She breathed hard, shut her lips tight to battle the sobs, and then her lips quivered. "I'm so sorry—"

"We're going to get out of here, alright?" I whispered. "I promise."

She shook her head, the tears dripping down her cheeks.

"Hey, look at me."

She shook her head again.

"Melanie."

She heaved, her chest rising and falling with the painful breaths she tried to suppress. She finally turned to look at me, her eyes wet but her skin dry.

"I promise." I didn't know how I was going to deliver on that promise, but I would, one way or another. "Keep your head down and do what they say in the meantime. But we will get out of here."

She gave a hesitant nod.

"They can take our bodies, but they can't take our minds. We will get out of here—and we'll make them pay."

───────────────

I HAD NEVER BEEN MORE exhausted.

The second I got to the cabin, I went straight to bed. My fatigue overpowered my hunger, and I knocked out fully clothed, sleeping in the dark.

The door opened later and stirred me from sleep.

I sat up immediately, jolted awake because my mind was so deep asleep that the noise was startling.

A tray was placed on the chair before she darted out.

My guard came in afterward and looked at me.

I rubbed the sleep from my eyes as I sat on the edge of the bed. I didn't look at him, still half asleep.

He moved to the nightstand next to my bed and placed a couple things there. A mug full of something warm and steamy, a plastic tube of lip moisturizer, a little bottle of body lotion, and a book. He stepped away but still looked down at me, as if he were expecting a reaction from me.

I stared at the book on the nightstand. *The Count of Monte Cristo.*

That was fucking ironic. "Why did you bring this?"

He grabbed the tray from the table and set it down beside me before he fell into the chair, getting comfortable as if he expected to be there for a while.

I hadn't had a hot coffee or anything warm since I'd arrived here. The food was rarely hot because it took so long to reach me after it was finished in the kitchen. So, I grabbed the mug and looked down inside, seeing the marshmallows floating on top. "Oh my god..." It was so minor, something I would have taken for granted in my previous life, but looking into that mug made me think of a lost childhood when my mother was still alive, hot cocoa in front of the Christmas tree. It made me tear up for just a moment, to think that she was looking down at me right now, rolling in her grave because of what had happened to her girls. I brought the mug to my lips and took a drink, enjoying the first taste of sugar, the warmth as it thawed my throat and stomach, the way the hot mug heated both of my palms as I held it close.

Then I grabbed the book and held it tightly. It was a book I'd already read, but I'd read it a million times just to be connected to someone going through the exact same thing as I was. He escaped...and so would I. He got his revenge.

And I would get mine.

"You tell me escape is pointless, but then you bring me this?" I held up the book and looked at him before I returned it to the nightstand.

"Coincidence." His deep voice brought warmth to my cabin, like he was the fire in an invisible hearth. He seemed to possess power I didn't understand, because he lingered when he shouldn't, because he always walked away as if he could dismiss himself whenever he wished.

"Why don't I believe you?" I grabbed the lip moisturizer next, squeezing the plastic tube to feel all the ointment inside. It was unopened—brand-new. I set it down and took another drink of the cocoa.

He stayed quiet.

I wanted to pretend these gifts meant nothing to me, but now that I had them, the cabin felt livelier, more bearable. They say the little things in life matter most...and I realized that was true. "Why did you bring these to me?"

"Why don't you thank me instead?"

I looked down into the marshmallows before I took a drink, purposely catching one in my mouth so I could chew it and let it dissolve on my tongue. "Thank you..."

He rested his head against the back wall, the only skin visible from his ungloved hands.

"But why? You know I'm trying to find a way to get out of here."

He didn't speak.

He never tattled on me; he never reported me. Come to think of it, he was the only somewhat kind guard in this camp. "You're a lot different now than you were when I arrived here." He'd shoved my face into the snow and tried to suffocate me into submission. He'd threatened to break my face.

Still, nothing.

I was hungry, but I wanted to enjoy every single sip of that hot cocoa before it went cold. I sat there and enjoyed it. He was probably staring at the side of my face, but since his eyes were hidden, I had no idea. But I could feel it...feel that piercing stare.

"Magnus."

I stilled at the way his deep voice cut through the silence, the way it commanded my attention so effortlessly. He had a powerful presence, so it made me wonder if he was higher on the food chain than everyone else here.

He abruptly rose from the chair and moved to the door.

"I want my sister...please."

He stilled on the doorstep, the door cracked so the cold air entered the cabin. "That's not going to happen."

"I'll do anything. I'll scrub toilets. I'll do laundry. Whatever you want. But please, just let us stay in the same cabin."

"That's not up to me—"

"I don't believe you."

He continued to glance outside, like he didn't want to see the pained look on my face that matched my voice.

"Please...I know you aren't like the others."

Silence passed as he looked out into the cold. "You couldn't be more wrong about that."

8

MAGNUS

THREE DAYS WERE SPENT DIGGING IN THE SNOW.

My legs were so sore, I could barely walk.

Magnus must have known how tired I was because he continued to bring me extra things, like a mug of hot chocolate, a couple cookies, and even a notebook with a pen...as if he knew I liked to write.

When those shoveling days were over, I was actually relieved to get back to normalcy, back to the boring job in the clearing.

I didn't look at the woman hanging from the noose. It was different now, because I knew what she'd looked like when she was alive. There was no snow beneath her because it had been shoveled away. A wooden cross had been placed there, like one of her friends had done something to pay homage to her life.

But I never looked directly at her.

I would never get used to the executions, regardless of what Bethany said.

Even if years passed, my feelings would never change.

Somehow, I'd escape from there and tell the police everything. I'd watch the murderer's trial, and then his imprisonment after he was convicted. I'd make him pay for what he did to the poor women who were simply in the wrong place at the wrong time.

Bethany ate across from me. "That was your sister?"

I nodded.

"You're the first pair to be brought here...that I know of."

I didn't mention the story, because it made my sister look bad. Right now, we needed to survive, and having as many allies as possible was the way to accomplish that. "Yeah."

"She's taking it pretty hard. Cindy is with her in the cabin, says it's been rough."

"I know."

"I'm sorry. That must be difficult. That's one thing I'm grateful for...being in here alone."

"Who did you leave behind?" I whispered.

She was quiet for a while, shoveling the food into her mouth with her eyes down. "My daughter."

My eyes fell when I heard those words. "I'm sorry..."

"I'm sure she's with her grandmother, but..." Emotion caught in her throat, and she stopped talking.

A guard passed, and we kept our eyes on our food.

"I'm going to get out of here. And then I'm going to burn this place to the ground."

"It's fun to fantasize..."

"No. I'm going to do it." I pulled the piece of metal from the snow out of my pocket and opened my palm so she could see it. It was a thin shard of metal, having broken off from the hinge of the busted crate. I returned it to my pocket.

She stilled for a second before she continued to eat. "What are you going to do with that?"

It was too small to be used as a weapon. It was too small to fight off wolves in the wild. But it could do one thing. "Magnus gave me a pen—"

"He told you his name?"

"Yes. Do they not do that?"

She shook her head.

I continued. "I think I can use both to pick the lock to my cabin."

She stopped to stare at me, so surprised that she didn't express her interest or disdain. "Then what? You'll never make it out there alone, in the dark... And who knows if you really heard that bell. It was in the middle of a storm, so the sound could have carried from anywhere. You might not even have the right direction."

The wind could have been blowing from several directions, so wherever its origin, it might be so far away that I had no chance of making it there at all, and I might be going in the opposite direction of the sound. But I held on to the fact that I'd heard it, that it was somewhere out there. "I'm going to explore the camp and see if I can steal some equipment. Maybe a map, a gun, some food and water to survive, flares if they have them..."

Bethany was still in shock.

"Just do some prep work before I run for it. I still have to get my sister too..."

"If you can make this work, you'll have to leave her behind."

"Why?"

"Because not everyone in that cabin is loyal to your cause. They could snitch."

That disgusted me. "Even if that means they could be liberated?"

She nodded. "You'll have to leave her, and if you make it...come back for her."

I couldn't leave my sister behind. We left together— we survived together.

"But I think it's a bad idea, because you'll probably get caught."

"Do they have guards out at night?"

"I have no idea, but I would assume so. If you get caught, you'll be the next victim of the Red Snow."

I suddenly lost my appetite.

"And if that happens, what will your sister do then?"

I didn't want my sister to see my lifeless body hanging there for a week. I didn't want her to live with the memory of my murder. "I know, but I have to try. Because if I don't try, then every woman will die here. They have drugs drop out of planes in the fucking sky. They know what they're doing, and they're never going to get caught by law enforcement or intelligence agencies. No one is coming for us, Bethany."

She dropped her gaze.

"We'll be filed as missing persons, and the police will assume we've been trafficked...which is brilliant. They're completely on the wrong track. These guys did that on purpose. They have women working in the camp because men are strong enough to fight back. You know what? We're strong enough to fight back—and I will."

She pushed her food around with her plastic fork, giving a slight nod. "For all our sakes, I hope you're right. I hope you can do this. I hope you can give us the freedom we all deserve."

"I will, Bethany... I fucking will."

AFTER DINNER WAS BROUGHT, I waited.

I didn't go to sleep, even though I would be exhausted the next morning.

I clicked the pen Magnus gave me, my thumb pressing into the pad at the top and making the tip emerge. Then I hit it again. Again. The click filled my dark cabin, my eyes on the ceiling, my heart racing because of my late-night plans.

I didn't have a clock, so I had no idea what time it was. I didn't even have a window, so I had no way of gauging life outside my door. All I had was my hearing, but my skills could only span to the front door and the patio right outside my cabin.

I was too anxious to continue waiting, so I got out of bed and pulled on my boots. My jacket was secured. Then I stuffed a towel into the crack of the door so I could turn on the light and dismantle the pen.

Piece by piece, I took it apart, until I got to the slender rod that I could use in the door. I left the remains tucked under my sheets before I pulled out the metal shard I'd picked up when the drugs fell from the sky.

I'd never done anything like this before.

But I'd seen it in movies, and there must be some truth to it.

I stuck the pieces into the small slit in the door and tried to feel around, sticking the shard inside to imitate the placement of a key, and then I used the pen to slowly turn the knob. Every time I tried, I could barely turn the knob an inch before it slipped.

"Ugh..."

I kept going, doing the same thing over and over, not giving up even though this seemed impossible. I didn't have the right tools like those guys in the movies. I wasn't some mastermind. I cursed under my breath then stepped back, pissed off that a stupid door would be my undoing.

I turned back to my bed to get under the sheets.

Instead, I stopped and stared at the book on my nightstand.

The Count of Monte Cristo.

He didn't give up. He planned his escape for years. He got out, returned with revenge, and made everyone pay.

I had to do the same.

I turned back and kept at it.

It took me thirty minutes, my hands got slippery and sweaty, so I had to remove my jacket, but I got it.

I fucking got it.

The doorknob went slack, turning with a twist of my wrist.

I stood back and stared in surprise. "Yes." I put my jacket back on, turned off the light, and pulled the towel from underneath the door. Now my heart was racing so fast, I could barely hear anything. The pounding blood masked everything around me. I was so terrified I almost didn't want to leave this cabin.

I was in Plato's fucking cave.

Far more afraid of potential freedom than sterile captivity.

I took a deep breath, tried my best to control my racing heart, and then cracked the door.

It was dark.

There were some lights around the camp, but very few, and the walkways were mostly hidden in darkness. I stood there and listened, waited for the sound of boots against snow, waited for a guard to pass.

But nothing happened.

If all the prisoners were locked in cabins with no windows, how would they escape? Maybe having a nighttime patrol was pointless, especially when fleeing in the dark wouldn't get you far.

I needed a flashlight.

I stepped out of the cabin and onto the wooden patio. The door shut quietly behind me, barely making a click when it returned to the doorframe. My eyes scanned left and right, only able to visualize the cabin in my mind because of the gentle lights sparsely spread out. I'd taken the walk to the clearing enough times to remember the way, and since we shoveled all the snow days ago, I shouldn't trip on anything.

I took the stairs and felt my boots hit the earth.

This was really happening.

I walked slowly, trying to feel the earth in front of me before I took a step, to make sure there wasn't an obstruction that would make me fall and break my nose, or worse, knock me out so they would find me in the morning.

Even if I wanted to escape that very moment, I couldn't. I'd walk out into the pitch-dark wilderness and just get lost. I wouldn't survive more than a few hours. I needed tools to survive, weapons, water, food...light.

I wasn't enough.

I moved farther into the camp, passing the cabins that I knew were there. There was a slight breeze, a gentle rustling of the branches in the tall pines that stood over me like wild skyscrapers. My warm breath escaped my mouth then came back and sprinkled across my face like I stood in front of a humidifier.

Even if I'd had a flashlight, I wouldn't use it. It was so dark here that any light would be a beacon. It made me believe there were no guards on duty—because they couldn't see anything.

I made it to the clearing. I could tell because the most lights were in this area, because boxes of drugs were still on the tables. I made sure to avoid that direction, because they cared more about their products than a girl escaping, so they might have eyes on that section.

I went around a cabin then moved past it, eventually reaching the larger building I'd noticed when we were shoveling snow. I stilled because the windows were lit up from lights inside the structure.

There were guards in there.

And if that was where the guards were...that meant there were supplies.

My heart had slowed down once I got used to the suffocating darkness, once I realized I was truly alone in the camp. But now that I detected signs of life, it started to pound once again.

I stared for a while, waiting to see someone walk past the windows.

Nothing happened.

I wanted to walk away and explore the rest of the camp, but I knew that building was the most likely location of the things I needed. Even if I could just get my hand on a gun and ammunition, that would really level the playing field.

I moved toward the bigger cabin and hit something.

My knee banged into the wooden rail that outlined the steps.

I shut my mouth and suppressed my groan, keeping silent even though that was so hard to do. Once I breathed through the pain, I made my way up, gripping the rail and keeping my footfalls silent. I reached the top and flattened against the wall, doing my best to listen.

Voices were audible, but I couldn't make out any words.

I slid closer to the window, standing right outside it, trying to hear exactly what they were saying. They could share information that would help me figure out where I was, if anyone passed through the area, if there was an obvious escape route that we weren't aware of.

But the windows were too insulated, and I couldn't translate anything. I heard several different voices, like there were quite a few guards together. What were they doing at this hour? Whatever hour it was...

I slowly moved closer and closer, facing the window, letting one eye move over the glass so I could see inside. I needed to know what was inside, to find out if the contents were worth breaking in at a later time.

Five guards were gathered around a round table. A lamp hung directly down from the ceiling, showing the cards on the table, the poker chips, the pile of euros in the center. They were in their long-sleeved black coats, but their cloaks were gone.

I saw their faces.

One guy had a thick, black beard. He was muscular and large, and I was pretty certain he was the guard who'd punched me in the face on my first day in the camp. Another guy was bald with a mustache. Every single one of them was muscular, not a scrawny guy in the mix. They couldn't be weak to do a job like this, physically or mentally. The guy directly facing me stared at the cards in his hand, his eyes down, his look impassive because he had a good poker face.

He had brown eyes, warm like the hot cocoa I'd had in my cabin, and he had fair skin with a hint of an olive tone, like he was French but also Italian. His broad shoulders stretched the fabric of his uniform, and while he was tall like the other men, he wasn't bulky. He was still for another moment before he laid his cards on the table.

"Motherfucker." The bald guy threw his cards down and took a drink from his beer.

The rest of the guys growled in protest and threw down their cards too.

The corner of his mouth rose in a slight smile, and then he pulled all the chips toward him, smug but also humble, because he didn't say a single word about his victory. He grabbed his beer, and when he lifted it to take a drink, his eyes moved to mine.

"Shit..." I ducked down instantly. "Fuck, fuck, fuck." I started to shiver in fear, because there was no doubt that he saw me. He paused his movements because he saw something in the frosty glass.

I was so scared that I couldn't move.

But I didn't hear any movement inside the cabin, footsteps heading to the door, loud conversations that led to shouts.

I didn't stick around to find out what happened.

I crawled under the windows and moved around the patio, careful over the floorboards, and maneuvered toward the back of the building, which was close to the forest. I could hide out there until they stopped searching for me. They probably didn't get a good enough look at my face to identify me. I just had to get to my cabin before they did.

I rounded the corner and made my way to the stairs in the rear. With my hand on the rail, I slowly crept to the bottom, my feet hitting the little mounds of snow that hadn't melted yet.

A hand grabbed me.

I was yanked up against the rise of the platform, my back hitting the wooden material that obscured me from view of the patio. It was dark so I couldn't see his face in the commotion, but now the light from the cabin above struck him perfectly, highlighting his face enough to make out his features.

It was the guard who'd spotted me.

He got out here fast—without making a sound.

I breathed hard in his face, paralyzed by my capture, so terrified that I couldn't move. But I found my strength and yanked my arm back to punch him in the face, to break free so I could run into the woods.

He overpowered me easily, like I was a child. His hands locked my arms in place, keeping me pressed down so tightly the only movement I could make was the steady rise and fall of my chest through my breathing. "What the fuck are you doing?" His deep voice was hushed in a whisper, but his anger was so potent that it felt like he was yelling, screaming at the top of his lungs. "Do you know what they'll do to you if they find you out here? You'll be the next victim of the Red Snow. Do you understand me?" He squeezed my arms hard, gripping me so tightly there would be two bruises there tomorrow. He pulled me then pushed me back into the wood, trying to strike some sense into me.

The threat instantly passed at the revelation. "Magnus?"

His nostrils made a steady line of vapor because he was breathing hard, full of rage. "You think you'd be alive if I were anyone else?" His brown hair was short but full, a little messy because it was the end of a long day in the cold. His jawline was sharp like glass, sharper than I noticed in the quick glances into his hood. The shadow across the bottom part of his mouth was gone, like he had shaved sometime after he delivered my dinner. The look in his eyes wasn't calm and knowing like it had been when he played poker with the guys. Now his eyes were wide—and on fire.

"I'm just trying to—"

"I don't give a fuck what you were trying to do. You need to get back to your cabin before they discover you. If they find you, I won't be able to help you." He finally released his grip on my arms and stepped back, like he needed to withdraw himself so he wouldn't really hurt me in his anger. "Go. Now." His eyes lifted up slightly, as if to check if one of the other guards had departed the cabin.

I was still paralyzed, unable to move.

His eyes dropped down and looked into mine again, just as fierce as before, that rage growing.

"Why are you helping me?"

His brown eyes shifted back and forth slightly, burning into mine as his chest rose and fell with furious breaths, the vapor trailing from his nostrils into the darkness and disappearing. This was the look he'd been giving me from the privacy of his hood for the past few weeks. He looked livid, but maybe he always looked this way. "Keep pissing me off, and I'll stop." He came back to me and lowered his voice. "I'll be gone for a few weeks. You'll be on your own. So, I suggest you be on your best behavior."

That church bell on the wind had been the first sign of hope in this desolate place. But this man was the bigger sign of hope, my saving grace. My hands shook, not from the cold, but from the comfort he brought me, the belief that there was some good in this place...even when wrapped in darkness. And losing that, even for a short period of time, was brutal. I couldn't let him go, couldn't lose this lifeline that God gave me. "What do you mean, you're leaving? Where are you going? When will you be back—"

"Go back to your cabin. And do not pull this shit while I'm gone."

I moved closer to him, my hands moving to his forearms because I wanted to touch him, to touch the only man in this camp who wasn't evil. "Take me with you..."

His eyes didn't blink as he looked into mine, as if he actually considered it, took a moment to figure out how he could make that happen, a plan to sneak me out of this horrible place. "I can't."

"Please—"

He yanked his arms from my grasp. "I said I can't."

"Magnus—"

"Go." He walked away from me, dismissing the conversation, taking the stairs back to the patio.

A man's voice sounded at that moment. "Are we playing another round or what?"

I immediately stepped back, hiding against the platform so the light couldn't shine on my body.

Magnus's response was curt. "Coming." He stepped in and shut the door loudly behind him, like he wanted me to know they were all inside—and the coast was clear.

9

TRENDSETTER

AFTER I MADE IT BACK TO MY CABIN, I COULDN'T sleep.

I tossed and turned until morning.

The guard who came to get me was nothing like Magnus.

"Get your fucking ass up!" My door flew open, and he startled me from sleep in the most jarring way possible.

I panicked so much, I ended up falling out of bed, hitting the hardwood on my hands and knees.

The guard laughed loudly. "We're gonna have some fun."

My knees ached from the collision with the hard-wood floor, and it took me a second to get up, to grab my boots from the floor and return to the bed to put them on.

"Go, come on." He smacked the back of his hand against his palm in my face. "Chop-chop. That coke isn't going to cut itself." He kept making the hand motion right in my face, over and over, like he was trying to get a rise out of me or make me burst into tears.

I ignored him and got my boots on then grabbed my jacket.

He grabbed me by the arm and shoved me outside before I could even get the jacket on.

I stumbled forward over the wooden patio and hit the rail, my jacket hanging from my body because I only had one arm in the sleeve.

He walked past me and headed down the stairs. "Chop-chop."

I glared at him as he passed before I righted myself. I took the stairs as I pulled on my jacket the rest of the way, zipping up the front and hugging what little warmth I had left to my body.

He walked ahead and escorted me to the clearing where I'd work for the day and strain every muscle in my body from lifting all the heavy boxes. Instead of leaving like Magnus did, he stayed, joining the others to keep an eye on our progress.

I turned to the table and started to prepare a box.

"You okay?" Bethany worked on her own box, her head down.

"I'm fine."

"Because you look like you're going to kill someone."

"I must always look like that, because that's how I always feel."

WE ATE OUR LUNCH, the guards circling around, hoping that someone would step out of line so they could punish us.

Because they were sick.

The Red Snow was tomorrow...and I couldn't go through that again.

"I snuck out of my room last night," I whispered.

Bethany was good at not reacting, and she didn't now. "What happened?" She stabbed her fork into the chicken and took a bite before scooping into her rice.

"I explored the camp, tried to figure out where they keep the essentials."

"And?"

"I found the guards playing poker in a cabin. When I peeked inside, one of them saw me…"

She stilled, her fork stationary. "Oh my god…"

"It ended up being Magnus. He came outside and told me to go back to my cabin."

"What?" Her voice rose a little.

I kicked her, telling her to be quiet.

She snapped out of it and kept eating.

We didn't talk again until the next guard came and went past us.

"What happened?" she whispered.

"He told me he was leaving for a few weeks… I asked him to take me with him. He said no."

"And he didn't report you?"

"I'm sitting here, aren't I?"

"I can't believe that..."

I still couldn't believe it either.

"He could have hung you right then and there. He should have reported you, and he didn't."

"I know."

"I guess they aren't all evil, but I've never seen a guard be anything other than evil."

It made me reflect on our first meeting, when he was rough with me. Maybe he only acted that way because the other guards were around. Or maybe he always did act that way, but something about me made him less violent. I really had no idea.

"Are you sleeping with him?"

"No," I said immediately.

"Has he tried...?"

"No." He never did anything like that.

"You think he's an undercover cop or something?"

Wouldn't that be nice? "No...because he would just tell me."

"I guess that's true."

"I have a new guard in the meantime. He's a fucking psychopath."

"They're all psychopaths, girl. Did Magnus say where he was going?"

"No, but the guards must have time off. They can't live here all the time. They must have lives outside of this place. Does your guard rotate?"

"Yeah. I've had a few different ones over the years."

I pushed my food around, thinking about the way those brown eyes burned into mine with an inferno of rage. When the hood covered his face, I never really cared what he looked like underneath, because all the guards were the same to me—monsters. I never imagined that was his appearance, with masculine angles to his face, a hard jawline, eyes full of authority, and a voice that could make the walls shake with its potency.

"Do you think he'll help you escape?"

"I don't know... I feel like he would have offered that already."

"True."

"Honestly, I really don't know him at all. I don't know his purpose here. I don't know who he is outside this camp. I don't know why he's kinder than the rest of them. I don't know how far his generosity goes..."

"Ask him when he gets back."

"Yeah, I will."

MY GUARD WAS DESPICABLE.

He treated me like a dog.

When dinner arrived that night, the woman didn't even come inside. The guard was the one with the tray. He came toward me, held it out to me, and started to whistle like I was a dog that needed to beg for my food.

"Speak." He whistled again. "Speak, girl."

Did he do this to all the girls or just me? If he tortured every single one, dinner delivery would take forever, but since he was stuck here, he probably had nothing else to do with his time. And maybe he remembered punching me in the face, and he'd hated me ever since.

He started to click his tongue. "You want a treat? Roll over."

I just stared at him, unable to believe this bullshit.

His voice deepened. "Bitch, I said roll over."

I'd rather starve than obey. "Fuck off."

"What'd you just say to me?"

I should hold my tongue because he wanted me to fight back. He wanted any excuse to punish me more. It was exactly what he wanted.

He came closer until the tray was right under my face. He shook it, making the roll vibrate then fall onto the floor. "You think you can talk to me like that?" He pulled the tray away then sat beside me. He pulled off his gloves.

I started to breathe harder, feeling his heat beside me, feeling the way he made the mattress shift from his weight. The adrenaline mixed with the anxiety and made a brand-new cocktail.

He ate with his bare hands, shoveling the food into his mouth, making a mess everywhere, looking me right in the face to watch my reaction.

I stared straight ahead and did my best to ignore him.

He got stains all over his clothes, chewed loudly and obnoxiously, his lips smacking, adding a loud burp just to disgust me. "Pretty fucking good." He finished the tray until it was clean. "Maybe if you listen, you'll get some next time." He rose from the bed, threw the tray on the floor, and then walked out.

My eyes shifted to the roll that sat on the floor, the only morsel I would get that evening. I was too stubborn to eat it, would rather lose sleep from the hunger than break my strength.

But then my eyes shifted to the book on my nightstand.

I had to bide my time, hold my patience, and then my chance would come...and I would get retribution.

But in order for that to happen, I had to stay strong. I had to eat. I had to stay calm. My eyes needed to remain focused on the prize that was far in the distance, the dream that would become a reality...someday.

I picked up the roll and ate it.

ANOTHER RED SNOW.

I didn't look, would never look.

But it was impossible to tune out the sounds, to listen to an innocent woman scream as she was dragged to the noose. Then the gag after she dropped. The knife to the stomach. The guttural sounds. And then the silence of death.

You couldn't block that out.

You couldn't keep it from your nightmares.

You couldn't protect your spirit...as it faded more and more every time.

Bethany said it got easier as time went on.

No—it got worse.

THE GUARD really got off on torturing me.

He continued to treat me like a dog, making me work for my dinner, like busting my ass all day wasn't enough to garner a meal.

He pulled the chair from the wall and placed it in front of me, where he took a seat.

Fuck. This. Shit.

He held up the tray. "Wow, this looks good...pot roast, carrots, sourdough bread...some strawberries..." He took a loud sniff before he lowered it again. "Just as good as the dinner we get."

The only reason I didn't fall apart was because this torture was temporary. Magnus would return eventually, and this nightmare would end. I would get my meals like usual, even get some nice company—and maybe if I could convince him, my freedom. I hated all the guards when I arrived here, including Magnus, but now he was my ally, just like Bethany was. He would return...and rescue me from this hell.

I kept my eyes on his dark hood, seeing his thick black beard stick out a bit. I knew what his face looked like now, after spotting him inside the largest cabin. At least I didn't have to look him in the eye now, just focus on the shadow over his face.

"No dinner every night... You must be hungry."

"Not particularly." Having to sit there in his presence chased away my appetite.

"Why don't I believe you?" A deep chuckle came from his throat because he was enjoying this way too much. He grabbed the fork and stirred the contents on the plate, moving the beef through the gravy.

My stomach growled.

I heard it.

He heard it.

I didn't need to see his smile to know it was there.

"I'll make a deal with you." He moved the tray forward and placed it in my lap.

I wasn't stupid enough to touch it.

"You can have all of that...if you do something for me."

I already knew where this was going.

"Eat my cock...and then you can eat this."

My goal was to stay strong, and in order to do that, I needed nutrition. I had definitely had a hard time working that afternoon because my body was at such a deficit. But there was no motivation that could make me agree to that.

I grabbed the tray.

He inhaled a breath, like he knew he was getting what he wanted.

I raised the tray higher then slowly tilted it, letting everything roll off the plate and onto the floor between us, my eyes on his hood the entire time, listening to the food splatter all over the floor in front of my bed. I turned the tray completely upside down before I released it and let it fall to the floor.

He was still.

There was a chance he would hold me down and force himself on me, but I took the gamble anyway.

He stayed in the chair for a full minute.

Bethany had never mentioned the girls getting raped by the guards, but there was no way it didn't happen, not when they weren't unafraid to beat us, starve us, enslave us. I was prepared to fight him, dig my nails into his eyes and make him blind.

He rose to his feet.

I flinched slightly, anticipating him charging into me and holding me down.

But he stood over me and kicked the chair back. "Looks like you aren't getting lunch tomorrow either."

Fine with me.

He walked out and slammed the door behind him.

I finally let the air out of my lungs, let myself breathe normally, relaxed now that the danger had passed.

The food was still all over the floor.

I didn't hesitate to eat what I could salvage.

———

My GUARD MADE good on his threat.

Everyone was given a tray—except me.

Bad behavior was punished with less food, but not no food entirely.

Bethany spoke when the coast was clear. "What happened?"

"My guard said he would give me dinner if I sucked his cock. You know what my answer was."

"I've never seen anyone get no lunch..."

"What can I say? I'm a trendsetter."

"Why does he hate you so much?"

"No idea."

Bethany put a piece of bread in her hand, like she was attempting to share her food.

"Don't," I whispered. "I'm sure he's waiting for you to do that. I'm fine, really."

Bethany put the bread in her mouth instead.

In truth, I was starving, and knowing I wouldn't get dinner tonight either made my stomach cramp. I'd salvaged the meat and potatoes from the floorboards, but now that I wasn't getting enough calories on a regular basis, it really affected my body's performance. It was harder to carry the boxes, and there were times I was so fatigued, I wasn't sure if I could pick them up at all.

It was exactly what he wanted.

So I would be the next victim of the Red Snow.

10

FRIENDS IN LOW PLACES

The guard never came.

There was no dinner...but there was no torture either.

I considered myself lucky, even though I was so hungry I actually started to feel sick. My muscles were tightening and turning stiff because I didn't have the electrolytes for healthy contraction.

I couldn't even sleep because I was so hungry.

It was a long night. I just had to tell myself that Magnus would return and make sure I had plenty to eat.

When the guard woke me up the next morning, he was still furious. "Bet some cock doesn't sound so bad now, does it?" He grabbed my boots and threw them right at my face.

I winced when the bottom of the boot hit me right in the cheek.

"Let's go."

I got my boots and jacket on then followed him to the clearing, but just the walk was difficult. I was out of breath, shaky, so weak... I didn't know how I would get through the day. When we made it to the clearing, he nodded to the table. "Get to it."

Bethany was already preparing the next box.

I went to the table and struggled just to slide it toward me. I opened the box and then slid it into my arms. But I lost my balance, and it almost toppled over, nearly spilling the cocaine everywhere.

Bethany steadied it before it could spill.

"Don't help her!" he yelled from the other side of the clearing, watching me like an experiment that was about to fail.

I returned the box to the table and breathed hard.

Bethany pretended to be working on her box even though it was ready to go. "What did he do to you?"

"I haven't eaten in days..." I took a moment to focus my brain, to tell myself that I could do this, that I had to do this. This was exactly what he wanted, to make me so weak that I would be the next victim on that noose...unless I gave him what he wanted.

"Fuck."

I used my entire body to pick up the box, swaying from the weight, and turned around and slowly made the journey to the table.

The other girls obviously had been watching, so when I came closer, the girl closest to me discreetly helped me get it onto the table, like they'd noticed I didn't get lunch yesterday and the guard was purposely starving me.

"Thank you," I whispered under my breath.

When I turned around, my gaze locked on Melanie.

She looked heartbroken, her eyes wet from the tears that quickly evaporated.

I promised her we would get out of here, so I had to keep going.

I had to.

When lunchtime came around, I didn't get a tray.

Again.

I watched Bethany eat.

She didn't try to slip me food, because my guard was waiting for the first opportunity to bring someone else down with me—and make me feel even worse. He even came over and stood at the edge of the table, just hovering over us, like he wanted to make sure Bethany didn't successfully give me anything.

Because he wanted me to break.

I probably wasn't the first woman he'd done this to.

He didn't get off on rape. He got off on submission.

If I didn't want to be the next victim, I'd have to suck his dick.

I literally had to suck his dick to save my life.

I wanted to tell myself that I could keep going, that I didn't need any food, but if I didn't get lunch or dinner...I would pass out.

We got back to work, and I was growing weaker by the second. I wasn't sure how I made it to the end of the day. Time passed so slowly. Every time it felt like three hours had gone by, it'd only been three minutes.

The girls rose from the tables and prepared to return to the cabins.

Bethany walked up to me, a few of the girls at our table coming close and standing nearby. Then Bethany emptied her pockets and stuffed food into my pockets, moving as quickly as she could without dropping anything.

I wanted to cry.

It all happened within ten seconds.

And then the girls walked away...like nothing happened.

———

IN THE PRIVACY of my cabin, I ate everything they'd given me.

It was way more food than the contents of a single meal, which meant that several women had given up parts of their meal and handed it over to Bethany to donate to me. There were several pieces of chicken, slices of bread, even a protein bar, grapes, and an entire apple.

Within minutes of finishing everything, I felt better.

I felt alive again.

If I didn't want the guard to realize what was happening, I had to pretend to be weak, but not so weak that I couldn't do my job. I couldn't be the strongest one in the herd, but not the weakest either.

I felt a bit guilty because by not being the weakest one, that meant someone else was, and that meant I would live...and they would die.

But I pushed the thought away. I had to survive.

I had to survive...for my sister.

At dinnertime, the guard entered my cabin with a tray of food. He obviously thought tonight would be the night I would cave. If Bethany hadn't given me the food, he would have been right.

He pulled up the chair again.

I lay on the bed and didn't get up, pretending to be too weak to sit up.

He set the tray on the edge of the bed. He sat there in silence, as if he expected me to sit upright and inhale the food. He'd counted his eggs before they hatched.

I turned over and faced the other wall.

He was still.

I didn't want him to figure out that someone was slipping me food, so I had to be weak instead of defiant, too weak to give him a smartass comment.

He rose to his feet, and then a loud crash sounded.

Because he threw the tray against the wall.

I jolted slightly but tried not to react.

He stormed out and left.

His anger was a blessing, because he probably regretted throwing that tray at the wall so there would be food on the floor, but he had too much pride to pick it up. He left it behind.

And bought me some time.

WHEN I GOT to work the next day, I felt strong again, because of all the calories I'd been able to ingest. I didn't hesitate to pick up all the food off the floor and eat it, because Bethany's food made me feel better, but my hunger hadn't been completely satisfied. Though, I still pretended to be tired.

Bethany stood at the table, working on her first box.

I stood beside her, doing my best not to get emotional, to give our game away. Bethany had shown me kindness in a world where kindness didn't exist. She made me want to live during the times when I thought living was pointless torture. "Thank you." I ripped off the tape on the box and folded down the sides.

"We got you, girl." She lifted the box and carried it away.

I stalled for a bit, masking the emotion on my face, and then turned around and got to work.

———

THE GUARD STOOD over us to make sure I didn't take Bethany's food.

He was paying attention to the obvious, when he should be paying attention to the less obvious. I could tell he wasn't the smartest guy in the world. He was probably the dullest tool in this shed.

There was a sudden change in energy all around us, like something was happening, something was coming.

I lifted my gaze to look at the other side of the clearing because all the guards faced that way, as if they expected something too. The girls knew better than to turn around in their seats to get a look, but the ones facing that direction stopped eating.

A man emerged into the clearing, flanked by two guards.

I immediately knew he was the boss.

Not because of his black bomber jacket with gray fur down the front. Not because he was in black jeans and boots. Not because he was accompanied by two guards who seemed to act as his personal entourage.

It was because he showed his face.

With short brown hair, dark eyes, and a thick shadow on his jawline, his face was completely visible to every single person there. His lips were pressed into a straight line, and his eyes seemed innately hostile even though he didn't speak a word. He stopped and looked at the body hanging from the noose, the snow beneath her a faint pink because the blood had dripped onto the ground, like a snow cone in summer. He shifted his gaze to us, watched us with those angry eyes, his gaze moving around the entire area like he wanted to look at every single one of us, commit our faces to memory, to survey his kingdom.

My blood immediately boiled.

This was the guy. This was the reason I was here.

Because of him.

The guards didn't speak to him.

The boss moved farther past the tables, examining our trays like he was curious about our lunch. His eyes scanned a few more times before he turned back the way he came, getting a different angle of the clearing.

He stared right at my sister.

I knew that was exactly what he was staring at because of her reaction.

She held his gaze for a moment, terrified, and then dropped her eyes, breathing hard.

He continued his stare, on the exact same spot, like he didn't want to look away.

I'd seen men stare at my sister enough times to read that look.

No.

He eventually turned away and crossed the clearing, escorted by his men.

He stepped into one of the cabins, the one Magnus usually walked into.

Once he was gone, the silence in the clearing remained, like we didn't know what to do with ourselves after what we'd seen. Then the girls started to eat again, the sound of forks scratching against trays, of chewing mouths, filling the area once more.

But the bumps were on my arms underneath my coat —and not because of the cold.

Because I was afraid...truly afraid.

BETHANY CONTINUED to slip food into my pockets when no one was looking. She gave me as much as could possibly fit, making my pockets so bulky it was a blessing that my jacket was too big for my body and successfully concealed it.

I wasn't getting lunch or dinner, so without it, I wouldn't survive.

But I worried how long this could go on.

Regardless of how stupid the guard was, he would eventually figure out that I was somehow getting food. There was no amount of willpower that would make me last over a week without food and continue to get my job done.

I just hoped he wouldn't figure it out before Magnus came back.

More days passed, and I knew I was on borrowed time. At any moment, the guard would figure it out. I did my best to seem as weak as possible without collapsing, but I suspected he'd done this before, and the women always caved when they reached their breaking point.

"Has he fed you yet?" Bethany discreetly asked the question at the table since we couldn't talk over lunch anymore, not with the guard standing right over us, watching us like a hawk.

"No."

She released a quiet sigh. "When do you think Magnus is coming back?"

"He didn't say, just that it would be a couple weeks."

"We're almost at two weeks, and this guard is gonna figure it out soon."

"I know... You should stop giving me food."

She kept working with her box. "You'll starve."

"Magnus will be back any day, and if I don't stop eating, he's gonna figure it out...and know it's you."

She released another sigh. "Not to make matters worse, but...Cindy told me that Melanie was removed from their cabin."

"What?" I couldn't stop myself from turning my head to look at her full on.

"Don't look at me," she hissed.

I forced myself to face forward again, but my hands shook as they gripped the box. "Where did they put her?"

"No idea. Just thought you should know."

"Did she do anything?"

"The girl's as quiet as a mouse."

The image of the boss came into my head, remembering the way he looked at her, and then I felt like I'd been punched in the gut.

I knew what happened.

I knew...and I had to do everything I could not to start sobbing then and there.

11

IF YOU MUST DIE, DIE BRAVELY

I leaned against the wall as I sat on my bed, lost in the dangerous thoughts clouding my mind. It was impossible to know the exact hour, not after my dinners stopped coming, when all I had was the light under my door to gauge the time.

My predicament was nothing compared to my sister's.

I knew exactly what had happened to her.

I tried to tell myself that there was another explanation, that she was rewarded for her good behavior with a nicer cabin, more space, more privacy...

But I didn't believe the lies I told myself.

She was beautiful. It'd been a blessing I'd always cursed. I used to be jealous of her years ago, the way she attracted every guy in her vicinity, including the guys I wanted for myself. The men I wanted to notice me forgot about me the second they met her. It didn't matter if we had more in common, beauty was always king, and I was second best.

But now I wasn't jealous at all.

I was ordinary in comparison, and that made me safer.

But she didn't deserve this.

She didn't deserve to be forced just because her beauty was intoxicating. She didn't deserve whatever was happening to her...night after night.

Tears welled in my eyes and fell down my cheeks.

I was too late. I should have rescued us sooner. I should have done something...

My bedroom door flew open, and the guard came bursting in. "Where is it?"

I jolted upright, jarred by the way he charged into my bedroom like an angry bull.

"Get your ass up!" He grabbed me by the arm and yanked me off, sending me to the floor. Then he picked up my mattress and looked underneath it. When he didn't find anything, he started to look for holes in the mattress. "Where the fuck is it?"

He knew.

When he didn't find anything, he moved to my night-stand, yanking out drawers only to discover nothing. He pushed the nightstand aside and found nothing behind it. He even picked up my book and flipped through the pages as if crumbs would fall out. Then he threw it on the floor before turning to me. "I know you're getting food, bitch. And once I figure out how, I'll kill everyone who helped you." He left my cabin a mess then stormed out as harshly as he barged in.

I sat up and looked at my destroyed room, the place that had become a substitute for home.

Bethany couldn't help me anymore.

I'd starve from now on.

And hope that Magnus came back in time.

———

THE DAYS PASSED, and I grew weaker.

Even with the food Bethany had given me before, I still wasn't eating enough.

So, I declined quickly.

I struggled to carry the boxes, struggled to even be cognitively aware of anything. My body shut down first and then my mind. I stopped being hungry after day three, because my body seemed to accept my demise.

I stopped craving food, stopped thinking about food altogether because it only made my situation more unbearable. If I did feel an appetite, I thought about dog shit. Otherwise, I would fantasize about the lunches Bethany ate in front of me.

When I glanced across the clearing to look at my sister, she never met my gaze. Her eyes were always down, like she wanted to be invisible. It seemed like she was purposely not looking at me...because she couldn't.

Because she wouldn't be able to hide her pain.

The night before the Red Snow, I lay in bed and looked at the ceiling, hoping that Magnus would walk in and bring me dinner, return my life back to the way it used to be. I actually missed those days, appreciated how good he had been to me.

But he never came.

No one came.

THE NEXT DAY was my fifth day without food.

And I was so weak.

Every time I had a box to move, I had to take a lot of deep breaths before I lifted it, and when I made my way down the table, I could only take one step at a time, because my legs shook from the exertion.

I groaned as I forced myself to take another step...and then another.

But then I tripped and spilled the contents everywhere.

No.

Girls immediately got up from their seats and quickly helped me, like that would draw less attention to my blunder.

"Get up!" The guard stepped forward, yelled at the top of his lungs, and made the girls sprint away like mice returning to their holes.

I was still on the ground, trying to scoop the coke back into the box even though most of it had been lost. It was mixed with snow, the powder turning into sludge.

His footsteps crunched against the snow as he came closer, taking his time like he relished every single moment. He kneeled so he could be level with me. "You know how much this costs?"

I already knew my fate before it happened.

I knew I was the name at the top of the list.

I'd waited too long for Magnus to come back...and I should have caved.

He grabbed the box and pulled it away from me. "This is ten million dollars...that you just spilled all over the fucking ground."

I was still, my eyes on the ground, the snow that made my knees frigid through my pants.

"Look at me."

There was no hope for me at this point. I should have just gotten on my knees and sucked him off. Now I couldn't save my sister. I couldn't save myself. I let my self-respect jeopardize my survival. I waited for a man to come to my rescue when I'd already learned not to expect shit from a man.

He lowered his voice so only I could hear. "Was it worth it?"

I kept my gaze down.

"Was a blow job worth your life?" He rose to his feet, holding the remaining coke inside the cardboard box. Then he turned it over and poured it all over me, just the way I'd dumped food onto the floor in my cabin. He raised his voice again. "The entire batch is ruined —and you'll pay for that."

IT WAS impossible to get through the rest of the day.

I was literally waiting for death.

My fate was sealed when lunch was delivered.

The guard didn't stand over us, because it didn't matter.

At the end of the day, that noose would go around my neck, they would kick out the crate from underneath my feet, and then I would be stabbed in the stomach, my guts spilling onto the ground as I dangled and gasped for air.

That was how I was going to die—like that.

I was a good person who always took care of everyone else. I did everything right, always lived a life of honesty and integrity, always did the right thing even when no one was looking. But that virtue didn't change my fate, didn't protect me from this cruel end. I didn't even save my sister, didn't sacrifice my life for someone else, so my death really was a complete waste.

Just as my life had been.

Bethany kept lifting her gaze to look at me, the pain in her eyes showing her thoughts, showing the turmoil she felt at my expense. She knew exactly what I knew. She knew my fate before they even announced it.

She would probably be the last person I ever spoke to. "Thanks for helping me."

Her eyes fell in a deeper look of sadness.

"Tell Melanie..." There was a catch in my throat, and it was hard to continue, not when my eyes were getting wet with tears, not because of my impending death, but because of how the event would torment her forever. "Tell her not to give up...and I love her."

She nodded. "I'll make sure she knows."

It was such a violent way to die.

I rehearsed it in my head over and over, how it would hurt, the rope against my throat and the knife in my belly. The only comfort I had was knowing how quickly it would end. The sounds stopped within thirty seconds.

I just had to get through those thirty seconds.

And then it would be over.

My body would hang there until they cut me down and added me to the pile of other corpses, and no one would discover my bones for a long time. There would never be a grave. I would never have children to honor my memory until they were gone. My death would be like my life...like it never really mattered.

But if those were the last moments of my life, I would go with my head high, wouldn't give them the satisfaction of my tears, of my pleas. I wouldn't make a sound while that knife plunged into my intestines.

They could take my body...but never my mind.

Darkness descended, and then the torches were lit.

The executioner stepped into the clearing, the metal plate over the bottom half of his face. Every single week, he took his time in selecting the victim, but I knew it was all just for show. They just wanted to scare the shit out of everyone before they got to the main attraction.

He started to do the same, walking down every aisle.

There was no doubt that I was the sacrificial lamb this week, and I decided to take the situation into my own hands. I decided to show some power, to be brave, to stand straight and tall instead of being dragged from my seat.

I chose to be fearless.

Silently interrupting him, I rose to my feet.

All the stares initially had been on him, but the women started to look at me. Row by row, they turned my way, no longer paying attention to him...but me.

I stepped out of the bench and moved to the edge of the table, standing tall, not shaking, not giving in to the fear.

Melanie started to sob. "No!"

The girls at her sides covered her mouth and silenced her.

The executioner stopped and stared at me.

I stared back. My body gave me the last thrust of adrenaline I would ever have. It gave me all the courage it could produce, because it knew this was the last time I would ever need it. My body did everything it could to make this easier, to let me die with as much honor as possible.

He remained still as he looked at me, his eyes filled with ferocity, as if my actions really pissed him off.

Good. "I'm the one you want, so cut the shit."

All the girls turned to look at him, to witness his reaction.

His eyes narrowed at my audacity.

I started to move to the noose on the other end.

Bethany's hand reached out for mine and gave it a squeeze. Tears burned in her eyes before they fell down her cheeks. "I'll see you on the other side."

I squeezed her back before I moved forward, wearing a mask of stoicism, staring at my killer like he should be afraid of me instead of the other way around.

He watched me walk toward the noose, like he'd never seen anything like this as long as he'd been here.

The guards didn't say anything either.

Then he moved toward me, his cloak billowing behind him, his monstrous eyes promising an even more painful death than usual.

I took it one step further and stood on the crate that they would kick from underneath me. My hands moved to my back, and I stared at the executioner as he walked toward me. "I know where I'm going, and we all know where you're going when it's your time, which means our paths won't cross again." I pulled the saliva from my throat then spat down at him, hitting him right on the metal plate.

The spit dripped down until it fell to the earth.

He grabbed a piece of rope and moved behind me, securing my wrists in place, tying the rope unnecessarily tight just to hurt me.

I didn't make a sound.

My heart rate was slow...for the first time since I got here.

Then he came back around and put the noose over my neck.

Melanie cried out again, and her friends silenced her the best they could.

I stared straight ahead, putting on a brave front, hoping to inspire these women into defiance.

Then he kicked the crate.

My body fell, and the noose constricted around my throat. My air supply was taken from me, and I swung slightly left and right. But my body hung limply, and I didn't try to resist, even though it was the most unnatural thing to do.

Not to fight.

At some point, my lungs would heave and I would automatically struggle, but I'd probably be dead from his knife before then.

He unsheathed his knife from his pocket.

I could feel my face already turning blue.

I wanted it to end already.

I wanted the pain to start so it could end.

My eyes became blurry, and I could make out his withdrawn arm as he prepared to stab me.

Melanie wailed.

Then I heard a voice I thought I'd never hear again.

"Stop!"

The executioner lowered the knife and turned to Magnus.

"What the fuck are you doing?" His voice was loud and scathing, full of a rage so fierce that it couldn't be subdued. I could feel the energy of his power, feel the way the guards responded to his outburst. "She's our best worker. Why are you hanging the strongest woman on the line?"

"Because she's a fucking cunt," my current guard said. "That's why."

This rescue was about to be pointless because I was slipping out of consciousness.

Then my feet touched the crate...and I could breathe.

I gasped for air, like I'd died and come back to life, like I'd crashed and the doctors put those paddles against my chest and shocked me until I returned.

"She's weak," my guard continued. "She dropped a whole box of cocaine. She's the slowest one on the line—"

"Because you starved her." Magnus pulled out a knife then cut at the rope.

I fell forward, landing on the snow and earth. I coughed hard as I collapsed on the ground. A knife cut the ropes from around my wrists. I reached for my already swollen neck and continued to heave, yanking that air into my lungs so my heart rate would slow once the oxygen had been replenished in my blood.

"You starved her like you've done to the others." He sheathed his knife but didn't lean down to comfort me. He stood next to me, addressing the guard who now got in his face. "She's my prisoner, and I know that she busts her ass every goddamn day. You poisoned her like you did to the others. We've all looked away up until this point, but no more. I won't let one of the strongest lifters on the line die just because you can't get a woman to suck your dick."

The coughs subsided, and I lay there, just breathing, feeling the flames from one of the nearby torches.

The guard stared down Magnus before he backed off. "Then we'll pick someone else—"

"There's no Red Snow this week." Magnus came over to me, and like last time I fell in the snow, he extended his gloved hand. "They've seen it enough times. They know how it goes. They've already seen the show."

I stared at his hand for a few seconds before I placed my palm in his.

He squeezed it before he pulled me up, squeezed me the way Bethany squeezed me, like he wanted me to know he was there...that he was my friend.

12

HERO TO ONE, VILLAIN TO ALL

WHEN I MADE IT BACK TO THE CABIN, I immediately collapsed on the bed. I was already so weak to begin with since I hadn't eaten in five days, but after the adrenaline rushed through me during that critical moment, I was even more exhausted. My throat ached like it'd been burned, and I still needed to cough here and there. "Thank you…" I'd thought my life was over. I'd thought my sister would have to listen to the sound of the knife stabbing into my body over and over. But at the last possible second, he returned.

Magnus walked out.

"Wait, where are you—"

The door shut and locked.

I stared at it, so disappointed that I didn't know what to do with myself. I wasn't sure what I expected, but at least a few words, a conversation...something. He saved my life, and then he just disappeared.

I lay on the bed and stared at the spine of my book.

It was as if it were talking to me, and not from the words on the page.

I grabbed it and pulled it to my chest, holding it like a stuffed animal, gripping it like a lifeline. Tears welled a moment later, a catharsis that came from nowhere. Every time I complained that my food wasn't right at a restaurant, every time I groaned when I had to walk to work in the rain, every time I was annoyed when my date showed up late...all of it felt so fucking stupid.

I never should have taken anything for granted.

Never.

Fifteen minutes later, the door opened again.

I immediately sat up and abruptly wiped my eyes with the back of my jacket, cleaning myself up, embarrassed that someone would witness a moment of weakness.

The woman who ordinarily delivered dinner came in even though it was earlier than usual. She brought a tray that was overstuffed with food, everything piled high on the plate and toppling over. There were two bottles of water there too.

The second I looked at it, my stomach rumbled.

It was the first time the woman actually looked at me. She was several decades older, as if she could be my mother, and her eyes softened like she pitied me, like she wanted to place her palm against my cheek and tell me everything would be alright. But a look was enough to convey that kindness.

She walked away.

"Thank you." I pulled the tray into my lap and ate at the edge of the bed, almost too tired to even eat.

Then Magnus entered, wearing the same jacket and cloak like the other guards. But this time, he lowered his hood once the door was shut behind him, revealing his face because I already knew exactly what he looked like.

I stopped eating.

He carried a mug of hot cocoa to my nightstand. Then he dug into his pockets and pulled out a tube of medicine to apply to my neck, a couple pain pills, and a medical ice pack. His head turned slightly, and he glanced at the book lying on the bed. "You're reading it."

"I've already read it. But I'm reading it again..." It was my bible, my therapy, my hope.

"Eat." He didn't look right at me, never giving me direct eye contact even though his hood was down. His brown hair was a little longer this time than it was weeks ago. His jaw was covered with a shadow because he'd ignored the shave for a few days. There were thick veins up his neck, like his skin was so tight that the rivers popped out. He moved to the chair against the wall near the door and took a seat.

His presence gave me more comfort than the food in my lap, but I was starving and weak, so I grabbed the fork and continued to eat.

He leaned back into the wall, his knees apart, his eyes looking at nothing in particular. He had masculine angles to his face, noticeable cheekbones, and his brown eyes conveyed a constant sense of indifference. He'd shouted in that clearing just minutes ago, but now he didn't seem angry.

I continued to eat, my eyes down most of the time, though I couldn't help but to sneak a glance at him from time to time.

He was still, as if he were encumbered by his thoughts. He didn't say anything to me, but he lingered like he might.

I liked having him there. After being terrorized by that asshole for two weeks, I didn't want Magnus to leave my cabin. He was the only power that I had, the only weapon in my arsenal. "Did you just get here...?"

He nodded.

If he'd arrived just thirty seconds later, he would have seen my dead body hanging from that noose, my guts spilled into the snow.

"Where were you?"

"Paris."

I steadied my fork and looked at him. "That's where I live. Well, where I *lived*..."

He kept his gaze on the wall. Despite his visual indifference, he remained.

"What were you doing there?"

"Work."

"You have two jobs?" I asked in surprise.

"It's the same job, just in a different place."

There was no way there was a labor camp in Paris, so he must do other things there. "Do you distribute the coke?"

He shifted his gaze to me, eyes cold. "Do you really care?"

I stilled at the look then turned back to my food. "I just... I guess I don't. I just haven't really talked to anyone for the last few weeks. It's been really hard... with you gone."

"And of course, the second I leave, you get yourself in the noose."

My head snapped in his direction. "I did nothing. Your..." I couldn't find the right word to describe that asshole. "*Colleague* decided to torture me the second you were gone. He treated me like a dog, made me beg for my food, told me I had to suck his dick or I would starve. I did nothing. I carry no blame."

He shifted his gaze away.

"He targeted me, for whatever reason."

"Because you're difficult to break." He shifted back to me. "So, it's fun to try."

That explanation disgusted me.

He removed the gloves from his hands and stuffed them into his pocket. Then his chin tilted down slightly, his eyes on the floor.

"Magnus?"

He wouldn't meet my look.

"Don't leave me again..."

He inhaled a breath before he lifted his chin and looked at me. The expression in his eyes was different this time, absorbent, as if he took time to digest the request.

"Don't leave me with anyone else but you." I didn't realize how much better my life was with Magnus. And just how I took things for granted back in Paris, I did the same with him. This man wouldn't hurt me. He wouldn't force me. He even protected me...

"I'm not a saint—trust me on that."

"But you're not evil either—trust me on that." I'd seen evil with that guard. I'd seen evil with the executioner. I'd seen evil all over this place. But with

Magnus...not really. He was guilty due to the fact that he worked here, but he didn't get off on torture.

He stared at me again, his brown eyes warm like coffee that I hadn't had in weeks. There were tendrils of vapor in his eyes, like the steam that rose from the surface of a freshly brewed cup of coffee on a cold morning.

I finished the mound of food on my plate, the most I'd eaten in any sitting, and set it to the side for him to take away when he left. I grabbed the mug of cocoa instead and brought it to my lips, feeling the warmth return to all my veins. "Help me."

He stared me down without blinking. "I already did."

"I know, and I'm grateful, but...please."

He knew exactly what I was asking for. He regarded me stoically, like my request had no effect on his heart. "I can't."

"Yes, you can—"

"I said, I can't." His voice turned sterner, hard like steel.

My lungs sucked in more air on their own, the devastation painful as if that knife really had pierced my belly. "I deserve more, and you know it."

"Doesn't matter what you deserve. A lot of people deserve a lot of things. It doesn't mean they're entitled to have them."

He wasn't a white knight in shining armor. He wasn't a hero. He just wasn't a villain. I didn't understand his motivation for things, why he helped me in so many ways, but he wouldn't help me in the way I needed most. "Please."

"I've done a lot for you. The only thing I should be hearing is your gratitude."

"And I am grateful—"

He abruptly got to his feet and headed to the door.

"Wait. Please."

He sighed loudly, like he hated himself for turning back to me. "I've got to deal with the aftermath of all this, while you sit here and sleep soundly tonight. I've got to justify my actions and somehow make it convincing, because a lot of women have been hung before you, women I've guarded, and I didn't do a damn thing." His brown eyes burned into mine, like the brown trees of a forest on fire.

My palms squeezed the mug between my hands, the cocoa still warm but the marshmallows dissolved. "Why? Why did you help me?"

He stared me down, and it was obvious I wouldn't get an answer.

"I'm going to get out of here whether you help me or not. But if you help me, I'm far more likely—"

"You won't make it." He dropped his hand from the knob and faced me. "The trip by wagon to get here is seven hours—and that's if you know the way. You need to get it through your fucking head that there is no escape from this place—"

"I heard a bell." I got to my feet and faced him, the mug still in my hands. "A church bell. I heard it on the wind... I know I did."

He was still, his look cold.

"Tell me where it came from—"

"The wind likes to play tricks, especially in a place like this. Don't put all your faith in a sound you may or may not have heard—"

"I heard it."

He clenched his jaw tightly, like he was annoyed with this conversation.

"If you tell me the way, draw me a sketch—"

"They will hunt you down so goddamn fast, especially down the road they've trekked for years. Even on horseback, at a full sprint, you won't make it. You can leave in the middle of the night, and it still wouldn't make a difference. Do you understand what I'm saying? There's nothing I can do for you."

"You can tell me another way. Somewhere through the wilderness where it'll be hard to find me—"

"You need to stop." He raised his hand and regarded me coldly. Then he dropped his hand and pulled on his black gloves like he was about to depart. "There is no escape from this place. None." He pulled up the hood to his cloak and grabbed the doorknob.

"If you won't help me, please help my sister."

He didn't open the door, but he didn't turn back to me either.

"This man came to the camp. I think he's the boss, because he doesn't wear your uniform and he doesn't hide his face..."

He slowly turned back to me, but he didn't pull down the hood again.

"They moved my sister out of her cabin. I think he took her. I think he's..." I couldn't finish the sentence. "If you won't help me escape, then help me get her out of there. Help me get her away from him."

He was quiet for a long time, as if he was thinking about my request, or thinking about something else entirely. Then he released a quiet breath. "I'm sorry about your sister, but there's nothing I can do about that either."

My eyes started to water in devastation. "I know you're high up in the hierarchy because of the way the guards respond to you—"

"You just confirmed that someone else is the boss. I'm not the boss. What do you expect me to do?"

"I...I don't know." I didn't know how he could intervene, get that man to be less interested in my sister and leave her alone. "You could help us both escape. I know you said you wouldn't, but that's my only chance. I'm going to try whether you help me or not. So, if you aren't going to tell me, then tell me where her cabin is."

He must have gotten fed up with the conversation because he opened the door to leave. "I'll say this once more. If you try to run, you won't make it. When that happens, they'll hang you. And when that happens...you'll be on your own."

13

SILENCE OF THE BELLS

MAGNUS COLLECTED ME THE NEXT MORNING and escorted me to my post, but he didn't say a word to me.

It was like he was angry at me.

I should be grateful I had someone to look after me, but I couldn't stop myself from wanting more, from begging him to get me out of this outdoor cage.

Once I was at the table with the boxes, he walked off and entered the cabin the boss had entered days ago. My old guard was there on the other side of the clearing, his gaze clearly on me even though the hood of his cloak covered his face.

I ignored him and turned to the table. I didn't feel helpless anymore, not when I had Magnus to look out for me. He'd stopped both the executioner and the guard, so I had someone powerful on my side.

Bethany spoke the instant I was beside her. "Girl, you okay?"

"Yeah, I'm good."

"I can't believe Magnus saved you like that..."

"I know."

"Are you sleeping with him?" She'd already asked the question, but she asked it again because she clearly didn't believe me.

"No."

"Then why is he helping you?" she demanded. "What incentive does he have?"

"I've asked him the same question many times—he never answers."

The guard yelled across the clearing. "What's taking so long?"

I quickly turned and carried the first box to the table, feeling much better than I had yesterday after all that food I'd scarfed down. I set it down then returned to the table to prepare the next one.

Bethany met me at the same time.

"I need your help with something."

"What?" she whispered.

"I need to figure out where my sister's cabin is. Do you know?"

"No idea. I could ask Cindy, but she's not going to know either."

I glanced over my shoulder to look at where my sister sat. Cindy was nowhere nearby, seated much farther down the line. I would ask Beth to ask Cindy to ask Melanie during the workday, but that didn't seem possible either.

"Are you lying to me?"

I stilled at the question and turned slightly toward her. "What?"

"Are you lying to me?" she repeated. "Because a guard wouldn't stop a Red Snow like that unless there was something going on. There's nothing to be embarrassed about. If I could have a guard to watch my back, I'd do it too."

I opened the next box and got it ready. "I'm really not lying."

"Then he must want to sleep with you."

"He hasn't asked. He hasn't tried."

"What will you do if he does?" she whispered.

"I...I don't know." I didn't want to give in to any man's demand, but Magnus was powerful, and if he wanted something from me, I wasn't sure how I could turn him down. But he didn't seem like someone who would only do nice things in exchange for sex, because he'd had weeks to make the demand and he hadn't.

"What does he look like?"

"He's got brown hair and brown eyes. Looks like he could be part French and part Italian."

"Is he attractive?"

I'd never really considered it because attractiveness was out of context here. How could there be any form of desire when every single day was horrific? "He's not bad to look at."

An uneventful week passed.

Magnus escorted the woman to bring me dinner at night, and while he usually brought me hot cocoa and some other surprise, he never stuck around to talk. For a man willing to risk his neck to help me, it didn't seem as though he liked me very much.

Or maybe he knew if he stuck around, I would just pester him to help me.

Magnus came to collect me one morning, and instead of escorting me to the clearing, he took me away from the camp.

I already knew where we were going. "Is there a drop today?"

He walked ahead of me, moving effortlessly through the short mounds of snow. "Sounds like you already know the answer." He escorted me to where the girls were waiting with the men and the wagons. Once he had me in sight of the guards, he turned away. "Don't do anything stupid." Then he walked back.

Beth and Cindy were both there, and they immediately walked over to me once Magnus turned away.

I instantly asked the question on my mind. "Cindy, do you have any idea which cabin my sister is in?"

She crossed her arms over her chest to fight off the cold. "No. They don't tell us stuff like that."

"At the end of the workday, do you ever see which direction she goes in?"

She shook her head. "I'm sorry."

The last girls were escorted to the meeting point, and then we moved farther into the plains in front of the camp. A layer of snow from the last storm still lingered, but it had slowly melted to a smaller size because of the clear weather we'd had. It was sunny and clear today, so I took advantage of the conditions to look into the distance, to see if I could spot a land- mark, some sign of human civilization.

There was none.

Like last time, the plane approached. It appeared from the Alps and came our way, the engine getting louder and louder. Then the crates fell from the sky, landing on the powder below. They dropped it as they continued to fly past, leaving a trail of cocaine- filled breadcrumbs.

Then the plane left.

"Move it," one of the guards barked.

We seemed to be out here at the same time as last time, so I hoped to hear that church bell again, that a priest rang it at the same time every day.

We moved to the crates and started to put everything in the wagons. I wasn't as lucky as last time, and there were no pieces of debris that could be used as a weapon. Even though my hands were gloved, they were still cold every time I stuck my hands in the snow to retrieve the smaller bags of drugs that fell out of their crates.

The men sat on their horses and watched us, their bows and arrows on their backs, their horses snorting in impatience.

We finally got everything onto the wagon and headed back to the camp, frozen and sweaty at the same time. I looked over my shoulder for a sign of life, for the hope that I would hear that ringing bell, to prove to myself that it hadn't been my imagination.

That it really happened.

A STORM HIT THAT NIGHT.

I'd been waiting for it.

Because if there was a storm, that meant there would be snow.

And we'd have to shovel that snow.

Magnus opened the door that night, let the woman put the food on the chair before she walked out. He had a mug of cocoa and set it on top of the tray. Then he turned to walk out, like always.

"Wait."

He stilled, standing near the door.

"Could you stay awhile?"

"No." He opened the door.

"I'm not going to ask you to help me escape. I just... want someone to talk to."

My assumption must have been correct because he pushed his hood down and revealed his face before he grabbed the tray and chair and came closer to me. He set the tray on the bed then took a seat across from me, keeping six feet between us like he never wanted to get too close to me at any given time.

His elbows moved to his knees, and he leaned forward, his chin down and his eyes on the floorboards. His jaw was free of hair, and his eyes were a little less hostile than usual. He pulled the gloves from his hands and stuffed them into his pockets.

I grabbed the tray and put it in my lap. After grabbing my fork, I started to eat.

He wasn't averse to a conversation, but he didn't put any energy into speaking.

"Where does that plane come from?"

He massaged his knuckles, like they stung from the cold. "Colombia."

I didn't know anything about the drug industry, but I assumed that was where the plants were grown. They must be processed and then dropped here so they could distribute the drugs throughout Europe. Without confirmation, I assumed I was working among the most notorious drug lords in Europe. "Do you live in Paris?"

"Mostly."

I ate my dinner, my eyes down most of the time.

"You said you lived there."

I nodded.

"You sound American."

"I am." I noticed he had a clipped French accent, but his English was flawless. Most of the French spoke English, but they sounded much sexier doing it with their accents. "I moved here for a study abroad program. But I liked it so much that I decided to stay." If I hadn't chased my dreams, I'd be living a quiet life in America...as a free person. Now, I would be forced to work until my body gave out...and I was hung. It would happen to us all; it was just a matter of time. "I had a little apartment next to this coffee shop that I love. The university is just a few blocks away. I made a lot of friends at school, most of them native French people, but some of them visitors like I was. I haven't traveled a lot, but Paris is really special. It's so romantic, so thrilling. Sometimes, I can still taste the wine and cheese...and the bread."

"I'm surprised you speak so highly of it after what happened to you." He raised his chin and looked at me, his hands together as they hung off his knees.

I pushed my food around before I took a bite. "It's not the city's fault. It's the people who took us."

"Us?" he asked. "They took you both at the same time?"

I nodded.

He rubbed his hands again, sliding his dry palms across each other. "That's unusual. They usually only take one girl at a time."

"Who's they?"

"The hunters."

So that man outside my apartment had had his eyes on Melanie, must have noticed her somehow. It wasn't his first time; he knew how to spot a submissive type, someone who would just do what they were told without causing a fuss. "I noticed one of the hunters staking out my apartment one night. He watched Melanie leave and walk down the sidewalk. But when he walked the other way, I thought I was being paranoid. A few nights later, we were in a wine bar. I was talking to my friend, and she was with some guys on the other side of the room. She's gorgeous, so she always attracts admirers. When I saw her leave with them, I recognized the hunter from outside my apartment."

His hands went still, and he watched me, holding his breath even though he knew how this story ended.

"I went after her, told her about the guy lurking outside her apartment, but she never listens to me...

so she ignored what I said. I lost my temper and said things I didn't mean—"

"What kind of things?"

"That I was tired of taking care of her...cleaning up her messes. Our mother passed away when I was eighteen, so I took care of her until she was an adult. But she makes terrible choices, over and over, and I was always the one who had to deal with it. When she was old enough, I moved to Paris just to have my own space." My eyes fell in shame, for saying those things, for thinking those things. What kind of sister was I? "That only hurt her feelings more, so she got into the car. I didn't know what else to do to keep her safe. There wasn't time to call the police, especially when I didn't even have any proof of my suspicions and they probably wouldn't send anyone, so I got in with her."

He held my gaze, his hands still, as if my story hit him deep down.

It was a stupid decision that led me to this insufferable existence.

"She must feel like shit."

She'd tried to apologize to me, but I never forgave her. "If I could change my decision, I wouldn't. I would have done everything all over again, because I couldn't live not knowing what happened to her. She's all I have left, and I'd rather die with her than live without her."

His hand started to move again, and he dropped his gaze, as if he were replaying that story inside his head over and over. "It makes a lot more sense now."

"What?"

"You're not the type of woman they go for. They want someone obedient. You aren't like that."

I stared down at my food and pushed it around even though I was hungry. "Is that why you like me?"

He didn't say anything.

When the silence continued, I lifted my head and looked at him.

He kept his head down, his eyes on his hand. "You do exactly what I would do...if I were in the same position."

I stared at him and felt my affection grow, felt a connection that hadn't quite been there before. It was the first time someone had showed me some kind of respect, complimented my disobedient qualities rather than trying to suppress them.

"And if there really is no chance to get away...would you still try?"

He lifted his chin and looked at me, those brown eyes shifting back and forth as he looked into mine. There seemed to be a lump in his throat because he swallowed, his hands still gliding past each other, the veins on the tops of his hands slipping under his sleeves. "Yeah, I would—because I'd rather die out there than live here."

14

THIEF

I ALREADY KNEW WHERE MAGNUS WOULD TAKE me that morning.

There was snow everywhere.

The storm had swept through the camp, returning it to disarray, the branches heavy with the snow piled on top, all the roofs coated, the stairs and railway covered in white powder.

It might look like a winter wonderland...if you didn't know what happened here.

I struggled behind him because I wasn't tall enough to navigate as quickly.

When I fell behind, he turned around. "Step over the snow. Don't push through it."

I took his advice, and it became a lot easier. "You don't do that."

He ignored what I said and escorted me to the same place as last time, where the shovels were leaned against the house, waiting to be claimed.

It would finally give me an opportunity to talk to Melanie.

But I also dreaded that conversation.

He nodded to the shovels and walked away.

A sense of emptiness always fell into my stomach when he walked away, like he was the jacket keeping me warm, and the second he was gone, I was exposed to the elements in just my skin.

I grabbed a shovel and searched for my sister until I found her.

She was shoveling snow the way I taught her, protecting her back and using her foot to generate the force instead of her arms. She scooped it up and carried it to the tree line.

I waited for her to return, pretending to struggle with the snow. That way, she and I could be on the same timing.

When she came back to me, she wasn't relieved to see me like last time. She had been dreading this moment, like she'd been thinking about this conversation for a long time.

I didn't have it in me to ask for details, to even address it.

It was just too fucking hard.

Maybe that made me a coward, but I didn't know how to be brave. "Where's your cabin?" I dug into the snow and scooped up the fresh powder.

She stilled at the question, surprised I'd skipped over the conversation neither one of us wanted to have. "Why?" She dug her shovel into the snow then carried it with her to the tree line, walking at my side.

"Because I'm going to get us out of here." I tossed the snow onto the pile.

She did the same. "I'm the last cabin in the northeast part of the camp."

That meant she was farther back, closer to the areas the guards used.

"Everyone is talking about how your guard helped you."

I walked back to the pile of snow we were working on. She moved beside me, keeping some distance so it wasn't so obvious we were conversing. "I'm not sleeping with him."

"Nobody would care if you were."

"I know. That's how you know I'm not lying." I dug my shovel into the snow.

"Do you think he'll help us escape?"

"No. I already asked."

We got more snow then walked back to dump it.

"Are you okay?" she asked. "Your throat looks better."

"I'm fine." She didn't need to worry about me, not when she was the one in distress. "I'm going to sneak out and collect supplies. When I've got enough stuff, I'll get you in the middle of the night, and we'll run for it."

She pushed her shovel into the snow but didn't lift it again. She just turned to look at me. "What do you mean, sneak out?"

"I found some tools to pick the lock. I've done it before."

"And you didn't get caught?"

Technically, yes. "No."

Her eyes were wide. "Oh my god..."

"Once I have everything, I'll let you know."

"How?"

"I'll have to wait until the next storm when we're shoveling snow. Then we'll go that night."

"How are we going to survive out there? How will we know where we're going?"

"I'll take care of all that, alright?"

She scooped the snow then started to carry it.

I joined her, and we moved to the tree line.

Her voice came out as a whisper. "Raven, I'm scared..."

"I know. But we have to be brave."

"If we get caught, they'll hang us. And watching you go through it once..."

I couldn't promise her we would get away. "I know. But we have to try. Because if we don't try, we'll be hanged at some point anyway."

"What if we wait until spring? When the snow is gone?"

"It'll just make it easier for them to find us. If we leave in a storm, it'll be a lot more difficult."

She nodded. "Yeah, that makes sense."

"I'll let you know when I'm ready. And on the first night of a storm...we'll go."

I snuck out that night.

It was dark like last time, the camp barely visible.

One of the things I needed most was a flashlight, preferably two. If it was dark here with a couple lights, then it would be pitch dark out there. I needed weapons, survival gear, and most of all, a map.

A horse would be essential too, but I couldn't steal that now.

I left later in the evening this time, hoping that everyone in the camp was asleep. I found the same cabin where Magnus had been playing poker with the other guards. There was no light from the windows.

Either no one was in there, or they were asleep inside.

It was a bigger cabin, but I found it unlikely that the guards all bunked in there. It was hard to believe that the guards all slept together anyway, because they probably wanted their privacy.

I took the stairs to the porch then stepped in front of the window. My eyes narrowed as I looked inside, making out the circular table that had been there last time. There was no movement inside. It was too dark to make anything out, so I wasn't sure if there were beds somewhere farther in.

I wouldn't know until I went inside.

I moved to the front door and pulled out the rod of my pen and the metal shaft. Gently, I inserted both into the door and tried to trip the lock. It took me a long time because I was still terrible at this, only had my own door for experience. My eyes glanced over my shoulder to make sure there was no one moving through the compound that might spot me.

Then it clicked.

Fuck yes.

I returned the tools to my pocket then gently turned the doorknob, moving as quietly as possible, not making a single sound. Then I stepped inside and shut the door behind me.

Jesus Christ, I did it.

I wanted to turn on a light so I could see better, but that was too risky, especially since the windows didn't have shades. I moved farther inside, past the table, and then listened.

I didn't hear anything.

There was a fridge next to the table, a counter with a microwave, as if this was a break room. I crept through the doorway to the rest of the cabin, and there were windows on the back wall, showing some illumination from the back porch light.

It was a living room, a couple couches angled toward the TV on the wall.

I saw another doorway, so I crept through and found a bathroom and another room. It seemed like no one was in the cabin, so I was a little braver. My feet moved a little quicker, and I didn't hold my breath so much.

The door was closed, so I had to turn the knob and crack it open.

Bingo.

It was a supply room. Bows and arrows were on the wall, along with other supplies, like first aid kits and medicine.

I was so grateful these windows had been lit up that night. It would have taken me forever to figure out which cabin to investigate without knowing where the guards were in the first place.

There was no window in this room, and that was probably by design. I shut the door behind myself and flicked on the light.

Yes, yes, yes.

I opened drawers and looked through everything, finding matches and flashlights. I pocketed both, getting a flashlight for both Melanie and me. The matches would come in handy if we needed to make a fire, something I didn't know how to do with just sticks. I wanted to grab extra things, like the medicine, but if I took too much, it would be obvious.

There were no guns...unfortunately.

Those must be under lock and key.

I stuffed my pockets with a couple bottles of water and bags of nuts. When I couldn't carry any more, I looked up the wall to where the bows and quiver of arrows were mounted. There were only four, so if I took two, it might be really obvious.

If I took one, it would be less obvious.

I didn't know how to use a bow and arrow, but I could practice in the forest with a flashlight. That way, we could hunt in the forest—even though I didn't know how to do that either. Or at least have a weapon if they hunted us down.

I took the bow and quiver of arrows, and since there was no way to stuff those into my pockets, I just slung them over my back.

If I got caught, I was dead anyway.

I turned off the light and left.

Before I walked out the front door, I locked it from inside and then took the stairs back to the ground. The walk back was uneventful because everyone seemed to be asleep. I made it the rest of the way, anxious and excited, eager to get back to my cabin so I could finally rejoice.

There was no map, but that was okay.

We'd figure it out.

I got back into my cabin, locked myself inside so even Magnus wouldn't know what I did, and then I finally released the breath I'd been holding. "Holy shit...I fucking did it." I emptied my pockets and put everything on the bed, including the bow and arrows.

But then I realized I had a problem.

Where was I going to hide everything?

I had no furniture. My mattress just sat on the floor. I had a nightstand, but that wouldn't hold everything.

I could hide it somewhere outside, but what if I couldn't find it again?

That only gave me one choice.

The bathtub.

There was no shower rod, but no one ever came to clean my cabin, so no one ever looked. Magnus never peeked. It was my only option because there was literally nowhere else.

So that was where I put it.

I turned off the light and got into bed, unable to believe my luck.

I had nearly everything I needed to escape. I just needed to pick the lock to the stables and grab a horse.

And then we'd be on our way.

THE DAYS PASSED EVEN SLOWER than before.

Because now I was actually anxious for the future.

I ignored the next Red Snow as best I could, but it traumatized me even more than usual, because I remembered exactly how it felt to have that rope around my neck. Listening to her screams made me stop breathing because it felt as if the noose were around my own throat, choking me.

Hopefully that was the last Red Snow I'd have to listen to.

I just needed that storm to come.

Another drop came, and we grabbed everything that fell from the sky and put it on the wagon.

There was no bell.

We returned to camp, unloaded everything, and then had a full day of work.

The sky was clear, so a storm didn't seem to be in the forecast.

At the end of the workday, we weren't dismissed as usual.

Instead, the executioner came out.

The torches weren't lit, and it'd only been days since the last Red Snow.

So, something different was happening.

He looked at all of us, as if searching for something.

I turned to Bethany, who was standing beside me. "Do you know what's happening?"

She shook her head.

The executioner started to speak. "One of you has stolen from us."

Instantly, I was sick, so fucking sick that I wanted to vomit right onto my boots. Blood pounded in my ears, and all the excitement I felt at my success was quickly taken away. My eyes darted to Melanie.

Her eyes were already on me.

The executioner scanned all of us, searching for a reaction.

I forced myself to keep a blank face, to hide just how fucking terrified I was.

"If anyone knows anything about this, come forward. You'll be rewarded."

Melanie was the only one who knew, so I was safe.

"Every cabin will be searched."

Shit.

"When we find what belongs to us, you'll hang." The executioner turned away, ending the announcement.

Fuck, what was I going to do? When I got back to the cabin, I would have to leave again, carry everything into the woods. But it was still light out, the sun setting, so someone would see me. Guards would be everywhere.

They must have noticed the bow and arrows were missing that morning before we collected the drop. They probably tried to find the missing set all afternoon, and when they couldn't, they realized someone had taken it, along with other items.

Why hadn't that storm come?

I hadn't anticipated this because the drops were unpredictable. Sometimes they came often, and sometimes they didn't come at all.

Fuck, I was so screwed.

The women rose from the tables and headed back to their cabins, immediately whispering to one another about the revelation. Before I turned away, I looked at Melanie again.

She looked at me—like she knew.

Magnus grabbed me by the arm and yanked me away. He was harsh, when he normally didn't touch me at all. "Come on." He marched me back along the route we took in the morning, keeping me ahead of him so he could walk behind me.

The blood was pounding so loudly in my ears that I couldn't hear my own boots against the snow. I felt neither cold nor warm, just alarmed, just full of anxiety for the mess I'd caused myself.

I was so lost in my head that the journey to my cabin took only a few seconds. I didn't even realize we were there until Magnus moved in front of me and entered the cabin.

I followed behind him.

He shut the door behind me and rounded on me so fast. "What the fuck is wrong with you?" He yanked his hood down, showing his red face, the vein pulsing in the center of his forehead. "How stupid are you? You really thought they wouldn't notice? Do you even know how to use a bow and arrow?"

I stepped back, breathing hard because I was scared of what would happen when they came to my cabin.

"I told you that you can't escape, but you pull this stunt?"

"You told me you'd still run for it."

"So I can die on my own terms. Not because there's any chance that I could make it a mile before they hunted me down." His hands moved to both sides of his head, and he dug his fingers into his hair, gripped his skull like he was furious. "You said you were sick of cleaning up your sister's messes? Well, I'm fucking sick of cleaning up yours." He took a knee on my floor and pulled out tools from his pockets.

"What...what are you doing?"

"Get the shit you stole." He pulled out a crowbar and stuck it between the boards, yanking it back so the wood would come free. "Come on. Quickly. We don't have time."

I grabbed the bow and arrow from the tub and then gathered everything else. "What if you just put it in the woods—"

"I can't walk out of here with all this shit. Dead fucking giveaway." He got on his stomach and started to tuck everything underneath the cabin, digging up the soil with his bare hands and placing everything underneath it until he smoothed it over with the dirt, hiding it from view. Then he returned the plank to the floor, putting a dab of glue between the boards so it wouldn't be obvious that one was loose.

The fact that he had all those things on him meant he already knew I was the culprit before the executioner had announced anything. He knew it was me without asking, and he knew he had to come prepared. Otherwise, I would be caught.

He saved my ass...again.

He got to his feet and dusted off his hands before he pulled his gloves back on.

Footsteps sounded outside.

He turned at the sound then quickly pulled up his hood to hide his face. "Sit. Now."

I did as I was told and sat at the edge of the bed.

The front door flew open, and the executioner came in with two guards.

Magnus did a remarkable job of looking innocent. "I checked the lock on her door, and it hasn't been tampered with. I checked her room but haven't moved the mattress."

They didn't seem suspicious of Magnus at all. One guard moved to look in the tub, while the other opened the drawers in my nightstand and searched there. The executioner came to me. "Move."

I got off the bed right away.

Magnus silently excused himself.

The men looked through everything in my room, upending the mattress, even moving the nightstand to make sure there was nothing behind it. They looked underneath the tub then undid the piping of my sink, as if I'd shoved some things there. They came up empty-handed.

The guards left without putting my stuff back where it was.

The executioner didn't walk out. Instead, he came up to me, looking down at me with those furious eyes. He stared for a long time, a minute straight, his look so intense that it terrified me.

I couldn't be as brave as I was last time. At that moment, I had accepted my death.

But right now, I had no idea what would happen.

Finally, he spoke. "He can't protect you forever. Next time he's gone, so are you."

15
_____

THE STORM

LIFE WENT ON.

There were no other announcements about the stolen items.

The girls knew the stuff hadn't been recovered because no one had been killed.

It seemed as if the executioner suspected me, but without proof, there was nothing he could do.

But I definitely had to make a run for it before Magnus left again, because once he was gone...I was done for. Every day was sunny and cold, and there was barely a breeze on the wind. We worked day after day, time blending together.

God, I needed that storm.

Melanie was surprised I hadn't been caught based on her shocked expression, but once the immediate threat passed, she didn't look so terrified. She actually looked a little hopeful, like we had a chance.

My dinner was delivered that night. It was placed on my bed, a pile of food on the plate, like the girls in the kitchen always made sure to give me extra after I'd been starved last week. There was a mug of hot cocoa too.

Magnus was my guardian angel.

We hadn't talked about what happened because he'd left my cabin the instant the food was delivered every night. It seemed like he wanted nothing to do with me.

But tonight, he stayed.

He shut the door behind himself, dropped his hood, and then pulled up his chair so he could face me, the way that asshole guard used to. His black gloves were removed, and he started to curl his fingers into his palm, as if working out the aches caused by the cold. "A storm is coming tonight. It'll be here around three a.m." He lifted his gaze and looked at me, staring at me with those brown eyes that were uniformly dark but somehow beautiful. He regarded me with suppressed concern, with a hint of annoyance. "If you leave before it hits, you'll get a lead on them."

I ignored my food, despite the fact that I was starving. The only thing that mattered was the words he spoke.

"When the winds hit, it'll cover your tracks."

My hands started to shake because the moment had arrived. This was really happening.

"But you won't make it, Raven."

It was the first time he'd said my name. I liked the way it sounded.

He shook his head slightly. "If you're lucky enough to evade capture, you'll get lost and die anyway."

"Unless you tell me the way."

He held my gaze, unblinking. "You know I can't do that."

"Please..."

"Even if I did, you aren't going to make it."

"Stop saying that. It's not true."

"Have you ever been out in the wilderness in your entire life?" His voice started to rise, his anger getting to him. "Let alone, in winter? You think those two flashlights are going to be enough to navigate in the pitch-blackness? In a storm? You're going to get yourselves killed."

"We're just going to ride straight through."

"Ride?" he asked incredulously. "Ride what?"

"A horse."

"And how do you plan on getting a horse?"

"The same way I got the other stuff."

He shook his head. "You can't pick the lock on the stables. They're bolted. That's not an option."

My heart did a somersault.

"You'll have to go on foot. And you definitely won't make it."

"Do you think you could get me—"

"Did you really just ask me that?" He raised his voice again. "After everything I've done for you? You have the audacity to ask me for anything?"

I bowed my head in shame.

"I'm tired of saving your ass. If I really thought you had a chance out there, I would tell you that. But you don't. You have no idea what you're up against. And here I am, yet again, trying to save you."

"I'd rather die out there than work for these monsters a day longer. My sister is gorgeous, and once the boss is done with her, it'll just be another guy... They'll force her until her beauty fades. She'd rather die out there too...with me."

"I don't see what the big deal is with her."

"What are you talking about? She's beautiful."

"On the outside. But she's weak on the inside."

I lifted my head and looked at him again.

His eyes were on me with the same intensity as before. "And I've seen better."

I was paralyzed by his words. All I could do was look at the brown eyes staring at me, look into the face of the man who held my life in his hands. My makeup had washed away shortly after I arrived here, and I hadn't even combed my hair since. There was no mirror, so I had no idea what I looked like, but even on my best day, I was nothing compared to Melanie. So, there was no way he was referring to me specifically...right?

"Even with several hours of lead time, they'll send all their guys out, on horses with hounds."

"There are dogs here?"

"They're inside because it's too cold."

So, we were forced to work outside in the cold every day, but the dogs got to stay inside? Wow.

"The snow will be piled high, so you'll have a hard time getting through. There are frozen lakes out there hidden under the snow, and one wrong move will send you under the ice. The wolves are hungry because everything is hibernating, and they'll smell you a mile away."

"Then we'll find a hiding place and wait it out until the guards stop looking for us."

He shook his head. "They'll never stop looking for you."

"I just—"

"Nothing I say will make a difference, will it?" He leaned forward slightly, looking into my gaze with a pissed-off expression, like he wanted to grab me by the neck and shake me. "Nothing I say will make you see reason, will it?"

All I could do was shake my head.

He dropped his gaze and released a heavy sigh, his fingers curling toward his palm as he made a fist.

"Do you really think I won't survive...or you just don't want me to go?"

He was still as if he hadn't heard the question, as if it didn't elicit a reaction. But then he lifted his gaze and looked into mine. "I don't want you to die, Raven. That's what I want." He rose to his feet and carried the chair back to the wall.

It was time to say goodbye...to the only friend I had here. Instead of rejoicing at my escape, I actually felt a twinge of sadness, like I was losing something special. "Thank you...for everything."

He pulled up his hood as he prepared to leave. He stared at the door, as if he had something else on his mind that he wanted to share, but then he came back toward me, his boots echoing against the floorboards. He reached into his pocket and pulled out a long blade, at least five inches. It was sheathed in a covering so it wouldn't slice him in the thigh. He gripped it by the handle with the blade pointed to the floor. "Don't hold it like this." He turned the knife and pointed it upward. "Hold it like this. We're trained to push down on the arm to force it into the thigh. If you keep the blade up, you have a better chance." He dropped it on the bed. "Good luck." He didn't look at me again before he walked out.

He didn't bother to lock the door...not this time.

I used the knife to access everything beneath the cabin. Then I returned the floorboard and hoped they wouldn't notice it. Not for my sake, because I'd either be dead or free, but because of Magnus.

I didn't want him to lose his head because of me.

With the bow slung over my back, along with the quiver of arrows, which I had no idea how to use, and all the supplies I'd stolen, I left my cabin and became absorbed into the night. But the camp wasn't abandoned like it used to be.

There were guards on post.

Shit.

They obviously expected whoever stole the supplies to sneak out of the camp. That was how they intended to capture the perpetrator—red-handed. Now I had to be even more careful than before.

I crept through the snow and headed in the direction of my sister's cabin. I noticed the speed of the wind through the branches overhead, the sounds of the forest as everything swayed with the coming storm. An owl screeched and made me jump a foot off the ground. The forest knew something was coming.

I stuck to the edge of the camp, using the different cabins for cover, always peeking around the corner to check if the coast was clear before I made my way to the next structure. Again and again, I moved, holding my breath, slowing my frantic heart.

When I spotted the cabin Melanie had described, I noticed the light through the crack beneath the door. It was the only light on in the camp, at least in this quadrant. That meant she was awake. Maybe she knew a storm was coming and that was her way of telling me where she was.

I peeked down the row of cabins and saw no one around, so I moved toward the cabin.

Then the front door opened.

"Fuck..." I quickly backed up, hoping the guy wouldn't see me.

Fortunately, his gaze was on the doorknob where he inserted the key to lock it.

That gave me enough time to duck back for cover.

When he turned around and walked off, I recognized him.

He wore the black bomber jacket on top of a pair of jeans, his face fully exposed to the elements. His boots crunched against the snow from his weight. He moved down the row of cabins until he turned the corner.

I was sick.

Now I knew, without a doubt, that was Melanie's cabin.

This was bad timing...but also great timing.

I had to put the revelation from my mind because now wasn't the time to dwell. I didn't have the luxury of becoming emotional, of having any kind of reaction not based on survival. This was our last night here—it was almost over.

I moved across the snow, and the instant I was exposed, I could feel the wind pick up.

It was going to be a harsh storm.

We had to get moving now.

I got to the door and stuck my tools inside, twisting and turning the locks to get it free.

Melanie's voice came from the other side. "Raven?"

"Shh." I looked down the row of cabins to make sure I was still alone. The coast was clear, so I kept messing with the lock, the shaft slipping from time to time. "Come on, don't be a bastard right now..."

Click.

"Oh, thank god." I opened the door and pushed inside.

Melanie stepped back, like she couldn't believe I was in her cabin.

The bed was rumpled like two people had been rolling around in it. There was a lone candle burning, a vase of flowers on the nightstand, a TV in the corner. At least she was given extra things and she wasn't covered in bruises.

Melanie breathed hard as she looked at me. "Oh my fucking god..."

"We've got to go. Got to get a head start before the storm hits."

"I..." She looked around her cabin, like she wasn't sure if she wanted to leave.

"I'm not sure if this will make you feel better or not, but I'm scared too."

Her emotional eyes shifted back and forth as she looked into mine.

I pulled the flashlight out of my pocket and placed it in hers, along with the bottle of water and the plastic bag of nuts. I kept the knife for myself. "We can do this."

"Did you get a horse?"

I shook my head. "It's bolted."

"How far can we get on foot?" She whispered even though no one was around.

"We just have to hide from them. They'll eventually give up...and we can take our time."

"Raven, we won't survive long enough to take our time—"

"I'm going. Are you coming with me or not?"

She hesitated.

"Don't make me leave you here...but I will." I wanted to get her out of here, but I couldn't force her, couldn't force her to be brave. I wouldn't stay just to be near her. I would roll the dice and hope for the best out in the wilderness. Just because she wanted to remain a prisoner didn't mean I had to do the same.

She finally nodded. "Alright." She put on her boots, pulled on her jacket, and then opened her drawers to stuff her pockets with the extra food she had lying around. She had an extra bottle of water, so she took that too. "Okay, let's go."

I looked at my little sister, seeing the same look of terror that she'd had in her gaze when we were growing up. She'd always been scared of the unknown, but that was just how she was. I never judged her for it. Magnus called her weak, but that wasn't how I saw her. I pulled her in and embraced her, hugged her for the first time since our capture. "We're gonna make it."

She clutched me hard and nodded against me.

"Let's go home." I walked to the front door, poked my head out to see my surroundings, and then nodded for her to join me. We shut the door behind us and headed for the tree line, the darkness of the forest, the loud creaking sounds haunting.

Melanie stayed at my side and gripped my arm once we stepped into the trees. "I can't see."

"It's fine. Keep going."

"Can we use the flashlights?"

"Not now. We're too close to camp." But we really did step into the pitch-blackness, and our only guide to our surroundings was the wail of the shifting trees. It was the only way to navigate and not strike a tree. There were no stars in the sky because a blanket of clouds covered it, so we couldn't use the starlight to distinguish through the silhouettes either.

With our hands held together, we moved through the darkness...and escaped.

WITH OUR FLASHLIGHTS ON, we navigated through the darkness, pointing at the bases of the trees to make sure we didn't crash into anything. Our feet fell deep into the snow with every step. It was hard to move at a decent pace because we continued to shuffle forward, our legs aching as we pushed through the cold resistance.

"Won't they see our tracks?" Melanie looked behind her, pointing her flashlight over the streaks in the snow.

"The storm is supposed to hit in a few hours. The wind will cover it."

"Hope so..."

I kept the lead, not knowing how deep this forest was. The trees were close together, so it would be difficult for the horses to come this way, but not the hounds. We had to keep moving quickly.

"Fuck, it's cold out here."

"Just think about a hot cup of coffee in front of the fireplace." I was too focused to feel cold, too determined to get the hell out of here to worry about the elements.

"Did Magnus at least give you a direction?"

"No." His help only went so far.

Melanie groaned as she trudged through the snow.

I kept going...unsure when this forest would end.

THE STORM HIT SO UNEXPECTEDLY. It was calm, and then suddenly, it was raging full force.

It was like being hit by a freight train.

Melanie fell several times, but I grabbed her by the wrist and pulled her up. The wind was fierce, daggers in our eyes, and our eyes began to smart, only to be dried out a moment later. Snow billowed all around us, covering our jackets and pants, falling around us like mini tornadoes, not the cute snowfall that sometimes happened in Paris.

This snow was spiteful.

"We shouldn't have left!" Melanie shouted to me, her voice carrying on the wind.

"Don't say that. We've got this. Come on!"

She continued to lag behind me.

It grew lighter along the horizon because sunrise had arrived.

They probably knew we were gone by now. "We gotta keep moving."

Minutes later, we reached the edge of the forest. Out in the open was a plain, a plain that reached far into the distance. It was totally open...totally vulnerable. With the snow as high and lumpy as it was, it would take us hours to get across. If they followed our tracks, they would probably get here before we made it across.

Melanie caught up to me then put her hands on her knees as she leaned forward and caught her breath. "Oh Jesus... We're gonna cross that, aren't we?"

I decided to steer clear of the Alps because the closer we got, the more dangerous the terrain would become. There might be lakes underneath the snow, dangerous animals, and the closer to the mountains we came, the less populated it would be. We need to stay on the flat lands. "Take a short break. But yes, we're gonna cross that as quickly as we can."

She slumped against a tree and sat in the snow, still breathing hard because the endurance we'd built in the camp wasn't enough to prepare for the journey. She opened a bottle and drank from it before digging her hand into a bag of nuts. "How are you not tired?"

"Never said I wasn't." I leaned against a different tree and sat in the snow. It felt like a cold pillow. The second I was on the ground, my legs ached from the exertion. I'd always been on the slender side, but living here for over a month had turned me into a strong machine. My legs were toned and tight, my arms too. I even had a six-pack, which I'd never had in all my life. I turned my head and looked at the plains, seeing the snow blowing across, the visibility poor because snow was everywhere. The world was white.

Melanie's hair kept flying around, so she tucked it inside her shirt then pulled up her hood. "Why aren't you drinking?"

Because we had to conserve as much as possible. "I'm fine." I expected this journey to be long. I didn't expect to get to the finish line quickly. It would take work, perseverance...and hope.

She put the bottle and snacks away but didn't get up to start moving again.

I gave her another minute.

Then she started to cry. "I'm so sorry—"

"We don't have time for this." I knew she needed to absolve herself of the guilt, but I wasn't ready to give it to her. I loved her with my whole heart, but all of this happened because of her stupidity, and I just wasn't ready to forgive her. I might never be ready to forgive her.

"Raven..." She wiped her tears away with her gloved hands. "I just—"

I got to my feet. "We've got to keep moving." I extended my hand to hers to help her rise.

She didn't take it. "You're never going to forgive me, are you?"

I stared down at her, my hand lingering. "Melanie—"

"We're probably going to die out here. I need you to know how sorry I am."

"I do know you're sorry."

With her arms crossed over her chest, she looked up at me, her eyes always dried from the wind. "I need you to forgive me..."

My hand shook as it remained extended to her, and not because of the cold. Then I pulled it away entirely and got moving, stepping into the open on the snow that was piling higher and higher by the minute. I'd been beaten. I'd been hanged. I'd been starved. I'd had to watch an innocent woman on the guillotine like this was 1789. No...I wasn't ready to give it to her.

THE TREES HAD GIVEN us cover.

Now, we had none of that.

I stayed in the lead, making a line in the snow that made it easier for Melanie to traverse. But we were walking against the wind, which made this so much harder. But it would also make it harder for them.

Freedom pumped in my veins, and that kept me pressing on.

I was fighting for so much, and I wasn't going to stop.

That gave me the strength to go on, to move despite the pain in my legs, to strive for the life I'd never really said goodbye to.

Melanie's voice came from behind me. "We have to go back!"

I turned around and looked at her, the hood of my jacket smacking into the back of my head. I stared at her on the ground where she'd fallen onto her hands and knees, the snow a wall on either side of her. "We're halfway there."

"We aren't going to make it! We have to go a different way."

I marched back to her and grabbed her by both arms until she was on her feet. "There is no other way. We need to cross this plain. Now, come on. You're better than this, Melanie."

"I'm so tired..."

I shook her. "Then stop being tired. You can do this." I turned and kept walking, and then a rush of wind hit me so hard that I fell backward.

"Are you okay?" Melanie came to me, her hand moving to my shoulder.

The collision with the ground immediately made my back sore, but I got up again.

The wind hit me again, and I fell.

Melanie was beside me, on her knees. "We have to go back."

I didn't want to admit that Magnus was right...but he might be. Sheer will and determination weren't enough to fight the unconquerable. I didn't want this storm to defeat me.

But it had.

Ring.

I instantly sat up, knowing I heard it, knowing I heard that church bell ring.

Ring.

"Do you hear that?" I shouted.

Melanie turned into the snow, like she heard it too.

Ring.

I got back to my feet, my boots planted firmly in the snow, keeping me upright even when a gust of wind hit me harder than all the others before. All the muscles in my body tightened and fought against the ferocity of the wind and snow.

Ring.

"Come on, keep going!" I took one step forward.

When Melanie didn't argue, I knew she heard it too.

This storm wouldn't defeat me.

Because I would be the eye of the storm.

We crossed the plain and entered another forest of trees. Once we were under cover, the wind wasn't so harsh. The storm seemed to be abating too. When I looked back the way we'd come, I couldn't see to the other side. I wasn't sure if the wind had covered our tracks, but with the amount of snowfall, it must have. And what would the dogs smell? The wind was taking our scent away, the snow piling on and hiding it.

I had a good feeling about this

There was less snow in the forest, so it was easier to move.

Melanie needed another break, so she took a seat. "I need to sleep."

"No sleep."

"What?" she asked incredulously.

"The guards have slept all night, so they're rested. If we stop, they'll catch up to us."

"I meant just an hour—"

"No."

She opened her water and took a drink.

"I couldn't sleep in these conditions anyway." I pulled out my water and took a drink before tucking it back into my pocket. Melanie had granola bars, so I ate a few of those.

"Where do you think that bell is coming from?"

"Not sure, but I hope we're on the right track."

"I wonder if it's close."

I didn't want to discourage her, so I didn't tell her the truth. During our trips in good conditions, I never heard the sound. Only in a storm could I hear the ringing of the bell, which told me it wasn't close and the sound carried to us from its origin on the high winds.

But it was still out there. "We'll find it." I took a seat against the tree. "If the wind covered our journey through the snow, they'll find never find us."

"I hope so…"

I pulled things out of my pockets to get to my water, including the knife I hoped I didn't have to use. I set it on the snow beside me.

"Where did you get that?" Her eyes admired the weapon that sank into the snow from its weight.

"Magnus."

"He just gave that to you?"

"Yes."

"So, he knew you were going to leave?"

I nodded. "He hid all my supplies under the cabin so I wouldn't get caught."

"How does a nice guy like that work in a place like this?"

I shrugged. "He never told me much about himself."

"Do you think he'll snitch?"

I shook my head. "No."

"The guy must be in love with you or something."

He didn't strike me as a romantic guy. He never said anything complimentary, and he never touched me, except when he pulled me to my feet. And he had classically good-looking features, like a strong jaw, pretty eyes, a very handsome face... Why would he be interested in a prisoner in a labor camp when he had a life outside that place? "I don't think so."

"Then what other explanation is there?"

I leaned my head back and looked up at the canopy of swaying trees. "I think he respected me." That was my best guess. He never initiated a physical relationship or expected anything from me. Besides, I looked like hell every single day. Not exactly my finest look, in the baggy clothes with unkempt hair.

"I don't think a man risks his neck like that for respect."

"This one does."

WE CONTINUED MOVING through the night.

I wanted to stay focused, but my mind started to grow fuzzy.

It'd been two days since I'd last slept.

Melanie moved even slower.

We were back to feeling around in the dark once again. The storm had passed, so now the world was quiet. That was both a good thing—and a bad thing. There didn't seem to be anyone on our trail, so we used our flashlights to keep going.

"What's the first thing you're going to do when we're free?" Melanie asked from behind me. "I'm going to take a shower, do my hair, have a pumpkin spice latte...get a burger."

"I'm going to the police."

"Well...besides that."

"And I'm going to kill that fucking executioner."

"I'm not sure how you're going to pull that off, but he'll probably be behind bars forever."

That wasn't good enough for me—not anymore.

Now that the wind was gone, it was much easier for us to speak to each other. The snow was stationary, so that made it easier to navigate too. The stars came through as the clouds passed, and the moonlight provided us some illumination.

We kept going, Melanie walking in my tracks so she could keep up.

The need for revenge was so paramount in my blood that it screamed in my ears. I wanted to burn that place to the ground, all the guards with the blaze.

Well, except one.

Magnus was guilty because he'd been working there for years, but I couldn't imagine reporting him—not when he'd saved my life so many times. But I had to report that camp and liberate all the women who didn't belong there.

"Raven...?"

I stilled at the fear in her voice. "What?"

She didn't answer.

I turned around to look at her.

She was looking back the way we came.

I saw it.

The lights. There were glimmers of light from flashlights. There were burning torches—like they were bringing the Red Snow to us.

They were right on our tail, like their hounds had picked up the scent.

Fuck.

"Move." I started to run, to push through the snow harder than before.

"We'll never outrun them, Raven! They're on horses!

"I said, move!" I knew we wouldn't get away. I knew we couldn't hide. The snow kept a record of our footprints, and now that the storm was gone, there was nothing to erase our trail. Our only chance was to get to safety before they could reach us.

Which seemed unlikely since they were on horseback...and we were on foot.

THE SOUND of the barking dogs carried to us.

They'd made incredible time.

"They know exactly where we are, Raven."

There was no chance of success, not when there was nothing we could easily reach. I turned back around and looked at her.

She'd never looked so terrified. "They're gonna hang us."

Yes...they were.

She looked over her shoulder then stared at me again, emotion in her eyes. "We should have stayed."

"I'd rather die on my own terms than be a prisoner to someone else."

She gave a slight nod.

"You've got to be brave, Melanie."

She nodded again, but this time, she sniffled.

"But it's not over yet." I pulled my bow off my back and grabbed an arrow from the quiver.

"What are you going to do?"

"Kill them." I put the bow on the string, pulled back my arm, and released the arrow.

It moved less than a few inches before falling to the ground.

"How many are there?" I picked up the arrow and tried again.

"I don't know." She turned to look behind her. "I see two flashlights...and two torches. So maybe four? And no idea how many dogs they have..."

I pulled the string back and tried again. The arrow went a little farther. It was an improvement, but not by much. "I need you to keep going forward. Go a hundred feet before you turn around and walk back along the same trail."

"Why?"

"So, they won't stop where we're hiding. We'll shoot them in the back." I pulled the knife from my pocket and handed it to her.

"What the hell am I supposed to do with this?"

"Kill anyone who comes near you."

"What about the dogs? I'm not going to kill a dog."

I didn't know what to do about them. "Then kick them until they back off. But I can probably shoot two of them. I'll need help with the other two."

She put the knife in her pocket and did as I asked, making a trail farther up ahead.

I kept practicing with the bow and arrow—like my life depended on it.

I HID behind a tree on one side of the trail.

Melanie hid on the other.

The guards were still in hot pursuit, all on horses, two dogs in the lead. They must have seen the trail continue up ahead because they ran right past us.

I'd never been so scared in my life.

Because I actually had something to lose.

Freedom was so close...so fucking close.

I was not letting these bastards take it from me.

I purposely waited until they came to a standstill because I couldn't hit a moving target. Then I moved out of the tree line, aimed right for the neck of one, and fired.

It pierced him right in the neck. Slowly, his body slumped sideways until he collapsed in the snow. He didn't make a sound because he was dead on impact. But his heavy body made a loud thud when it hit the ground.

I didn't stop to celebrate and quickly grabbed a new arrow, pointing it at the guy who had turned to look at his fallen comrade. "She's behind us!"

I pulled the arrow back, held my breath and focused, and then released it into the air.

It hit him right in the chest.

He fell to the ground, the horse immediately stepping away like it could sense death.

The other guys quickly turned around and kicked their horses to come after me. Their dogs started to bark in panic, German shepherds that sprinted toward us with their jaws open, their teeth bared.

I got another arrow and aimed, but they were charging me down, so I missed. "Fuck."

"You fucking cunt!" The guard jumped down and pulled out his bow to shoot me.

I sprinted away even though there was no way I could outrun them.

A dog got me quickly, biting into my leg and making me fall to the snow. Then an arrow pierced my arm.

"Ahh!" I fell and gripped my arm, the arrow piercing right through my flesh.

"Enough, boy." The guard's footsteps were audible as he approached me, as was the gloat in his voice.

The dog got off me.

I lay there, bleeding all over the snow. When I looked up, he stood over me, his arrow pointed right at my face.

The other guard stood over me too, his hood off because he didn't care about hiding his face at this point. "Where's the other girl?" He spat right on my face.

"She died." They had nothing on me anymore. They were going to kill me, so I'd lie through gritted teeth until it was over. There was no amount of torture that could get me to give it up.

The man with the bow kicked me hard. "Liar."

I groaned as his heavy boot hit my stomach.

"Tell us or—" He stumbled forward onto the ground, a scream erupting through the forest.

Melanie was on top of him, stabbing him in the back.

I moved, lunging at the guy with the bow while he was confused. I charged him to the ground and slammed my fists into his face, beating him to death, wild with insanity because I had to survive.

It was him or me.

And it was going to be him.

Both dogs jumped onto Melanie, and she screamed in pain.

I left the guard and rushed to her aid, to get those dogs off before they could kill her.

The guard came up behind me and slammed his fist so forcefully into my head that I fell hard into the snow, dizzy, confused, unable to move.

"Down!" The guard knew I was out of it, so he went to my sister, grabbing her by the neck and pinning her down. Then he tied her wrists with rope.

"No..." I could barely talk. There was only one of him, so I could take him out. If only I could lift myself up...I could stop this.

When she was bound, the guard moved to me next.

I tried to twist free, but he put a knee in my back so I couldn't move.

Melanie looked at me, wriggling to be free, but it was no use. "Raven, are you okay? Talk to me."

I couldn't. I couldn't think. My wrists were bound.

Then I noticed the torches coming closer, a man in the lead on a horse...in a bomber jacket.

And then I slipped under.

16

CRACK OF THE WHIP

I WOKE WHEN MY BODY HIT THE GROUND.

I was jolted awake, the panic immediately hitting me like a bucket of cold water had been dumped on my head, and that was when I became aware of the ropes around my wrists, the flames from the torches in the clearing.

I was back at the camp.

I didn't escape.

I got us both killed.

My little sister was going to die...because of me.

The other prisoners weren't there and it was dark out, so it was some time in the middle of the night. I had no idea if it was the same night as before, how much time had passed, nothing.

Melanie's body fell next to mine a moment later. Her eyes narrowed when she realized I was awake. "Raven..."

"Melanie." I groaned when the guard kicked me.

"We'll hang the other girl first...and make this one watch."

"No!" I started to writhe free of the rope that bound my wrists. "No, it was my idea—"

"Just this one." Boots came into my line of sight before I saw a man lean down to look at Melanie. Only his back was visible, but I recognized the black bomber jacket. The backs of his fingers moved to her cheek, and he gently stroked her...like she was a pet.

"Don't fucking touch her!" I tried to fight the ropes again. "You motherfucker!"

The guard kicked me again.

The boss ignored me. "Get her up."

The guards helped Melanie to her feet.

The boss grabbed her wrists in a single hand, standing behind her, over her, possessively. He looked down into her face, watching her panic at his touch. "You trying to leave me, sweetheart?"

She just breathed.

"I'll take you with me tomorrow, then." He nodded to his guards. "Take her to the cabin."

Take her where? I wanted to scream again, but at least she wouldn't be hung.

The guards escorted her away.

But she fought their hold, trying to get back to me. "Raven!" Her cries pierced the night, her tears hot in her throat. "No! Please! Please don't do this." She continued to fight as they dragged her away.

Then her cries went silent.

The boss turned to me then kneeled, right over me. With brown eyes, thick hair all along his jawline, and fair skin marked by a single dark mole on his cheek, he stared me down, indifferent to me. His eyes were wide and unblinking, and he examined me like he didn't know what to make of me. "Congratulations." He had a deep voice that was even but innately terrifying. "You've made it farther than anyone. I hope it was worth it...but I imagine it wasn't." He got to his feet then nodded to the guards.

They yanked me to my feet.

I didn't fight anymore since Melanie was safe. I'd already been prepared to die once before, and I could do it again. I could face my death bravely—with no regrets. I stood upright and looked at the guards in the clearing, the men who must have been part of the second search party.

Then the executioner came into view. His mouth was covered—but it was obvious he was smiling. "I'm really going to enjoy this." He looked down at me then shoved his large hand into my chest, making me fall back to the ground. An arrow was still stuck in my arm because they never removed it.

Just get it over with.

I knew Magnus wouldn't help me this time. He'd warned me, and I didn't listen.

"Up." The executioner kicked me.

I tried to rise, but with my hands bound, I couldn't.

"I said up, bitch." He kicked me again.

"We aren't hanging her." A beacon of hope came from nowhere, shining down from heaven, my savior giving me a lifeline with just his voice.

The executioner turned around to look at him.

"Not this time."

Magnus had his hood down, so his face was visible, his features lit up because of the torch that illuminated his face. Even though the executioner was much bulkier, Magnus didn't look the least bit intimidated. "She's the strongest worker we have—"

"No." The executioner stepped toward him. "She stole from us. She tried to escape. She killed two of our own. How dare you stand there and ask for her to be pardoned." The guards stayed back, watching the two of them stare each other down.

"I'm not asking for her to be pardoned. She should be punished."

The executioner stepped closer to him. "She deserves to be executed. Your dick is not part of this discussion."

Magnus hadn't blinked once. "She'll be whipped."

"No." The executioner turned back to grab me. "You can't save her this time."

My body relaxed as he came toward me because I knew it was over. At least Magnus would be there till the end...so I wasn't alone.

Magnus turned to the boss and looked at him.

He looked back.

The executioner got me to my feet, pulling the back of my hair like I was a dog being grabbed by the neck.

Magnus continued to stare at the boss, silently having a conversation with him. They were of the same height, even had the same colored eyes. Then he spoke quietly to him, their voices hushed. I couldn't make anything out. Only one audible word came out of Magnus's mouth, and it was the final word he said. "Please."

The boss stared him down, a bored look on his face, like this conversation was pointless and uninteresting. But he gave a slight nod.

The executioner released a loud sigh in frustration but didn't speak a word in protest. He shoved me forward slightly and released the hold on my neck. Then he grabbed me again, cut the rope binding my hands, and then moved me to a tree trunk.

One of the guards retrieved more rope.

The executioner yanked off my jacket then pulled out his knife to slice through my shirt, opening my back to the cold, the frigid air immediately making all my muscles tighten in protest.

The guard threw the rope over a tree branch and then tied my wrists above my head, my feet still touching the ground, my front against the tree trunk.

Then I heard the executioner speak. "You want her to be whipped? Then you do it."

All I could look at was the tree trunk, but I imagined what was happening behind me. I imagined the executioner walking up to Magnus and staring him down, shoving the whip into his chest because the punishment would be much more painful coming from him instead.

The executioner spoke again. "And you better do it right. Because if you don't, I'll start over—and do it all again."

It was quiet.

All I could do was stand there, my arms suspended over my head so I couldn't move. I could swing left to right if I wanted to, but not by much. Melanie had slipped his knife back into my pocket at some point, but I couldn't reach it and cut myself free.

All I could do was stand there and take it.

The quiet continued.

I stared at the bark of the tree, the glistening of the ice crystals embedded between the pieces. I knew what whipping entailed, but I had no idea how it would feel, if it would be better than the Red Snow.

Maybe it would be worse.

The executioner yelled so loudly that he must have woken up every prisoner in the camp. "Get on with it!"

I knew why he hesitated as long as he did. He didn't want to do this to me. He didn't want to hurt me. He'd suggested the punishment to spare me from the Red Snow, but the executioner was only interested in my death, not a short-lived torture.

His boots shifted in the snow as he positioned himself.

I stared at the bark, my breath escaping as vapor in front of my face.

And then a whip cracked against my back.

I did my best to silence the groan that came from my lips, but I couldn't. It was a quiet scream, a whimper from my lips, a shock so potent my entire body didn't know how to absorb the whip that bit deep into my skin. I swung forward slightly, getting closer to the trunk, my reality pausing for a moment to process what had happened.

I didn't have time to accept it before the whip bit into my skin again.

This time, I shut my mouth and swallowed the scream that wanted to burst from my lips.

He hit me hard—because he had to.

I wanted to be brave like I was for the Red Snow. I didn't want them to claim my terror. But I also stayed quiet to make this easier for him.

How long would this last?

He kept striking me, aiming for different parts of untouched flesh. The leather whip cracked into my skin, made the blood drip down my body and over my pants, making the snow turn red at my feet.

My back suddenly felt red-hot, all the flesh inflamed and pulsing.

It lasted forever.

My body swayed forward with every hit, and I kept my eyes on the bark for concentration. It would end soon. I just had to wait, had to be patient.

He continued to strike me, the whip making a loud crack every time it hit my flesh.

I tried to stay quiet, but I couldn't. I started to whimper with every hit, my feet slipping on the snow because I couldn't hold myself up anymore. The arrow was still in my arm, and I was weak from the punch I'd received to the head. I wasn't ready for this, ready to survive this with dignity.

Then it stopped.

"Oh, thank god…"

"No." The executioner's deep voice was a threatening growl. "Harder."

I closed my eyes and felt the tears drip down my cheeks because I couldn't take much more of this.

Magnus hesitated.

"Or would you rather I do it?" the executioner challenged.

God no.

Magnus struck me harder than before.

I cried out and swung forward from the momentum of his hit.

He didn't take pauses between hits anymore. He just fired them off, one after another, hitting me repeatedly and giving me no time to breathe.

It was excruciating.

Either from the loss of blood or the overload of pain, I knew my feet couldn't support me anymore, and I just started to dangle there, my head dropping, my gaze losing focus.

"What are you doing?" the executioner asked. "Keep going."

Magnus lost his temper. "She's not even conscious anymore."

"And neither are the men she killed!"

Was I going to die like this, hanging from a tree?

"Enough." Magnus's footsteps approached me, his boots hitting the snow.

Thank fucking god.

The rope above my hands was cut, and I fell forward, landing in his outstretched arms.

I collapsed against him, so weak I couldn't stand, in so much pain that I couldn't focus on anything else.

He tried to get me to stand and walk.

"I can't..." I fell down onto the snow, landing in the powder, the ice feeling a little better on my back. But my mind faded in and out, like a weak radio signal the antenna couldn't pick up because of poor reception.

Magnus stared down at me for a second, as if deciding what to do. Then he kneeled, scooped his arms underneath my body, and lifted me from the ground. He turned me into his chest and carried me away from the tree, past the executioner and the guards standing under the lit torches.

I kept my gaze focused on his chest, refusing to look at the men who watched one of their own carry me away.

The brightness faded as we left the clearing, as we walked down the path that we took every morning to work on the line. The only sound was his boots crunching against the new powder that had come in with the storm that was supposed to mask my escape.

I was in so much pain.

My arms circled his neck, and I pressed my face into his body, feeling safe for the first time since the last time we were together. The only thing stopping those men from ripping me apart was the man who carried me when I could no longer walk. He was the only reason I was still alive.

He held me a little bit closer, protecting me from the cold.

When we got to my cabin, he carried me inside and set me on the bed.

I collapsed, writhing in agony.

"I need you to stand."

"I can't..."

"Yes, you can. Come on." He pulled medical supplies out of his pockets, including a roll of gauze.

I forced myself off the bed and onto my feet, suddenly aware that my top had fallen off at some point. I stood naked from the waist up, my tits visible, my back covered in my blood. But I didn't hide my nakedness because I just didn't care.

Magnus didn't seem to care either because he didn't look. He started to unroll the gauze and wrap it around my body, making me wince at the pressure. He started at my waist and slowly moved up higher, covering every single injury as he moved over my breasts.

I hadn't noticed the pain when he'd lifted me, but I definitely noticed it now.

His eyes were down on his movements the entire time, his brown eyes steady and focused, like that scene that just happened in the clearing didn't affect him emotionally. He taped the gauze into place then opened my nightstand to pull out new clothes. "Get dressed."

I couldn't do it, so I just lay back on the bed, still in my bloody pants and boots.

He stood over me.

I turned on my side to get the pressure off my back. My brain was in shock, but once that wore off, I would feel the pain even worse. There was no way I would get through the night, at least not if I intended to sleep.

Magnus stared at me for a few seconds before he sat on the bed next to me and unlaced my shoes. He got them loose then slipped them off before he moved to my pants. He untied the strings and got them off too, leaving stains of blood on top of the comforter.

I was in too much pain to care about what he was doing.

Then he carefully pulled the sheets from underneath me and placed them on top of me, tucking me in like my mother used to when I was a child. He moved to the nightstand and pulled out some pills. "Take this. You'll feel better."

"What is it?" I turned to look.

"Good shit."

Since it would make me feel better, I found the strength to sit up and swallow the pills dry.

"These too." He had more.

"What is it?"

"Antibiotics."

I took those too before drinking half a bottle of water. I collapsed on the bed and just lay there again.

Magnus looked me over, as if searching for something else he could do for me.

I closed my eyes, my brain shutting down, both from fatigue and pain. Then I heard the movement of the chair as he positioned it in front of my bed. I opened my eyes and saw him sitting there, his hood down, his eyes on me.

He didn't have a range of emotions like most people. He was either angry or nothing at all. Right now, he seemed to be nothing. "It was the only way I could save you…" A hint of remorse was in his voice, showing an emotional depth he'd never expressed before. He dropped his gaze, as if ashamed.

"I know… Thank you."

He lifted his gaze and looked at me again.

I couldn't hold on to consciousness any longer. His face was the last thing I saw before I slipped under… and fell into my nightmares.

17

THE DEMAND

When I woke up, I had no idea what time it was.

But I somehow had slept through the remainder of the night. I felt rested, so it seemed like I'd been asleep for a long time, but Magnus never retrieved me for work. When I tried to sit up, I was hit with the pain I'd forgotten about. The medication must have worn off. My eyes looked under the door to see the light coming through.

That still didn't tell me what time it was, but it was definitely past early morning.

On my nightstand were more pills along with a note.

· · ·

YOU'RE EXCUSED from work for three days. That's the most time I could buy you.

I SWALLOWED the pills with water and noticed the tray of food sitting there. Breakfast wasn't served to prisoners, so this must be whatever the guards had in the morning. It was crepes, a croque monsieur sandwich, and a baguette with jam.

And there was coffee.

It was cold now, but still, it was the first time I'd had coffee in a long time.

The fact that I had an appetite showed just how much I'd starved over the last few days. All the food was cold, so it had probably been sitting there for hours. I ate everything, and I was almost finished when I thought of Melanie.

What had happened to her?

The boss said something about taking her...taking her where?

THE MEDICATION MADE ME SLEEPY, so I took a nap until dinnertime. The sound of the opening door woke me up.

Now that I'd pissed off every single guard in that camp except for Magnus, I was on edge. I was afraid one of them would come into my cabin to kill me, and I was too weak to fight back. Magnus had stuck out his neck for me enough times that I didn't think he could protect me anymore.

But it was Magnus.

Even with his hood up, I recognized him at this point. I'd stared at those shoulders enough time to identify the way they moved. His height was easy to remember. The way he carried himself, confident, strong, and with a distinct "I don't give a fuck" attitude.

I was happy to see him. "Hey."

He set the tray on the nightstand, along with a mug of hot cocoa. "You're feeling better."

"I think it's just the good shit you're giving me."

He turned to leave my cabin, as if delivering the food was the only reason he'd come.

"Wait."

He stopped in front of the door but didn't turn back to me.

"Aren't you going to stay?"

His head faced the door, and his chest rose and fell slowly. A long pause ensued, as if he were so deep in thought that he didn't even realize how much time had passed. When he spoke, his voice was quiet. "Do you *want* me to stay?"

"Why wouldn't I?"

His hand moved to his hood and pushed it down, revealing the chiseled jawline of his masculine face, the shadow that had grown over his bare skin. He turned back to me, his brown eyes full of a slight hint of anger, but it wasn't clear what he was angry about. He grabbed the chair and pulled it closer to my bed.

I sat up, wincing slightly in pain, and then set the tray on my lap, my feet over the edge.

He leaned against the back of the chair with his gaze slightly tilted down to the floor.

I didn't know what to say to him, but I felt a lot better with him there than when he was gone. He was the only person in this camp as loyal to me as my own sister. He was the only person looking out for me, the only reason I'd survived two executions. "I thought we could make it."

He lifted his gaze and looked at me. "I warned you."

I had no idea how terrible the elements would be, how Mother Nature would defeat me. My lack of experience quickly became apparent. My grit and determination weren't enough to overcome my lack of knowledge.

"You shot the guards but didn't kill the dogs. Why?"

"Because we aren't going to kill dogs. They're just doing what they're told. They don't know any better."

"You might have gotten away if you had. You could have killed them, taken one of the horses, and ridden as hard as you could."

I looked down at my food and twirled my fork through the pasta. "I will do whatever it takes to survive, but not if that means I have to kill the innocent. Then I wouldn't be any different from the guards."

He stared at me with that dark and serious expression.

I placed the food into my mouth and chewed. "I thought you said you wouldn't help me again."

He didn't respond to that. A stare ensued, with no reaction at all.

"I hope I haven't put you in a difficult position." He definitely had more power than the average guard, but I had no idea why. He could go directly to the boss and make requests that were granted—and the rest of the guards couldn't say anything about it.

He still didn't say anything.

"I won't try again..." It pained me to give up, to accept an abominable life when I deserved so much more. But I'd already done everything I could, and now that I'd seen the wild myself, I realized I really stood no chance. In summer, I would die from heatstroke. Without the snow in spring, they would just hunt me down even quicker. Unless we were liberated by the police, I had no chance.

His eyes narrowed slightly at my words. "You don't have that luxury."

The food was forgotten once I heard him say that.

"You have to try again...because the guards are going to find any reason to kill you. The second I'm gone, it's over."

The executioner had already warned me of that. "Then don't leave—"

"I have to. My position requires me to be elsewhere."

I set down the fork and gripped each side of the tray to set it aside because I was no longer hungry. "I won't survive out there, even with a horse—"

"I'll help you this time."

My hands balled into fists as the emotion rushed through me, the high of the hope and the low of the fear. I stared at the man who had been my saving grace, my lifeline, the raft in the middle of the ocean. "What...?"

"Because if I don't help you, they'll kill you."

Every time my life was on the line, he intervened. Now, he was doing it again, doing something he hadn't wanted to do in the first place.

"We'll wait until you're strong again. I'll draw you a map to get where you need to go."

Was this really happening? Was I really getting what I wanted above all else? "But...what will they do to you when they know you helped me?" I wanted my freedom above all else, but not if it meant he would be killed.

"Don't worry about me. I have a plan."

WHEN I RETURNED TO WORK, every guard stared at me.

I could tell, even without seeing their faces.

I moved to the table beside Bethany, still in pain, but able to function.

"Girl, are you okay?" she whispered. "What happened?"

"Long story... I'll tell you later." I prepared the box.

"Melanie hasn't returned."

I immediately looked over my shoulder to where she usually sat—and she wasn't there. I looked at the box again, at the powder that was more valuable than every prisoner in that camp.

The boss took her away, and I had no idea how to get her back.

Even if Magnus got me out of there, how would I find her?

Bethany whispered to me, "They're looking. Move."

I carried the box to the table and kept my head down, doing my best not to attract unnecessary attention from the men who already despised me. I was walking a fine line, on thin ice, and any excuse they had to snap my neck was a good one.

I returned to the table.

"Did you guys try to escape?" Bethany whispered.

"Yes."

"Oh my god...how are you still alive?"

All I needed to say was a single word. "Magnus."

"How did he pull that off?"

I still had no idea.

"I'm glad you're still with us."

"Yeah, me too."

"What happened to Melanie?"

"The boss took her..." In the limited interaction I had witnessed, I knew he saw her as a pet, like he owned her...when he had no right to own anyone. Now that she was a flight risk, he removed her from the camp. I just hoped her second destination was better than this.

"Took her where?"

"No idea...but not here."

A WEEK HAD PASSED and Magnus continued to drop off food, but he rarely stayed for a chat. He was either busy in the camp, or he just didn't want to talk.

I was much better than I had been a week ago, but the gauze was still wrapped around me, and I was still taking the antibiotics he left for me. The pain medication stopped, and I was relieved to find that I didn't need it.

When he came to deliver dinner one night, he pulled up the chair.

I cared more about the conversation than the dinner, so I sat at the edge of the bed and left the tray on the nightstand.

He pushed his hood down, revealing that handsome face. He didn't look like the kind of man who needed to work in a place like this. He wasn't cruel enough to do this job like the others. He wasted all his potential at this camp when he could have been doing something better, living a normal life, settling down with a woman just as beautiful as he was.

"Do you know where my sister is?"

The only response he gave was a stare.

"Please tell me where she is..."

"What good would it do?" he whispered. "Even if you get out of here and escape, there's nothing you can do for her. This camp is just a small piece of this operation. There's an entire militia out there. Just as you thought your ambition was enough to get out of here and it knocked you on your ass, it'll happen again with Melanie. Let it go."

I could never let it go, but I didn't tell him that. Once I was free, I would go to the police and report this camp. We would burn it to the ground and then hunt down the man in charge. I didn't need his help to do that. "I'm strong enough to go." I was ready to get out of there, to leave this place forever.

He shook his head. "Not yet."

"Why?"

"We need to wait for the right weather conditions."

"And how is now not the time?" It was snowing almost every day. It wasn't a storm, but the snowflakes were constantly adding to the powder and making it difficult to traverse.

"Because now that you know where you're going, you need to get there as quickly as possible—and not leave tracks."

"Won't the dogs smell me?"

"Not if you cross a river. They'll lose the scent."

Why didn't I think of that? But then again, I didn't even see a river, so...

"We need to wait another week. It's supposed to be sunny and warm, and a lot of that snow will melt. If you ride hard and don't stop, you can get there within a few hours."

I squeezed my hands together, needing to convince myself this was really happening. "I knew that bell was real."

He didn't acknowledge what I said.

"Is that where I'm going? To the bell?"

After a long stretch of silence, he gave a nod.

"Oh my god..." My hands immediately covered my face, and I felt the tears well in my eyes. That bell had kept me going. It'd been calling me home. It'd been the light in the darkness. "Is it a church?"

"A chateau."

"So, when I get there, I just—"

"You wait for me. I'll be there a few days afterward."

"You're...you're joining me?"

"We're far away from Paris, and that's where you want to go, right?"

"Yes."

"Then you're going to need help getting there."

"I can't just ask someone?"

He shook his head. "The chateau is still in the middle of nowhere."

"Then how does the bell ring?"

"A timer."

"How do you know so much about this—"

"Because it's mine." He looked slightly irritated by all the questions. "We need to focus on getting there, not what we'll do once we do."

"Are you fleeing the camp too?"

"No. That's where I'll go when I'm scheduled to leave."

I couldn't believe this was happening. I felt guilty that I would be escaping while the others didn't. I felt terrible I couldn't even tell Bethany that I was leaving, just in case she said something to someone she shouldn't.

"I'll tie up a horse in the forest with everything you need."

"How will you do that?"

He looked annoyed again. "Let me worry about it. After dinner that night, you'll take the horse and run. You'll need some daylight to see where you're going to get past the river. Without it, you'll never make it across. But once you get past that, you should be able to make it in the darkness. You made it as far as you did the first time, so this shouldn't be hard for you."

For the first time in my life, I was speechless. All I could do was stare at this man who had risked his own neck for me countless times. He was rough around the edges, but good underneath. He rarely had nice things to say, rarely issued a compliment, but his soul was pure. He had a conscience, unlike everyone else in that place. "I don't know how to thank you...for everything." If the folklore was true, I would be the only woman to escape this camp in years, and it wasn't happening because I had plotted a master plan that got me free. It was because a man cared enough to do the right thing.

He dropped his gaze. "You can thank me by making sure you get across that river."

Days passed.

The sun was out, and the snow melted.

I had no idea what the date was, but I suspected it was the end of January, maybe February. Perhaps spring was coming early. Or maybe it was just a long pause before another storm.

But I knew my time here was drawing to an end.

Any day...it would happen.

Without a mirror, I wasn't unaware of the condition of my back, but I felt better. I didn't have pain, and I didn't spot any more drops of blood. The gauze seemed unnecessary, so I removed it.

I'd been eating everything on my plate, making sure I got plenty of sleep, remaining mentally prepared for the undertaking I was about to make. But my heart constantly beat harder than it should, because I was nervous. If I was caught...that would be it. I was a cat with nine lives, and I'd already blown through the first eight.

I sat up in bed and leaned against the wall with the *Count of Monte Cristo* in my hands. I'd read this story a dozen times before, but I read it again because it took on new meaning.

Because I would make it out of there.

The door opened, and Magnus walked inside with my evening tray. The woman never delivered the food anymore, as if he didn't want anyone to interact with me besides himself. His hood was pushed down, and he carried the tray to the nightstand. Then he grabbed his chair and took a seat.

I closed the book and set it to the side as I scooted to the edge of the bed.

He glanced at the book, the cover visible. "Tomorrow."

Every day felt like the day it could happen—but now today was that day.

"The horse will be in the forest behind your cabin. I'll leave you a flashlight so you can find her. A bag will be tied to her saddle with everything you need inside."

I dropped my gaze for a moment and looked at my hands, my breathing ragged because it was really happening. Freedom was so close, but I was also terrified because I still had to go back out there...and survive. The darkness, the cold, the fear of the guards behind me...it was traumatizing.

"Ride hard. Don't look back." He pulled out a paper from his pocket and unfolded it. "Here's the map." It wasn't a professional one created with a computer. It was hand-drawn, showing the camp, the forest, the path to the river, and then beyond. He turned it over and showed me the individual steps I could take to figure it out. "Keep the forest on your right. As long as you do that, you'll hit the river. When you cross it, the chateau is farther to the left, so you'll have to look at these landmarks to help you."

I took the paper from him, studying his notes to see if I had any questions.

It was detailed enough that I didn't have any. "Will I have a gun?"

He shook his head. "The only way to retrieve those is with a code, so if they notice it's missing, they'll know I took it. I didn't give you any weapons—because that would be too obvious. But you shouldn't need them because all you have to do is get there as quickly as possible. If they did catch you, a weapon wouldn't help you."

Probably not.

I folded the paper and stuffed it into my pocket.

Now we sat together in silence because there was nothing left to say. A part of me thought he would have a change of heart because everyone would assume he'd orchestrated my escape. But he didn't.

I stared at him, looking at a face I would never forget, even if I was fortunate enough to grow old. My memory of my young life would fade, but the memory of this man never would. I shouldn't regard him as a hero for saving me, because he worked there in the first place. But he was definitely my hero.

A few minutes passed before he spoke again. "I'm not doing this out of the goodness of my heart." His brown eyes drilled into mine with invisible force, burning into me, digging deep past my eyes and further down into my soul.

My breathing immediately slowed because I could feel the tension in the air, the sudden increase in heat, the implication of his words. Not once had he asked me for anything. Not once had he expected something in exchange for his kindness.

But he'd been keeping receipts...and he wanted to collect.

"I want you." He was unapologetic about it, extremely candid. Now there was no misunderstanding, not there really had been since he'd first admitted it. There had never been a time when he looked at me like he wanted anything more than a conversation. His eyes didn't roam over my body the way the other guards did. Most of the time, he didn't even act like he liked me. But he had a remarkable poker face. Maybe this had been his plan all along, the extended buildup to this moment.

"No."

His eyes immediately lost their confidence, slowly filling with disappointment.

"I refuse to believe you'll only help me if I sleep with you. You'll help me because I deserve to be free. You'll help me because you know it's the right thing to do. My answer is no."

His eyes slowly dropped, resignation coming over his face. It was one of the rare times when he showed something other than his stonelike stoicism or his anger. There was no response to my decision. He didn't force himself on me. He didn't leverage my freedom to coerce me. He accepted my answer.

I watched him glide his palms past each other, his head bowed slightly to the floor. "But I'll sleep with you...because I want to."

His hands stilled, and his body went rigid. Seconds later, he lifted his chin to look me in the eye again.

It was impossible not to feel a connection to this man. I'd spent my life taking care of other people, and it was the first time I had someone to take care of me, to clean up my messes, to fix all my mistakes. The second his hood had dropped and I saw his face, I had been stunned by what I saw, because he was beautiful. He was the kind of man I could never have in the real world, because he could have someone much more beautiful than me. He would chase after Melanie or someone like her. But in this different reality, we were connected by something deeper than looks. We witnessed things other people couldn't possibly understand. He was a man who needed more than a pretty face to fulfill his desires. He needed something deeper.

He maintained his stare, his eyes different than before, giving me a look he'd never expressed in the past. It finally possessed emotion, overt reactions that were like words on a page. With deep intensity and masculine desire, he stared at me like there had never been a woman he wanted more than me.

I'd never felt so beautiful. I hadn't worn makeup, hadn't even combed my hair, had only worn the most unflattering clothes, but I was somehow the woman he would do anything for.

He continued that piercing look, like my answer was so powerful he didn't know what to do with himself.

With my eyes on his, I pulled my shirt over my head. My body was slim and tight because of my physicality in the camp. I'd never been so active, so I was in the best shape of my life. But I did have some bruises and scars from my mistreatment.

He looked at me like he didn't see anything except unblemished skin.

My boobs were firm and my nipples hard because I was instantly cold...and tense. My dark hair fell down my shoulders and over my chest, but I pushed it back so it would hang down my back, so he could look at me.

His eyes remained on my tits, and he released a deep breath, his jaw tightening slightly.

I knew my back was scarred and ugly, so I didn't turn my back to make him see it.

I untied the string to my pants then stood up so I could push them over my hips and let them slide to the floor. My legs were hairy because I hadn't shaved in over a month. My underwear were the generic ones they issued to us, so they weren't sexy by any means.

But his breathing increased, like he couldn't wait to watch me take them off.

My thumbs dug into the waistband and then pulled them down, the bush of hair visible because I couldn't groom my appearance. We weren't allowed razors, probably because we would slice our wrists.

My hair was curly and dark, covering the sight of my clit and opening.

But he didn't seem to care in the least.

When my clothes were gone, I sat on the edge of the bed again, my knees pressed together, my hands in my lap, my nipples still hard because I was anxious. His chest would be warm against my body, and the momentary coldness would be replaced by sweat.

He stared at me for another few seconds before he unclasped his cloak and let it slide into the chair and then onto the floor. Underneath was a long-sleeved black vest with little markings in it, the fur lining the edge of the sleeves. He gripped the back of the garment and pulled it forward over his head, revealing a black shirt underneath.

I watched him, waiting to see what he looked like underneath. He looked muscular through his clothing, and now that I could see his arms, I knew how strong he was. He had big arms, with lots of different muscles that made them bulky and smooth at the same time. His skin was fair like he hadn't seen the sun much, probably because it'd been freezing for a long time.

He did the same with his shirt, pulling it forward and revealing muscular perfection.

I inhaled a breath at the sight of him.

In the center of two strong pectoral muscles was a patch of dark hair. His stomach was carved with lines, his abs distinct and strong because there wasn't a layer of fat on top to hide them. Even when he was sitting, he didn't have a gut. He was ripped, with a thin line of hair below his belly button that disappeared into his pants.

My eyes roamed over his body, seeing a real man sitting before me, with muscles and hair. His collarbone popped out from his skin because he was so tight, so trim. His shoulders were muscular and broad. I'd never been with a man that looked anything like that...except in my fantasies.

I swallowed the catch in my throat before I lifted my gaze to look at him.

He studied my reaction, like he wanted to watch me want him, to see me want him as much as he wanted me. He loosened his boots and got them off before he pulled the string of his pants then rose to his feet so he could drop those next. He pushed them over his hips and thighs, his muscular legs too sculpted for the pants to just drop down like mine did. His thighs were thick with different muscles that made them tight and strong like tree trunks. They were covered with dark hair. He grabbed his black boxers next and pushed them down, revealing a big dick that was drooling at the tip. He wasn't groomed either so there was a lot of hair around his balls, but it was sexy.

I stared at his dick and felt my throat go dry at the sight of him. Instead of being stuck in that cabin in the middle of nowhere, I felt like I was somewhere else, in my bedroom with a man I'd noticed across the room in a bar...someone I wanted to take home the second he bought me a drink.

He stared down at me, watched me watch him.

I scooted back up the bed, my head reaching the corner of the mattress between the two walls. My thighs automatically parted for him to get on top of me.

He looked between my legs before his knees hit the mattress. He moved down and on top of me, his thighs scooping underneath mine, his face level with mine. He released a deep breath right against my lips, a quiet moan barely audible, deep and masculine. His eyes were warm like a summer day, and his skin was already flushed in arousal when he'd barely touched me.

My hands started at his stomach and moved up, over his hard pecs, to his shoulders, one hand moving to his jawline so I could cup his face. I stared at his lips and imagined how it would feel to kiss him, to feel those lips glide past mine, to feel his facial hair rub against my soft skin.

He stared at my lips before he leaned down and kissed me, a soft embrace, a gentleness that he never showed. He was callous and cold, but he kissed me like I was delicate, like he wanted to explore me before he took me.

The softness didn't last long, because both of my hands dug into his hair and I deepened the kiss, feeling a tightness in my stomach, an electric flush throughout my body that made me feel like I was somewhere far away. The chemistry was as hot as a lit torch, and the closeness I shared with this man made me desire him more, made me crave his touch deeper and deeper. The kiss turned urgent and frantic, both of us wanting each other more desperately as the minutes went on.

He pulled his lips away so he could grab his base and direct himself inside me, moving through my hair and landing in the wet slit that was ready to take him. He didn't lick his hand and moisten his tip because he didn't need to. With eyes locked on mine, he groaned as he felt my desire, groaned louder as he sank deeper and deeper.

My hands glided up his back as I pulled him closer to me, feeling a fullness between my legs that made me moan with hot breath. My hands dug into the backs of his shoulders as I secured him on top of me, feeling the chemistry between our wet bodies ignite and explode.

My ankles locked around his waist, and I enjoyed the first pleasure I'd received since coming to this terrible place. This man was my savior, the one looking over my shoulder when I forgot to check myself. He had my back when I only had my front. He was always there for me, keeping me alive, saving my ass when I thought it couldn't be saved again. He gave me everything, selflessly.

He was the reason I would get out of here.

He was the reason my fate had been different from the others who weren't so lucky.

He was the reason...for everything.

He closed his eyes and groaned as he felt me, his dick deep inside me, surrounded by the wetness that my body produced in copious amounts. Without a single kiss or touch to my clit, he made me soaking wet. He opened his eyes and looked down into my face as he started to thrust, pushing fully inside before he pulled out again, moaning every single time like he couldn't believe how good I felt.

My nails clawed at his body, and I breathed against his mouth, feeling his chest hair moving between my tits, feeling his body heat thaw me like I was next to a fire in the hearth. My ankles yanked on his ass as he moved inside me, pulling him a little deeper, wanting as much of him as my body could handle.

His hand moved into the back of my hair, and he fisted the strands, tilting my chin up so he could kiss my neck, smothering me with hot kisses from his hungry lips. His mouth moved between my tits, and he kissed me everywhere, enjoying my body like it was flawless, like I was the most desirable woman in the world.

My nails dug into his flesh, and I held on to his frame, getting lost in the haze of desire, of sweaty and sensual sex, of the way he made me feel good when I'd felt so bad for so long. The passion was hot as a fire, like it was the first time we'd given in to our desire, but our bodies were so in sync, it was as if we'd been lovers for years.

He raised his head then moved his arms behind my knees, pinning me back so he could thrust into me while looking down at my face, pumping his dick inside me deep and hard, with full and long strokes.

My hands held on to his arms, and I bit my bottom lip as I looked into his face above me, seeing the flushed color of his beautiful skin, the potent desire in his expression. Uncontrollable pants came from my lips, and then I writhed. "Yes...yes."

He lay beside me on his back, his hand resting on his chest, naked because we'd never gotten under the sheets. His eyes were on the ceiling, his mood dark once more after our passion was over. His hair was messy from where I'd fingered it, and his powerful chest rose and fell gently because his breathing had returned to normal minutes ago.

I lay beside him, the sheets pulled to my shoulder because I was cold once he was gone.

He didn't show affection. He didn't hold me close. It was back to how it was before—coldness.

He sat up and got out of bed.

I watched him stand straight and start to dress, sheathing his strong body in the clothes, his beautiful skin disappearing underneath his uniform. The cloak was the last piece of clothing, and he secured it in place like nothing had happened.

I didn't expect him to stay. He couldn't sleep there, not when people would assume where he spent his night. I didn't wait for a kiss goodbye or an affectionate touch, because I knew that night was a one-time thing.

He had to be a one-time thing.

He sat in the chair again and pulled on his gloves.

I sat at the edge of the bed, and even though he'd already seen me naked, I covered my body with the sheet. "Can I bring something with me?"

He finished with his gloves then regarded me coldly, like the heat of our passion didn't thaw his heart.

I grabbed the book by the edge. It was my bible. It was the story that mirrored my own, that made me feel connected to someone outside the four walls of this cell. It gave me hope when I was alone.

He eyed it in my hands before he lifted his gaze and looked at me again.

"This book has gotten me through a lot, and I want to keep it."

He rose to his feet and extended his hand to take it.

I gave a silent goodbye, my hands aching the second I released it.

He tucked it inside his pants and pulled his shirt back down.

I watched him head to the door—and walk out.

18

THE CHATEAU

I sat across from Bethany in the clearing, eating one of my final meals.

I wasn't coming back.

And if I was...I wouldn't sit here ever again.

I was guilty about the women I was leaving behind. While I would make it past the river and to the chateau, their lives would go on like nothing had changed. My successful escape might encourage them to rebel since there were far more of them than the guards. It might give them hope. It might give them strength to fight back.

I felt terrible for leaving my friend behind, after everything she'd done for me.

But if our situations were reversed, she would do the same.

"Do you know when Magnus is leaving again?" she whispered.

"In a few days."

"What will you do then?"

I wouldn't have to worry about it. "Not sure…"

She kept her head down and continued to eat.

"Thank you for everything." I needed to express my gratitude, to tell her how much her friendship meant to me before I never saw her again. "You're a good person, Bethany."

She lifted her gaze and looked up. "Don't talk like that. You've survived this long…"

I WAS DRESSED and ready to go.

I waited for the sound of footsteps, waited for my final meal to be delivered.

His feet climbed onto the porch. They came closer before he opened the door.

I turned to look at him.

He shut the door behind himself then sat across from me. There was no hot cocoa this time. There was just the tray of food. He handed it to me before dropping his hood and revealing his face.

I started to eat even though I wasn't hungry.

"Take your time. We need to wait thirty minutes."

"Why?"

"You'll see." He kept his gloves on with his head bowed, barely looking at me.

I ate the dinner in my lap, sitting close to the man who had bedded me the night before. That fire hadn't returned, probably because we were both focused on the next part of this plan. "If I don't get a chance to talk to you again...I really appreciate everything you've done for me."

Like always, there was no acknowledgment of my words.

I shouldn't have to thank him for what I was entitled to—freedom. But that was the world we lived in.

I finished everything on my plate then set the tray on the nightstand.

Now we just sat together, the minutes trickling by.

"I'm afraid." I let the words escape my lips, abandoning all pretense because he knew me inside and out at this point. He knew me in a way no one on the outside did, not even my sister.

He lifted his chin and looked at me, his brown eyes trying to read further into my words.

"I'm not afraid of dying. I'm not afraid of pain. I'm afraid of losing this...of losing this chance."

He regarded me with his signature hard gaze. "Then cross that river."

I gave a slight nod.

"You have the map?"

I patted my thigh.

He rose to his feet and returned the chair to the wall.

I knew it was time.

He moved to my tub and pulled out a tool from his pocket. Then he started to slam it down onto the faucet, breaking it from the wall until the metal clanked into the bottom of the basin.

"What are you doing?"

He grabbed the faucet then turned back to me. He came closer to me until he grabbed my hand and placed the piece of metal within my grasp.

Still confused, I never took my gaze off his face.

"Dinner is finished so there shouldn't be any guards around. But someone will find me sooner rather than later."

"Find you...?" My voice broke because I already suspected where this was going.

"When I open the door, you're going to have to hit me with that." He spoke so plainly, like this wasn't a big deal at all. "Hit me in the head. Knock me out. Then go."

I lowered my hand to my side. "No..."

He released a deep sigh. "It's the only way—"

"I'm not going to hit you!"

"If you don't, they're going to assume I helped you escape. You need to hit me, and you need to hit me hard enough to make this believable. I'm a strong guy, so it would take a lot to slow me down."

My eyes watered because I was disgusted by the price of my freedom. "No..."

"You're protecting me. The way I protected you."

I shook my head, the water welling up in my eyes until I formed tears. "It's not the same—"

"It's exactly the same."

"If I hit you with this thing, I could kill you."

"I could have killed you."

I shook my head, tears dripping down my cheeks. "Please don't make me do this. Please don't make me—"

"It's the only way."

I quickly wiped my face with my hands, fighting the panic spreading through my body.

"I'm leaving in a few days—so this is your only chance."

I took a deep breath and forced my tears to stop. "The last thing I want to do is hurt you. I *can't* hurt you. I just can't do it..." This man was the only thing separating me from execution. He was the only reason I still breathed.

He stepped closer to me, his hand moving to my arm, giving me a strong squeeze. "You can do this. Do it to protect me. Everything is already set up, and I can't go back and hide it. This needs to happen now—for both our sakes."

I raised my hand and looked at the faucet he'd beaten off the wall.

"I can handle it. I've had worse."

I lifted my chin and looked at him again. "I'm so sorry..."

"Don't be." His eyes were a little warmer now, like my pain softened him. "Hit me a couple times until I'm down."

How could he say that so nonchalantly?

"I already took some pills to make it easier for me."

I was going to be sick.

"Hit me in the back—so you don't have to look at me."

If he had told me the plan beforehand, I never would have agreed to it. "You didn't tell me before on purpose."

He didn't confirm my suspicion because it was obvious. "One final thing... I'm going to be down for a day or so. So, if you get caught, I won't be able to help you again."

Now the stakes were even higher.

"Don't get caught." He stepped away and headed to the door. After one final look, he gave me a nod, telling me to do it once he stepped outside, and then walked out.

I gripped the bathtub faucet in my hand and felt a rush of nausea because of what I had to do. Not only did I have to hit him, but I had to hit him until he lost consciousness. I had to make it look real, like I really did sneak up behind him after he delivered dinner and beat him to a pulp. It would make him look innocent in all this, that I stole his keys and got the horse because I thought he was dead.

I had to do this.

No turning back now.

He stood outside and faced the camp, waiting for it to happen, knowing it would happen at any moment.

This was my savior...and I had to hit him.

I slept with this man...and I had to hit him.

Now I knew exactly how he felt when he had that whip in his hand and stared at my bare back, knowing he'd have to whip me bloody. If he didn't, I would die.

I told myself he would be okay. He was a strong man who would bounce back. If I survived the whipping, he could survive this. I walked up to him and held up the metal pipe. My hand shook before I did it.

I hit him.

He scuffled forward slightly but remained upright, not making a sound.

I did it again...and again.

Until he collapsed.

He fell on his side, blood dripping from the back of his head to the floor.

I looked at the strongest man I'd ever met and cried. Tears filled my eyes and dripped down my cheeks, bringing salt to my lips before they fell down my chin. My chest heaved with the need to sob.

I felt so sick that I didn't want to leave.

I kneeled next to him and looked at him, seeing his closed eyes. My hand went to his chest and felt it rise and fall with his breathing. I wanted to patch him up, put a blanket over him, but I had to leave him like that. "I'm so sorry..." I left the pipe beside him and leaned down to kiss him on the lips. "I'm sorry." I spoke against his lips, crying because of what I'd done to him.

But I couldn't linger. Light was fading, and I was working against the clock. "I'll see you in a few days..." My hand touched his cheek before I rose to my feet. I took a look around, seeing no one in sight. The guards who were posted last time weren't there anymore because I was no longer considered a flight risk.

They were wrong.

I left and didn't turn back again, because if I looked at him one more time, I might not have the strength to leave.

I moved into the forest and followed his guidelines until I found the place where the horse was tied up. She was saddled and ready to go, the reins tied to a low tree branch. Her huge eyes immediately looked at me approaching, vapor coming from her big nostrils. "Hey, girl..." I rubbed her snout before I gave it a kiss. "Can I get a ride?" I loosened the reins then pulled myself into the saddle.

I'd never ridden a horse before. It was terrifying being this high off the ground, on top of a strong beast that could buck me off if she didn't like me. But

I'd never get there quickly enough on foot, so she and I would just have to trust each other.

The camp was on my right, so I dug my heels into her belly and clicked my tongue. "Let's go." She started at a walk, which was comfortable, but I knew I had to get there quickly, so a walk or a steady gait wouldn't be good enough. I knocked my boots into her again, telling her to run.

Then she took off.

"Oh my god..." The reins were wrapped in my hand, but I gripped the pommel because it was the only thing to hold. "Jesus." My whole body shook as she ran into the forest, moving around tree roots and choosing her own path away, deeper into the wilderness. But I held on and watched the light start to fade over the horizon. The snow had melted in the past week, so the land was mostly flat. The horse could see where we were going and avoid the obstacles. I started to loosen up when I got more used to it, but it was still one of the scariest experiences of my life. "I trust you, girl..."

IT WAS PRETTY MUCH DARK, the sky slightly blue like I had a minute or left before I plunged into complete darkness.

"Where the fuck is this river?" I had my flashlight out, scanning the landscape, listening for the sound of rushing water. "Do you hear it?" I'd started to talk to her like she was my friend, because she was the only thing I had right now. And she was literally getting me there.

She suddenly slowed down, going from a run to a walk. Then she stopped in front of the river.

"Yes!" I clapped my heels against her belly. "Let's go."

She released a neigh and wiggled her ears.

"I know it's going to be cold, but we have to do it."

She still wouldn't move.

Then I heard a distant bark.

"Oh fuck no..." I turned in my saddle and saw the far-off burning of torches. "Girl, we've got to do this." I clicked into her saddle again.

She didn't budge.

I got off the saddle and moved to the river. The water was wide and moving slowly, but I knew the current could be swift underneath. He never told me where to cross, probably because that was too difficult to detail.

I looked back behind me then grabbed the reins. "I can't leave you here, so you're coming with me." I started to pull her toward the water. I put the flashlight in my mouth and pointed it forward to see where I was going. Then I stuck one foot in the water. I groaned with the flashlight in my mouth.

Jesus Christ, that was cold.

But I didn't have time to take this slow. I had to just get through. I moved deeper into the water and pulled her with me.

She wouldn't budge.

I turned back to her, the water up to my thighs. "Girl, I know this fucking sucks, but you've got to do this. Please." I gave the reins a gentle tug.

Her eyes twitched.

I clicked my tongue and started to pull her.

She let me this time.

We both moved into the water. It was deeper than I wanted it to be, reaching all the way to my neck. But I kept going, fighting the current of the stream, and focused on the other side so I wouldn't give in to the cold, in to the fear.

If it went any deeper, I wouldn't know what to do. The current would pull me away.

But it started to become shallow.

"Oh, thank god..." My body emerged out of the water, even colder when it was exposed to the dry air. I began to shiver as more of my body was revealed. "Almost there..." I made it to the other bank, the water dripping from my clothes and onto land, the shivers taking me hard.

The horse came with me.

I was so cold I almost couldn't move.

She neighed and looked at me.

"God, I'm so cold..." I looked behind me and saw the distant torches. The hardest part was over. They would probably assume I didn't cross the river, because if I didn't find shelter soon, I would die. Magnus never told me if they knew about his chateau, but if they didn't, they would never suspect anything.

I just had to live long enough to get there.

I pulled myself into the saddle and dug my heels into her sides. "L-let's...g-go." My teeth chattered so much that my jaw ached. I could barely get the words out.

She started at a run, and that was enough to jolt my heart to life and get me going again.

———

I BROUGHT the horse to a stop, unfolded the soaked map, and then nearly dropped my flashlight.

The ink had run.

I could barely make it out.

"No..." I pointed the flashlight at the details, trying to make some sense of it. When I turned it over to look at his notes, I could barely read anything. "Fuck me..." I held the flashlight close and tried to make sense of it. There were only a few words here and there. "He said there's a forest to the east, hiding it from view...something like that. Something about rocks..." My heart started to race because I was fighting a different clock now.

I would freeze to death if I didn't get to shelter soon.

It was pitch dark, so I couldn't see. All I had was the compass he packed for me.

At least I knew what direction I was going.

"Let's keep going this way and hope for some trees." I folded the map and pointed the flashlight ahead so she would be able to see where she was going. The only sounds around us were the creepiness of the wind, the rustle of the grass and branches below her hooves, and the random neighs she would make.

My mind drifted back to Magnus.

They had obviously found him, and he was probably warm in his cabin. He probably already received medical attention. He was probably asleep...and alive. He would meet me in a few days. All I had to do was make it.

Then I could apologize for the horrendous thing I'd done.

And we could move on.

The horse slowed down when we made it into a line of trees.

"Okay, this has to be it..." She moved at a slow walk, her neck bobbing up and down with her progress. I shone the light into the trees and scanned the area, looking for the chateau where the bell tolled every morning.

We walked for a long time, but there wasn't the same urgency anymore. Every time I looked behind me, there were no torches in my view. There were no more barks from the dogs hunting my scent. They must have reached the river and turned a different direction to continue their search.

That meant I got away.

I fucking did it.

I just had to get inside quickly.

I couldn't feel my arms and legs, and I was shaking so violently that I could barely stay upright in the saddle.

And I was getting sleepy...so sleepy.

When fifteen minutes passed, I knew I wasn't going to make it.

I could barely keep the lights on in my head. The flashlight drooped in my hand. My body started to slide.

Then she stopped.

It made my body jolt forward slightly, jerking me awake.

And there it was.

I lifted my flashlight and looked at the tall structure, the ancient architecture. "Oh my god...we fucking did it." That rejuvenated me enough to guide the horse around the side, looking for the front door. Magnus had given me the keys, so I just had to find the way inside.

We moved to the front, and that was when I spotted the double doors of the entrance.

There were no lights on at all, not even landscape lights, so it was hidden in the darkness. "This is it..." I got off the horse, pulled out the keys, and then my hands shook as I inserted them into the lock. The flashlight stayed in my mouth so I could see what I was doing.

Then the lock came free.

I stilled for an instant, celebrating my victory while stunned by the accomplishment.

I opened the second door so the horse could come inside. "Come in..." I grabbed the reins and guided her into the chateau. It was freezing outside, and I didn't want to leave her out there. If I tied her up, wolves would get her. And if I didn't tie her up, she would get lost in the cold.

I immediately shed all my clothes because they were still soaking wet and cold, so they didn't do anything for me anyway. My flashlight moved along the wall until I found the switch. I flipped it on, the foyer coming into sight.

It wasn't what I expected.

It was made of stone, there were no pictures on the walls, no decorations. It felt abandoned.

I closed the doors behind us and locked them. Then I went into the kitchen and found a big pot on the stove. I filled it with water then carried it back to the horse. When I set it on the floor, she immediately started to drink like she was thirsty.

There was a large sitting area downstairs with old furniture, like something from the Victorian era. The window on the wall was colored stained glass, like something out of a church. A huge stone fireplace was below the windows, so I grabbed the matches from the saddle and lit the logs in it on fire.

The flames were low at first, but once all the wood caught on fire, it brought brilliance and warmth into the room. A large staircase led higher up, and there was more to the chateau to explore, but I didn't want the lights on up above, just in case they'd crossed the river to search for me.

The horse gulped in the foyer, the sound echoing against the stone interior.

There was a blanket on the back of one of the couches, so I grabbed it and wrapped it around my body. A rug was on the floor in front of the fireplace, so I pulled the cushions from the couch and made myself a bed next to the fireplace. I was still shivering, my bones frozen, so I snuggled in by the fire, as close as I could get without burning myself, and I lay there...thawing.

The shivering lasted a long time...for hours.

But the heat moved back into my skin, my muscles, and then my bones. Blood started to circulate once more. My knees were pulled to my chest, my arms wrapped around my upper body, and I gripped myself tightly until the jerking stopped.

I did it... I made it.

Hooves echoed against the stone as the horse came into the sitting room. They became louder and louder, muffled once they hit the rug. A loud neigh sounded, like she came close to feel the fire. Then she bent her legs and lowered herself, taking up the spot behind me, just like a dog that came over to snuggle.

I smiled and reached for her mane behind me, feeling it along the back of her neck. "Thank you..."

WHEN I OPENED my eyes the next morning, the fire was gone, the sunlight was coming through all the windows, and the horse was gone.

I stared at the ashes in the hearth, the previous night slowly coming back to me. It was hazy at first, but then flashes returned, riding the horse in the darkness, crossing that frozen river, the distant sound of a barking dog on the wind.

And then I realized...it was the first time in months I'd woken up as a free woman.

I quickly sat upright, the blanket falling off my naked body, the realization hitting me so hard that I sobbed. The grand sitting room echoed my tears back at me, amplifying them, giving me the most cathartic experience of my life.

I made it.

I didn't wake up on that shitty mattress. I wasn't marched to work in the cold. I didn't sit there at the table and eat my lunch in silence, sneaking in conversations because I'd lost my right to even talk to someone.

It was over.

The horse neighed loudly.

That silenced my tears. I turned to look at her.

She stood nearby, her neighs echoing against the stone.

I wiped my tears away with the back of my arm. "You must be hungry, huh?"

She neighed as if she were answering me.

I got to my feet and tied the blanket around me like a toga. "I doubt there's anything in the kitchen..." I walked inside and looked around, seeing the old-fashioned decor, the kitchen island made of solid wood, the small fridge that looked as though it was installed sometime in the sixties. The kitchen wasn't built for a fridge, so it stuck out like it didn't belong.

She followed me to the door, shifting her neck but not stepping into the confined space.

"What do horses eat?" I moved to the pantry and started to open doors. It was mostly canned goods. "Hay? Oats?" I kept looking, finding old boxes of cereal, mostly expired products. Then I found a large container of plain oats. "Yes!" I held up the container to her. "Look what I found."

She stared at me blankly, her eyes wiggling.

I found another large pot and emptied the entire container inside before I carried it back to her pot of water, which was empty. There were horse droppings around, along with puddles of urine. My living conditions had been terrible, so I didn't blink an eye over it. "Here."

She walked over, dropped her neck to smell it, and then started to munch.

"I'm glad you like it." I rubbed her neck while she ate. "I need to give you a name. I'm sure you already have one, but they probably named you something stupid." I searched for something pretty, because she was a beautiful brown horse with a light-colored mane. "How about Rose? That was my mother's name."

She continued to eat.

I patted her on the neck. "No objection? Rose, it is."

19

ROSE

I was too afraid to let Rose outside because the guards might still be looking for me, so I continued to give her water and scavenge for things to feed her. When the droppings and puddles became too much, I cleaned them up and threw them outside, but she always seemed to be making droppings, so I could never really stay on top of it.

I explored the rest of the chateau, which was two stories tall. It was like stepping into a history book, moving through narrow staircases, outdated bathrooms, the hard stone covered with rugs that seemed just as ancient as when the place was built. The bedrooms had four-poster beds with comforters with floral prints. When I ran my hand across them, dust covered my palm until it was black.

This place was extremely untouched.

There were old paintings on the walls, mainly of landscapes, or French aristocracy long before the new world had been fully explored. I searched through the house and examined everything because I had nothing else to do.

Every time I went upstairs, Rose waited at the bottom and remained until I returned.

I hoped to find a laptop or cell phone. The only people I could call right now were the police, and I didn't even know where I was to give them directions. Magnus said he would return me to Paris, so that seemed pointless. But I did have friends who were worried about me, so they'd like to know I was okay. But I didn't have their numbers memorized, so that wouldn't work either. Using the internet to send someone a message would be my best chance at contact.

But I didn't find anything.

I discovered the room Magnus used because it was the only room in the house where the bed was unmade. It was a master suite with its own bathroom, and it had windows that overlooked the tree line. I pulled back the curtains to take a look from this elevation.

In the daylight, I could see the trees and the plains. I could even see the river. But everything beyond that was a blur. There were patches of snow everywhere because it was too cold to melt it all away, and a lot of the trees still had the white powder on their branches. I closed the curtain then explored the closet.

It was empty.

Then I started opening the drawers in the dressers.

There was some clothing, but not much.

There were a couple pairs of fresh boxers, so I pulled one on. I found black sweatpants, so I put a pair of those on too, along with a gray t-shirt. Everything draped down my body like a curtain, and the pants struggled to stay up, so I had to tie them as tight as possible and make a double knot to keep them in place.

He had toiletries in the bathroom, like a razor, shaving cream, shampoo and conditioner, a comb, and a hair dryer. The chateau had mirrors in every bathroom, so it was the first time I actually saw my own image.

I didn't recognize myself.

The weight loss had changed the shape of my face. The fatigue caused slight bags under my eyes. The direct sunlight for hours at a time gave my skin a tan I didn't normally have. When I lifted up my shirt to see my stomach, I saw the outline of a six-pack, a curvature of my body that made me look ready for the beach. I'd never been in shape in my entire life, so it was a different look for me. When I turned around to look at my back, I stilled at all the scars from where I'd healed. I was covered in bumps and streaks from the way the loose skin healed together.

It was ugly.

I didn't look again.

I should be thankful I was alive. I should be thankful I escaped.

My appearance was insignificant.

I took advantage of the toiletries to really wash my hair, comb it, and dry it.

My hair felt so much lighter. It framed my face differently and improved my looks too.

It made me feel like me again...a bit.

I looked through the kitchen and made whatever I could find. The food wasn't as good as it was at the camp, but I'd gladly eat expired soup as a free woman than a gourmet meal made by my captors.

I came across a bag of carrots. There was no expiration date, but they weren't covered in mold, so they seemed good enough to me. "What do you think?" I pulled out a carrot to show it to Rose.

She neighed.

"Let me wash them first." I stood at the kitchen counter and scrubbed each one to make sure it was clean before I patted them dry and fed them to her.

She ate quickly and went through the whole bag in a couple minutes.

"Good?"

Her nostrils released a loud sigh.

"I'll take that as a yes."

I spent my evenings downstairs in front of the fire. I'd found other hearths in the house with dried wood sitting inside, so I confiscated those to use for myself. It was so cold and wet outside that I doubted I would find any dry wood that would burn and not create a ton of dark smoke, so I didn't bother with that.

The days trickled by, and I waited.

The high I felt from escaping faded away quickly, because now I was worried about Magnus.

What if he never came?

What if he'd died? Or what if they'd killed him?

Rose and I could make it the rest of the way on our own, especially with no one chasing us, but I worried about him...my friend.

On the fifth day, there was a loud pounding on the door.

I was on the floor in the sitting room, reading the book that survived the journey in the saddlebags. It managed not to get wet, so it was still intact. I turned at the sound, my blood spiking with both excitement and adrenaline.

Rose turned too.

I got off the floor and came to her side. "It's probably him, right?" What if the guards were outside? What if they'd figured it out?

I moved to the door and realized there wasn't a peephole.

The knock sounded again. "Raven?" It was his voice —I'd recognize it anywhere.

He must have given me his only set of keys. "I'm here!" I turned the lock and yanked the door open.

He stood in his uniform, his hood down so the daylight could highlight his features. His eyes shifted back and forth as he looked at me, like he immediately noticed the difference in my hair.

I lunged into him and wrapped my arms around him, squeezing him hard in an embrace that made me so warm I forgot what it was like to ever feel cold. I felt his muscled frame under my grip through the clothing, my touch immediately familiar because I'd held him before. My face moved into his chest, and I closed my eyes.

He didn't hug me back—like he had no idea what was happening.

I pulled away and looked at him again. "I'm so glad you're alright." I examined his head where I'd hit him, seeing a scar that he would carry for the rest of his life. "I was worried about you the entire time."

His eyes continued to take me in. "I told you I would be fine."

"Doesn't matter. I'm so sorry that I did that to you."

After holding my gaze for a few seconds, he moved past me and entered the house. "I'm surprised you're still here."

"What do you mean?" I shut the door behind him.

"I thought you would take off. You're free now."

The thought never crossed my mind. "I had to wait for you, to make sure you were alright." He told me he would be there in a few days, but I probably would have waited weeks before I accepted the horrible truth—that he didn't make it.

He stared at me again, his guarded eyes slightly dropping in hostility. When I hadn't answered the door right away, he must have assumed that I didn't bother to wait for him, that I got what I wanted, so he was insignificant. When he realized that wasn't the case, his frozen eyes started to thaw. When he turned to step farther into the chateau, he halted when he saw Rose standing there, staring straight at him.

Rose neighed as she looked at him.

"Why the fuck is there a horse in here?" He turned to me, accusation in his eyes.

"It's too cold outside."

He looked around the room, noticing the droppings.

"I've been cleaning it, but Rose goes a lot."

"Rose?"

"Yeah, I named her."

"Why didn't you put her in the stables?"

"There's a stable?"

He sighed loudly then walked to the stairs. "Take her down there and clean this place up."

"Where are you going?"

"Shower." He moved the rest of the way until he disappeared.

I turned back to Rose. "Sorry, it's not you. He's just... kinda grouchy."

She stared at me, warm breath coming from her nostrils.

"Let's go." I took her by the reins and guided her outside. It was a sunny day and there was less snow, so I spotted the stables farther down the hill. It was the first time I'd been outside since I arrived, so I took a look around. There were gardens on the property, but now they were wild because no one had taken care of them in decades. The bushes were overgrown, flowers mixed with weeds, and the patio furniture made of iron had rusted to a blood-orange color.

I walked her to the stables and found another horse there. "At least you'll have someone for company." I walked her inside then found the bucket of hay. I poured it into her trough so she could eat. I shut the door then turned to the other horse. He was solid black, so his eyes disappeared into his coat. He stared at me in stillness—just like his rider. I could tell he wasn't friendly like Rose, so I didn't bother trying to pet him. I made sure he had food and water before I returned to the chateau.

WHEN MAGNUS CAME BACK DOWNSTAIRS, it was evening.

The light had faded from the windows, so the lamps were the only illumination in the area. I sat on the cushions on the floor and ate my bowl of old soup. I looked up to stare at him.

His jaw was clean because he'd shaved, his hair was neat, and he was in sweatpants and a t-shirt...the first time he'd ever worn regular clothes around me. He was dressed entirely in black, barefoot. He stared at me for a few seconds before he turned around and walked off again.

I went back to my soup.

He reappeared minutes later with firewood he'd retrieved from somewhere and carried it to the hearth. He set each log in place before he lit the fire with a bunched-up piece of paper. The flames were big instantly, bringing light and heat to the sitting room.

Then he went into the kitchen.

Now that we were outside the camp and he was in different clothes, I almost expected him to have a different personality, but he was the same brooding man who seemed perpetually unhappy.

He came back a moment later, a bowl of soup in his hand. To my surprise, he took a seat beside me on the floor, pushing away the cushions. His spoon moved through the bowl, and he served his mouth the warm liquid, getting chunks of potatoes and noodles.

It was quiet, our utensils tapping against the bowls.

I looked up and stared at him, seeing the chiseled jawline that I'd kissed, the full lips that had kissed me in places besides my mouth. His shoulders stretched out the cotton of his shirt, and the veins that ran down his arms were like webs under the skin. I'd only seen him outside his uniform once—when he was naked. But seeing him in sweatpants and under a roof different from a cabin made him look like a normal person.

Like we were normal people.

The fire cracked and popped in the hearth beside us, keeping us so warm it practically felt like summer. "What happened?"

He kept his eyes on his food. "Not sure. I was unconscious for a few days."

I cringed and looked back into my bowl, feeling guilty for what I'd done.

"The search party gave up after a couple days. They think you may have crossed the river, but if you did, you got wet, and if you got wet, you wouldn't survive for more than an hour."

That was true. I almost didn't survive. "Did they suspect you?"

"No. But they did give me shit about it, for covering your ass when you stabbed me in the back."

It offended me, because nothing could be further from the truth. I was loyal to him. The only reason I'd struck him was because he forced me to.

"They said they hope I learned my lesson."

"Have you ever helped another prisoner escape?"

He stilled at the question, his spoon going stationary in the bowl. Then he lifted his gaze to look at me, his eyebrows slightly raised in subtle perplexity. He never answered, like it was a stupid question. Then he returned to eating, dismissing my question like I hadn't asked it.

"Then why me?"

He kept his eyes down on his food. "Does it matter?"

"You saved my life. It does matter."

He finished the bowl until it was empty. He set it aside, farther away on the rug. Then he lifted his knees and rested his elbows on top, his gaze on the fire. His eyes were the same color as the firewood, the pieces that didn't burn with red embers. "You deserved better."

"Why didn't the others deserve better?"

He shrugged. "Because they don't act like it. They accepted their fate. From the first day you arrived there, you never did. You were always out of place. You were always the prisoner we talked about. Once you told me how you got there, it made me realize you weren't supposed to be there in the first place." His eyes stayed on the flames, as if he were reliving every single moment in his mind.

"The other women don't deserve to be there either. They keep their heads down because they're smart. It's not because they're weak," I thought of Bethany, who plotted with the girls to get me food. "They're brave in ways the guards don't notice. My life isn't more valuable than theirs. Every single person there deserves to live their life freely."

He turned his head to regard me. "Let's get something straight. There's nothing you can say to make me feel sympathetic to the rest of the women in that camp. Even if they were liberated, a new batch would arrive to replace them. That camp has been there for ten years, and it'll be around for decades to come. I'm a hero in your story, but I'm still the villain in theirs." He turned back to the fire, his eyes shifting slightly as he watched the flames dance, following their movements until they popped. But he didn't flinch at the sound. "Be grateful that I helped you. But don't expect more from me."

I was disappointed because I did expect more from him. There was still a soul deep inside that hard chest, humanity the other guards didn't possess. He had potential—even if he didn't see it. "You aren't like the others."

"Doesn't mean I'm like you."

I stared at the side of his head, his handsome face illuminated by the brilliance of the fire. His beautiful complexion looked angelic in the light. "You can pretend not to have a heart, but I know you have one...a big one."

He turned back to me, his eyes cold despite the warmth hitting him in the face. "You don't know me."

"I disagree." I knew him in a way no one else did. His heroic actions were done in secret, so they weren't for show. He'd freed me at great cost. He'd stuck his neck out for me, stuck it into the noose of the Red

Snow. "What is your purpose there? Everyone has a place—except you."

He turned away and didn't answer.

"Why won't you tell me?"

"Because I don't owe you anything. You're the one indebted to me. So, I suggest you thank me for what I've done instead of interrogate me."

"I'm just trying to get to know you."

"Why?" He looked at me again. "After I drop you off, you'll never see me again."

I expected us to part ways without obligation to each other. But I still expected more from him. "I'm going to go to the police when I get home... You know that, right?"

He stared at the fire.

"So, if you get out now, you'll save yourself. I'm trying to help you."

"Yes, I know exactly what you'll do. Go ahead."

Was I missing something here? "Why does that not scare you?"

"Because you have no idea how the world really works." He clenched his jaw slightly, like this conversation annoyed him the longer it continued. "I suggest you go home and live your life. Be grateful every single day that you survived something no one else ever has. Honor those you left behind by living life to the fullest. That's my advice. Go to the police if you want—but it won't make a difference."

"If you think I'm not going to try to free those women, then you don't know me very well."

"Then try. If it'll clear your conscience and help you sleep at night, then do it."

Even as a free woman, I was starting to feel powerless. Magnus was getting me to safety, but he didn't have any concerns about the consequences of that action. It would never come back and bite him in the ass.

Maybe I really didn't understand what I was dealing with.

"We'll leave tomorrow. Sleep on the floor if you want —but there are beds upstairs." He got to his feet and picked up his bowl.

I stayed in front of the fire.

He walked away into the kitchen.

I stared at the flames for a moment longer before I went after him.

He rinsed out his dish then left it in the bottom of the sink. "How are we getting there? There's no car."

"Horse."

"All the way to Paris?" I asked incredulously. I had no idea where I was, but I knew we were nowhere near the city.

"To the place where I store my car."

"And what will happen to the horse?"

"I'll leave her there until I come back."

"Are you going to return to the camp with two horses?"

He turned around and leaned against the counter as he stared at me. "Why are you asking so many questions about this?"

"Because I don't want Rose to go back. And if you do bring her back, they'll know you helped me. So, what are you planning to do with her?"

He shrugged. "Not sure."

I loved that horse and felt weird parting with her. She was my friend. "Can I keep her?"

He regarded me with a cold stare. "You said you live in an apartment."

"I can rent her a place with a stable."

"That's expensive."

I didn't have much money to begin with. "I just... can't say goodbye."

He pushed off the counter with his hips and sighed. "What if I keep her?"

"This is no place for a horse. There's no fence."

"I have other residences."

Residences? As in plural? "Do you already own horses?"

He nodded.

"But then I'll still never see her..."

"But you'll know she's taken care of. Isn't that enough?"

Rose had carried me away from that terrible place and got me to safety. She became my friend. I didn't want her to be sold to some stranger. And I didn't want her to return to that camp. I wanted her to have a good life...with lots of oats. "You'll take good care of her?"

He nodded. "I will."

"Okay." I turned back to the foyer, still unable to believe that I was leaving tomorrow. I should be more excited, but I started to fear what he had said, that there was nothing I could do for the others.

He came up behind me and headed to the stairs. He stopped and turned to me, like he knew I had something else to say.

"My sister..." I knew I couldn't ask him for anything, not after everything he'd already done for me. I should just be grateful I'd escaped. Melanie got us into this mess in the first place, so it was entirely her fault. But her mistake didn't deserve an eternal punishment. She didn't deserve to belong to someone else, to be an animal in a cage. "Please."

"How dare you ask me that, after everything I sacrificed for you." He stared me down coldly, no longer looking at me the way he used to, like there was always a subtle hint of affection behind his cold stare. But that whisper of warmth was nowhere to be found.

"She's my sister. I can't just go back to life and forget about her."

"You're going to have to."

"Please—"

"No." He raised his voice, the sound reverberating off the walls. "Don't ask me again."

20

PARIS

We left the chateau on horseback.

I sat behind him on Rose, and we made the trek down the path, moving through the countryside in a direction only he seemed to know. We hadn't said much to each other after our contentious conversation the night before.

My feelings toward him were conflicted. On the one hand, he was the man who saved me, he was the man who risked everything to get me out of there, who had goodness inside his soul when the others didn't. But on the other hand, he wouldn't do more than that. He would return to that cabin like nothing happened.

After a few hours in the countryside, we approached a small house. It was a single story, almost like a shack, and it had a small stable there. There was a garage, where his car must be hidden. He put Rose in the stable then grabbed his backpack.

I stared at her, knowing I would never see her again. "Thanks for everything, Rose..." I stood in front of her and rubbed her snout, let her lick my face like she knew this was goodbye. It was hard to turn away, but I managed to do it.

How did I become so attached to something I barely knew?

Magnus watched me, his eyes kind, his human side coming out for the first time since he'd arrived at the chateau. "She's in good hands."

I looked up at him and gave a slight nod.

He walked ahead, passed the front of the house, and then opened the garage.

Inside was a black Bugatti.

I stilled at the sight of it.

He wasn't just some guard at the camp.

This guy had money—lots of it.

He pulled out a piece of fabric from his backpack then walked toward me while holding it up.

I stepped back. "Whoa, what are you doing?"

"Blindfolding you."

"Why?"

His eyes narrowed in annoyance. "You can't know the way."

I didn't want to sit in the car for hours without seeing anything, but he was right. That was exactly what I would do.

"It's nonnegotiable."

I didn't want to return to the camp, so I stepped closer to him and sighed.

He secured it around my face, making the material fall all the way to my nose so there was no chance I could get a peek of anything. Then he guided me to the passenger door.

"You don't think people are gonna call the police when they see a woman blindfolded in the passenger seat?" I reached for my safety belt and struggled to lock it into place. It took a couple tries before it clicked.

"Tinted windows." He shut the door.

After the car came on, he pulled out of the driveway and then headed to the main road. Then we started the drive, the car smooth, like we were flying instead of driving down a country road. I was excited to go back home, but I also felt empty at the same time.

Hours passed, and nothing was said.

He didn't turn on the radio or make conversation.

I couldn't believe I was sitting in a car with my former guard, taking a drive. The car didn't make a single stop in that amount of time, so I knew we were far in the middle of nowhere, taking backroads through vast amounts of nothingness.

"Is that chateau yours?"

"Did you see anyone else there?"

I rolled my eyes even though he couldn't see me. I felt my eyelashes rub against the material covering my face. "It just looks like it's fallen into ruin. A lot of things don't work, and the whole exterior doesn't seem to be cared for. So, did you just decide to squat in it?"

"Squat?"

"When you move in to an abandoned residence and make it yours."

"No...not a squatter."

"Then why did you buy it? You own a Bugatti, so you can afford something up to date."

"I didn't buy it."

"Then...you stole it?"

"Family heirloom."

"You inherited it?"

He didn't say anything.

"How do you inherit something like that? Isn't that something that belongs to old, aristocratic families?" There was no way he fit the bill, because he wouldn't work at a labor camp processing and distributing drugs if that were the case.

"What's your address?" He dodged the question altogether.

"Are we close?"

"No. We still have hours to go."

I leaned my head back into the seat and groaned. "I'm gonna have to pee."

"Hold it."

The car returned to silence again.

Minutes later, he spoke. "Got a boyfriend waiting for you?"

I turned my head at the question even though I couldn't see him. "Would I have slept with you if that were the case?"

"There are no rules when you're a prisoner."

I stared forward again. "You have a girlfriend?"

"Do I look like the kind of guy to have a girlfriend?"

"I don't know. You don't look like the kind of guy to save me...but you did."

He didn't have a response.

"You said your mom passed away. What happened to your father?"

"He ran off after Melanie was born."

There was a long pause. "I'm sorry."

"I'm not. We didn't need his help."

"Did you ever see him again?"

"Nope. What about you? Are your parents still around?"

He never answered the question.

"So, you can ask me whatever you want, but I can't ask you anything?"

"You can ask whatever you want. Doesn't mean I'll answer you."

I KNEW when we were in the city because of the sound of nearby cars, the constant braking, the honks from irritated drivers. "Are we in Paris?"

"Yes."

I pulled the blindfold off since there was no reason to keep it on.

Raindrops were on the windshield, pedestrians were on the sidewalk carrying their umbrellas, the sky was gray because the sun was low and the clouds blocked the light from coming through. We were on the street where my apartment was located.

I took off the safety belt and sat up, my fingertips touching the cold window, my nose pressed against it because I couldn't believe what was right in front of me. My favorite coffee shop passed by. "Oh my god..." My eyes filled with tears as the city's glory hit me right in the face, the place that had become home the second I left the airport. Memories washed over me, of romantic dates that fizzled out after a short fling, of nights out with my friends from school, quiet mornings when I went for a run before the streets and park were packed with people. My vision blurred from my tears, looking like the windows covered in raindrops.

He stopped at a light.

I faced forward and looked around, the Eiffel Tower in the distance.

His head was turned my way, and he watched me, his gaze intense, like he was absorbing my reaction so it would be a memory for him to replay on a lonely night. He'd given this to me—and it obviously meant something to him.

I covered my mouth to hold in my sobs, to force my lungs to relax instead of gasping for air.

The light changed, and he moved forward again.

A moment later, he pulled over to an available spot—right in front of my apartment.

I pushed the door open and immediately stepped into the light rain, my hands out to receive the water, to let the rain wash away the memory of my heartache. It washed away my bruises and scars, washed away the former life that had been hell.

I fell to my knees on the sidewalk and pressed my hands against the wet concrete, unable to believe this was real. The passersby glanced at me but continued on their way.

A hand moved under my arm and gently pulled me upright.

My hand immediately grabbed his, and I pulled him up the steps to the main door.

My name was still there, like I hadn't been evicted. I took the stairs to the third floor, pulling him with me the entire way, my hair and clothes wet from the rainfall. I made it to my front door and saw envelopes in the crack underneath the door. I grabbed one and opened it.

It was a reminder that my rent was late.

That meant my stuff was still inside, exactly where I left it.

I tried the door, but it was locked. "Shit..." All the things I had with me had been confiscated when I was abducted.

Magnus pulled something out of his pocket and opened the door easily, like it was a universal key.

I didn't ask questions before I walked inside.

Dishes were still in the sink, the smell noticeable because they'd been sitting there forever. The light over the kitchen table was still on. My laundry was on the edge of the couch with the laundry basket on the floor. I grabbed a shirt and brought it to my chest, feeling my old clothes in my fingertips. I dropped it and explored the rest of the place as if Magnus weren't following me. "Everything is still here..." I took the stairs to the second floor, to the office where I did all my work.

The Eiffel Tower was there—exactly how I remembered it.

The pictures were on the walls, of my mother, of my friends...of my sister.

She stared back at me...beautiful...innocent.

The flowers in the vase were dead.

Magnus grabbed the book sitting at the edge of the desk...my copy of the *Count of Monte Cristo*. He stared at it for several heartbeats before he lowered it and looked at me, like he could really feel what I felt, understand how overwhelming this was...because it was written all over my face.

"Thank you..." When I blinked, more tears fell. I never thought I'd see this city again, be in this apartment again, and it was given to me, like I was back in time.

The longer he stared at me, the more his eyes softened, turning warm like a cup of coffee.

"Thank you." I moved into him and wrapped my arms around him, embracing him like a friend. I held him close and let my tears absorb into his shirt.

This time, he hugged me back. His arms wrapped around me, his chin resting on my head, his breathing escalating...like my emotion permeated his soul. He held me with his strong arms, holding me in front of the window that showed the Eiffel Tower in the distance.

When I pulled away, his hands slid over my body as he let me go, but his fingertips stayed on my hips.

I looked into his eyes, thinking about that picture of Melanie looking at me, smiling in her usual beautiful way. It would haunt me forever, knowing she was somewhere she shouldn't be, that I was drinking coffee and working on an essay, while she was...god knows where. "Please help me..."

His eyes didn't harden into anger this time. They remained soft, remained warm, remained...beautiful. His hands stayed on my body, and he studied my face, his eyes shifting slightly back and forth, like that request moved past his brain...and into his heart.

"I need my sister back, and you're the only one who can help me." Tears poured down my cheeks, in both happiness and despair. My life had been returned to me, but it would never be the same without her. "She's all I have...the only family I have."

His eyes dropped for just an instant, a subtle reaction. They flicked back up just as quickly, like he wanted to hide the movement, like he didn't want me to know those words hit him exactly where I wanted them to. "Okay."

The rain started to fall harder, pelting the window with large drops of water. It blurred the lights from the city, from the Eiffel Tower that was lit up in the distance. My arms remained around his neck and shoulders, and my eyes were still, looking into the sexiest brown eyes I'd ever seen.

I couldn't believe he said that, said what I wanted to hear.

He didn't blink as he looked at me, studying my reaction, like he knew how I felt without needing me to describe it in words. He knew me through my worst, knew me in the coldest winter, with my back lashed and blood dripping onto my sheets, so he knew every expression I made, even when I was happy, even if he'd never seen it before.

My heart beat frantically, and my surroundings felt like the background of a vivid dream. This was real, even if it didn't feel that way. He gave me what I wanted and didn't deny me again. My life was given back to me, one piece at a time, because this man wanted to give it to me. My breathing grew labored and deep, my eyes wetter than they were before. My hands slowly glided down to the crooks of his arms.

He stared down at me, giving me a look I recognized instantly. It had happened once before, alone together in a cabin in the snow, and he'd said the bluntest words a man had ever said to me.

Now it was my turn to say them. "I want you." My eyes moved to his lips just a moment before he kissed me, watching them come toward me and press against my mouth. His hand slid into my hair at the same time, and instead of starting out slow, he gave me a passionate embrace, like we were picking up exactly where we'd left off. He already knew my mouth, knew my body, knew the way I reacted to specific touches everywhere.

His hands gripped me aggressively, squeezing my arms, my ass, the back of my neck, his mouth kissing me the way men kissed the women in movies...the way I'd never been kissed. Whenever his hands moved to my back, he was always gentle, always aware of the scars he'd given me, like the wounds were still fresh and bleeding.

I was still in the baggy clothes I took from the chateau, but he kissed me like I was in a mini dress and heels. My hands moved underneath his shirt that had drops of rain on the cotton and pulled it over his head, revealing the rock-hard chest that had been on top of me before. I was already familiar with his physique, so I touched the places I already knew, the hard muscles of his chest, the powerful abs of his stomach, his searing-hot skin, like he'd just run a mile in the summer heat.

His tongue was in my mouth, gliding past mine in an expertly executed kiss, taking my breath away before he sucked my bottom lip, tilted his head, and did it again...taking my breath away once more.

Other guys did *not* kiss like this.

They did *not* look like this.

They did *not* touch me like this.

His hands grabbed the material of my shirt and pulled it over my head, his mouth moving to my neck the second he got it free. He kneeled and kissed my collarbone, the hollow of my throat, his hand fisting my hair and knotting it. One of his large arms moved over my ass, and he lifted me off the floor and into his body, taking me from the office and moving to the closest bedroom.

My bed was unmade from the last time I'd slept in it, dirty panties on the floor that never made it into the hamper. My nightstand had an alarm clock that showed the time along with a tube of lipstick I had left there.

He laid me on the bed while moving on top of me, getting my sweatpants and panties off in one single pull. Clothes didn't drop slowly like last time. We were both anxious, eager to have what we already knew was good. He kicked off his shoes and got his own jeans and boxers off before he moved on top of me, getting between my legs instantly, like he couldn't wait another second to have me, like he'd wanted me for days, when it seemed like he'd been indifferent to me throughout that entire time.

He shoved himself inside me, knowing I was wet before he even touched me.

I moaned at his entrance, reunited with the physical bliss that made me forget every bad thing that had ever happened to me...for a time. My nails clawed into his shoulders, and my ankles locked together in the middle of his back as he ground against me, pressing my body into the mattress as he dominated me, gave it to me deep and hard, like everything we were doing wasn't enough, like he needed more of me regardless of how much he had.

I couldn't kiss him because I was breathing too hard to do so. He panted in my face, moving deep inside me every single time, anxious and desperate, like this was the first time rather than the second.

It was more passionate than last time.

I held on to him, cupping his face to mine and bringing our lips together as I came, whimpering and writhing like I didn't know what to do with myself. Tears spilled from the corners of my eyes because it was so good, causing both sets of toes to cramp because I'd tightened my body in so many ways.

His eyes were on me, and he gave it to me harder, thrusting my body into the mattress like he wanted me to be swallowed by it. He moaned as he made me come, like he could sense how good he made me feel.

My nails clawed at his back, feeling the mosaic of muscle that comprised his powerful frame. I rocked with him until I was finished, until the tears stopped falling and settled onto the pillow underneath me.

My ankles loosened around his back, and then I rolled him over so I could be on top.

He hesitated, as if he didn't expect me to do that. The confusion remained on his face, like he liked to be in charge, liked to do the fucking while I just enjoyed it.

But once I started to roll my hips, take his dick while palming his chest, his expression changed.

He closed his eyes for an instant, groaning like he really enjoyed it.

I'd never been adventurous or one to take charge in the bedroom. Most of my lovers were short-term, and there'd never been enough time to have anything this passionate. But with him, I didn't think twice about my actions...I just did them.

He propped himself up on one elbow and placed his open hand against my stomach, like he wanted to feel my body tighten and move, feel the way I rocked back and forth with the muscles I'd built up working in the camp.

Seeing the way he clenched his jaw like he'd never been fucked so good made me want to work harder, made my body get wetter because it was a turn-on. I leaned forward and arched my back, my face above his, our slick bodies moving together at a new angle.

He closed his eyes again and inhaled a deep breath. His hand moved to one ass cheek, and he gripped it hard, moving my ass up and down like he wanted a little more, like this was exactly what he wanted and how he wanted it. Then he made a loud groan as he finished, his face getting flushed and red, so fucking handsome.

It made me come again.

It was different from last time.

He didn't get up to leave.

There would be breaks of silence in between, and sometimes I would doze off, just to be reawakened with him on top of me. There was no discussion of the last thing he said to me, that he would give me what I wanted, and we chose to put that off until morning.

I turned on my side away from him and faced my nightstand, my eyes so tired I could barely make out the time on my clock.

It was 4:19.

We didn't snuggle after sex. He stayed on his side, and I stayed on mine.

But he grabbed my arm and gently rolled me to my back.

I looked over my shoulder at him.

He lay on his back, his head turned my way. But then he looked at the ceiling again, his eyes eventually closing.

I rolled over again, unsure what that was about.

He grabbed me again and this time pulled me harder.

"What are you—"

"I don't want to see." His hand released me and returned to his stomach.

"Don't want to see what?"

He closed his eyes.

Then it dawned on me.

My back.

I turned on my side the other way, my back displayed to the doorway.

He lay there, his breathing deep and even like he was relaxed.

I watched him, seeing how gentle he looked when he was relaxed, like he was a good man...who had a different life. We were two regular people in bed together, meeting in a coffee shop in the most romantic place in the world.

I saw the scar located behind his ear, the line from where the metal pipe had struck him and made it bleed. It was hard to look at it, reminding me of the pain I'd caused him with my bare hands.

I understood how he felt.

I moved into him and pressed a kiss to the scar, trying to replace the violence with affection.

He opened his eyes and looked at me.

I returned to my spot, keeping some space in between us, the rain still hitting the outside of the window.

His eyes watched me for a while, impossible to decipher. Minutes passed and the look continued, as if he didn't understand what I did or why I did it. Then he turned his face back to the ceiling and closed his eyes.

21

THE BOSS

I<small>T WAS THE FIRST TIME</small> I <small>SHOWERED IN MY</small> apartment.

I stepped out and looked at myself in the mirror, seeing how much I had changed in the familiar light. My skin had tanned so much that my old foundation was no longer the right color, but I still did my eyes and lips, made my hair full and nice, the way it used to be.

I almost didn't recognize myself.

My clothes fit a little loosely because I'd lost some weight. My body was fit now, so everything was tight. I pulled on a pair of jeans, little booties, and a sweater before I headed downstairs.

It felt like a regular day, like nothing had happened.

I opened one of the drawers and found some extra cash before I left the building.

It was lunchtime for most people, but I'd woken up late after my long night, so it was still morning for me. I took the walk to my favorite café a block over. I walked past the windows, saw the people inside with their laptops and coffee. The counter held displays of their cookies and pastries, their assortment of freshly baked breads and cheeses.

I stopped at the window and looked inside.

The sound of cars was loud behind me, the bell on a passing bicycle, a dog barking at another dog farther down the sidewalk. It was an overcast day, and the sidewalk was still damp from the rain that had fallen last night...but it was the most beautiful day of my life.

I couldn't believe it was real.

I stepped inside and placed my order, nearly forgetting how I liked my coffee. It was strange to talk to a real person, someone who had no idea what I'd survived. I stood there and waited for my food, listening to the blender, a customer talking obnoxiously loud on his phone, and the sound of quiet chatter as friends and family enjoyed lunch together.

I felt like I wasn't really there, but a ghost instead.

When my food and coffee were ready, I walked back to the apartment.

Walked there...because I had the freedom to do whatever I wanted.

Everything in my apartment was moldy and expired, even the coffee, so I'd had to fetch something from the outside world. But even if there had been something to eat, I probably would have left anyway.

I returned to my apartment and set everything on the counter. Magnus was still asleep, and I had no idea how long he would stay that way. I went upstairs and placed the coffee cup at his bedside so it would be there when he opened his eyes. I crept inside and gently set it on the nightstand.

He opened his eyes and looked at me, his gaze sleepy like he was still out of it.

"It's not hot chocolate, but it's warm."

He propped himself up on one arm, his hair messy from rolling around all night. His eyes were still heavy from sleep, but he looked me over, his eyes starting at my legs and slowly moving up until he looked at my face.

I knew I looked totally different, in a way he'd never seen before. I'd even shaved in the shower, so if he saw me naked again, I'd look different there too—not that I expected that to happen again.

His large arms were flexed and covered with veins, and his broad shoulders made the mattress dip underneath him. The sheets were at his waist, showing the chiseled abs and line of hair. A more beautiful man had never been in my bed before. Without blinking, he regarded me. "Beautiful."

I didn't know how to react to those words…the only compliment he'd ever given me on my appearance. "I have breakfast downstairs whenever you're ready." I left the coffee behind and ventured downstairs. The house was a mess and would be a pain to clean, but I was grateful to be there, so I refused to complain. I started on the dishes because that seemed to be the most pressing.

The chair pulled out from the kitchen island.

I stilled when I heard him behind me. I turned off the faucet, and I dried my hands. When I turned around, he was sitting on the stool, the same place where my sister had sat, shirtless with the coffee in his hand. He brought it to his lips and took a drink, watching me at the same time.

I opened one of the containers and gave it to him. "It might be cold…"

He pulled it toward himself and immediately started to eat, like he didn't care if it was frozen solid.

I drank my coffee, the cream and spices an explosion of flavor on my tongue, the pumpkin reminding me of holiday parties and celebrations. It was something I'd thought I would never have again. Now I wanted it every single day until it was no longer on the menu.

He ate in silence, his hair still messy, the dark patch of hair between his pecs a little darker than the hair on the top of his head. He took bites and chewed, his eyes on me all the while.

I realized it was one of the few times I'd ever seen him eat.

I was always the one eating.

Silence passed and we didn't speak.

Sometimes it was tense between us, but there was always this underlying comfort, like we didn't need to speak to feel connected. We could enjoy the silence and eye contact without filling it with point-less conversation.

I waited until he was finished eating before I got down to business. "How are we going to do this?"

He brought the coffee to his lips and took another drink, the empty tray in front of him. "Be more specific."

"My sister. What else could I be talking about?"

He regarded me for a moment, taking another drink, his elbows on the counter, his muscular arms in full visibility. "Let me figure it out."

"No." My sister's life was in the balance. I wasn't going to let him execute this plan without telling me the details. "I'm a part of this."

He set his cup on the counter and stared at the surface.

"Do you know where she is?"

He nodded.

"So, can we just go there and grab her?"

He shook his head. "Not exactly." He lifted his gaze and looked at me. "I'll go to his residence and talk to him. There's no guarantee this will work. I told you I would help you. I didn't guarantee I would be successful."

"You *have* to be successful." I kept my voice controlled, but I wanted to burst into a scream because failure was not an option in this.

He sighed before he straightened, sitting fully upright. "This is a lot more complicated than your life at the camp. Believe it or not, but the outside world is far worse than that place."

I couldn't believe that. "You've never been a prisoner, so you have no idea."

"You don't know me. You don't know what I've survived." He didn't raise his voice, but his cold calmness was somehow more ominous. "I will do my best, but I can't make him do whatever he doesn't want to do. Honestly, I can't think of a sound argument for getting him to comply. I'm gonna have to wing it."

"Can you just steal—"

"No." He shook his head. "I can't rescue her from that place the way I rescued you. Going behind his back and betraying him is not an option. A conversation, man-to-man, is the only chance we have."

"But what can you possibly say to convince him to let her go?"

He dropped his gaze and was quiet for a while. "Right now...I'm not sure."

I looked down and started to breathe hard, terrified that I'd have to live the rest of my life without her, knowing she was out there and I couldn't help her. "If you can't do this, I'm just going to do it myself."

"You'll be killed."

"Then I'll be killed..."

He studied me, his brown eyes the same color as his coffee. "Your sister would want you to live your life. She wouldn't want you to die for her. I will do my best to give you what you want, but if it doesn't work, you're going to have to learn to let this go."

"Would you let it go?" I snapped. "What if this was your sister?"

His eyes burned into mine, turning slightly hostile, like something I'd said struck a nerve. When he spoke, his voice was shaky, as if he used all his energy to control his rage. "I don't have a sister..."

I didn't understand what happened, what I said to provoke this reaction from him, but I knew to steer clear...because I'd triggered something.

"I said I would do my best, and you should appreciate that I'm willing to try at all. You have no idea what I'm putting on the line by going to his place and making a request like this. You have no idea how pathetic, how weak it will make me look. But I'm doing it anyway—for you."

———

HE WAS in his black jeans, boots, and his black t-shirt.

He looked good in black, especially with that dark hair and those brown eyes. He had a wallet in his pocket, and the outline of the front of his jeans showed his phone. He never took it out around me, and it was crazy to actually see one again.

He moved to the front door.

I followed him.

He turned around and looked at me, his eyebrow raised.

It was seven in the evening, so it was dark outside, and there were more raindrops on the window. "What?"

"What are you doing?"

"Going with you."

He turned to face me head on. "I go alone."

"No."

His eyes darkened in anger.

"That's where my sister is, and I'm going."

"You have no idea what you're doing."

"I need to come. Because if you get her out, I need to see her then and there. And if you can't, then I want to make my own argument—"

"You do not speak."

I couldn't stay in that apartment and just wait. "Please..."

"You have a lot of nerve—"

"Please." I moved into him and gripped his arm. "I can't just sit on the couch and wait. I'm not a coward. I can look him in the face and plead with my eyes. Maybe that will make him feel—"

"It will make him feel nothing."

"Magnus, come on..."

After staring at me for a while, he closed his eyes and sighed.

I knew I'd gotten what I wanted. "Thank you—"

"You do not speak. If he says no, you say nothing. You understand me?"

I nodded. "Yes, absolutely—"

"Your word. After everything I've done for you, breaking it would be a pretty shitty thing to do. I'm putting my trust in you. Don't make me look like an idiot."

I intended to fight to get her out of there if I didn't get the answer I wanted, but when he put me on the spot like that, I couldn't betray him. If I gave him my word, I had to keep it...even though it killed me.

"Your word."

I bowed my head and sighed. "Yes...I give you my word."

WE DROVE in his Bugatti through the rain.

His phone kept vibrating and lighting up in his pocket.

There was no music on the journey.

We left the city of Paris and ventured slightly into the countryside. The large estates were lit up from the roads, surrounded by cobblestone walls and iron gates. The Eiffel Tower was still visible in the rearview mirror.

When the car slowed down, I knew we arrived.

Far up the drive was a three-story villa, slightly visible through the iron gates. He turned and made the drive, moving past the large bushes that stood tall like trees. When we arrived at the gate, there were armed men outside, small buildings on either side of the gate, like tollbooths.

My heart was racing.

Magnus came to a stop and rolled down his window.

One of the guys came closer to speak to him, making an exchange in French.

The guy kneeled and looked at me in the passenger seat. "*Qui est la fille?*" *Who is she?*

Magnus stared him down coldly.

"*Allons, tu sais bien que je dois le signaler.*" *You must tell me.*

Magnus responded, still irritated. *"Mon invitée."* *Friend.*

The guy seemed scared because he backed away and motioned to the guards.

The gates opened.

Magnus drove farther inside, and it was another long road to the three-story Parisian mansion, moving down the winding road through the fancy gardens and the brilliant lighting.

"What did he say?"

"I told him you were my guest. End of story." He made it to the roundabout, parking on the cobblestones next to a fountain surging with water. He unclicked his safety belt and turned off the car at the same time.

I looked up at the historic landmark, knowing it'd been there since the Renaissance. It reminded me of the chateau, a piece of real estate that must be valued at over one hundred million euros. It was beautiful, but that didn't make me less afraid to go inside.

He turned to stare me down.

I met his look, breathing harder than I wanted.

"You gave me your word."

"I know…"

He got out of the car.

I joined him, standing in my heeled boots, the cold air immediately making my lungs tighten.

He moved ahead and didn't wait for me.

I followed behind him, unsure what to do with myself. I wasn't to speak, so all I could do was stand there and hope the desperation in my eyes would be enough for him to take pity on me…even though he didn't seem like an empathetic person. He wouldn't run a labor camp and conceptualize the Red Snow if he had a single ounce of kindness in his heart.

He rang the doorbell then turned to look at me. "You want to wait in the car?"

I shook my head.

"You look like a ghost."

"Because I've never been so afraid in all my life."

He studied me, his eyes dropping in subtle softness. "Nothing will happen to you when you're with me."

I was too anxious to cherish his words. "I'm not worried about that...I'm afraid to leave here without her."

The door opened and sabotaged our chance to speak.

It was an older man in a tuxedo. *"Bonsoir, monsieur. Comment allez-vous?" How are you?*

"Très bien." Good.

He opened the door wider and ushered us inside.

I walked with Magnus, seeing the bright chandelier hanging from the ceiling at the third level, the French paintings on the walls, the grand piano in the corner...like this was a room to host grand parties. A high table was in the center, showing a sculpture of a ballerina.

It wasn't what I expected.

The boss seemed like someone who lived in a cave or something.

The butler walked ahead, conversing with Magnus in French like they were well acquainted. He escorted us into a large sitting room in the rear, the sophisticated artwork on the walls worth more than the value of Paris as a whole. There were couches, a large hearth, another chandelier, and sculptures and art pieces that showed his incredible wealth.

I didn't know money like this existed in real life.

It made me a little sick to know I'd paid for some of it with my labor, as did the others.

And some paid for it with their lives.

The butler said a few more words before he departed.

Magnus stood there, looking out the windows to the incredible landscaped backyard, the large patio, enormous pool, and the gardens that stretched for acres, all lit up to be seen in the darkness.

At least my sister was in a beautiful place.

Footsteps sounded a moment later, heavy against the large pieces of tile on the floor. They weren't light and careful the way the butler's had been. They came from behind us. Magnus didn't turn right away.

I wasn't sure if I could turn at all.

The boss spoke. "*Qu'est-ce que c'est?*" He spoke in French, but his voice was slightly hostile, like he didn't like the evening visit. *What?*

Magnus turned to face him. *"Le moment est mal choisi?"* He said something back, matching his tone. *Inconvenience?*

I finally found the strength to look at him. I stayed behind Magnus because I didn't want to be closer than necessary. He was exactly as I remembered, with short brown hair, brown eyes that possessed a wildness that was fiercer than the woods I'd had to survive. His eyes were on me, drilling into my face, dissecting my features as if his eyes were two daggers. He stepped closer to me to get a better look.

Magnus moved slightly in the way, stopping the boss from getting too close.

Would the boss be furious when he recognized me? When he realized that one of his men had helped me escape? Magnus didn't seem worried about it.

The boss shifted his gaze to Magnus. *"Ils m'ont dit qu'elle s'était échappée."* He spoke in quick French. Living in Paris had given me some vocabulary to understand his words, but by no means was I fluent. I could only pick up enough to deduce a couple things. Something about my escape. So, he did recognize me. He shook his head. *"C'était toi."* *You.*

"Les hommes n'en savent rien. C'est tout ce qui compte." Men. Nothing else matters.

He stood in sweatpants low on his waist, and he'd skipped the shirt, like he didn't give a damn who saw him this way. He was bulky and strong, with lots of muscles in his chest and arms. He looked like a bull. *"Tu m'as piégé. Tu es venu ici pour jubiler?"* Trick. He raised his voice, growing angry.

Magnus was as calm as ever. *"Non."*

His eyes shifted back and forth as he looked at me. *"Si tu la voulais, pourquoi tu ne l'as pas dit?"* He barked at Magnus, so hostile it was unclear if we would walk out of there. *Why didn't you tell me?* He'd said something like that.

"Parce qu'elle a énervé tous les hommes...et ça aurait été une trahison." Betrayal to the men.

I suspected the boss had asked Magnus why he went through the charade of helping me escape instead of claiming me the way he claimed Melanie. But it surprised me that it was even an option for Magnus. Then Magnus said I pissed off the guys too much, and they would riot if I got an easy way out. But I wasn't entirely sure.

The boss was quiet and stared him down, his eyes showing his ferocity. He was having a standoff with Magnus, as if waiting for a concrete explanation for his actions. "*Comment ça?*" What?

"*Pour demander une faveur.*"

His anger slowly faded as his eyes narrowed. "*Quoi donc?*" What?

Magnus stared at him for a long time as he considered how to craft his words. "*Melanie est sa sœur...et je veux que tu la relâches.*" Sister.

It took the boss a moment to react, as if he didn't absorb the request right away. He shifted his weight, dropped one shoulder slightly, and regarded Magnus with skepticism. "*Et pourquoi je ferais ça?*" Why?

Magnus turned quiet for a while. "*Parce que je le demande.*" I couldn't make that one out.

He shifted his gaze to me and stared me down.

I stopped breathing.

Then he looked at Magnus again. "*Tu viens chez moi et tu me demandes ça? Elle m'appartient, t'as aucun droit de demander sa libération. Comment oses-tu venir ici pour demander une chose pareille?*" He fired off in French, talking so quickly it was hard to make anything out. *You ask for her release? How could you?* "Cette salope devrait plutôt me remercier d'être encore en vie. Elle devrait être reconnaissante que j'ai des choses plus importantes à faire que la ramener là où elle devrait être." *She shouldn't be alive right now.*

I started to breathe harder. I didn't want to be scared, but it was hard not to, not when I was standing in the home of the man who had enslaved my sister and me.

He spoke again. "*T'es amoureux de cette fille?*" He glanced at me and looked at Magnus again. *Woman you love?*

Magnus answered immediately. "*Non.*"

"*Alors c'est quoi ce bordel?*" *Fuck you.*

Magnus spoke again. "*Je tiens à elle.*" *I feel affection for her.*

The boss shook his head, as if disgusted. "*T'es faible. Pathétique. Comment tu peux te pointer devant moi et me demander une chose pareille? Elle t'a manipulé pour la faire libérer. Elle t'a manipulé pour que tu l'amènes jusqu'ici. Et maintenant, elle te fait négocier la libération d'une prisonnière. Où sont tes couilles, Magnus? Je ne t'ai jamais aussi peu respecté qu'en ce moment. C'est elle l'homme — et t'es la gonzesse.*" *Weak...not a man...no dick...you let her use you.*

Magnus was quiet.

"*Non.*" No. "*La réponse est non.*" He turned to walk away. "*Fous le camp de chez moi.*" Leave.

My eyes immediately watered, but I kept my mouth shut...because I promised.

Magnus watched him go.

I grabbed his hand and squeezed, silently asking him to do something...anything.

He sighed before he pulled his hand away and walked after the boss. "*Mon frère.*" Brother.

I sucked a big gulp of air into my lungs, making a quiet gasp.

He stopped but didn't turn around.

Now I noticed the resemblance. The hair...the eyes... the handsome features. Now that I knew the truth, I couldn't unsee it. And everything made sense... everything. Now I understood why Magnus had powers others didn't. I understood how he could come here without announcement and ask something like this without getting shot. I understood how he spared me from the Red Snow when everyone wanted me dead.

Magnus spoke again. *"C'est ce que je veux... et je ne te demande jamais rien."* I never ask anything of you.

The boss slowly turned around, his eyes wild in disbelief.

"Je te le demande comme ton frère...pas ton associé." Your brother, not your partner.

He stared at Magnus longer, his eyes unblinking, possessing the same intense stare his brother did sometimes. After holding his silence for seconds, he walked back to his brother, his eyes glued to his face. *"Je ne veux pas la relâcher. Demande-moi ça, et tu ne me demanderas plus jamais rien. Compris?"* I do this...then I owe you nothing.

Magnus gave a slight nod. *"Oui."* Yes.

The boss walked away and headed upstairs.

Magnus remained still.

"Does—"

He flashed me his stare, telling me to shut my mouth, even though I'd only whispered.

I closed my mouth again.

He stared at me for several seconds before he returned to the grand foyer, where there was a tall staircase on either side. He stood and waited, his eyes down.

A moment later, a door opened and closed.

Then Melanie appeared at the top of the stairs, her eyes visibly wet even from this distance. He gripped the edge of the stairs and looked down, right at me.

"Raven..."

It took all my strength not to speak. I started to heave with the breaths that wanted to escape my lungs. I went from stern seriousness to a sobbing wreck. Tears dripped down my cheeks like rivers, and I shut my lips as tightly so I wouldn't make a sound.

Melanie was in a black dress, wearing a piece of clothing worth more than anything we owned in our closets. She took the stairs, gripping the handle as she quickly moved down.

The boss appeared behind her, looking at his brother.

Melanie reached the bottom then darted toward me, crashing into my arms, bursting into tears just as I did.

I held her tightly and cried into her shoulder, feeling my little sister once more, the only family I had in this cruel world. "Baby sister..." I ran my hands down the back of her hair and whimpered in pain at our reunion.

The boss reached the bottom of the stairs and stared down his brother.

I didn't feel bad for the tension I'd caused between them, because I got what I needed.

Magnus turned to me and spoke in English. "Let's go. Now."

I pulled away from Melanie at his command, knowing I had to listen if I wanted to make it to the finish line and not trip. "Let's go home." I grabbed her hand and pulled her with me to the door where Magnus stood.

But she pulled her hand free.

I turned back to look.

Melanie stared at her captor.

He stared back, his expression cold.

She lingered, continuing the stare.

I had no idea what was happening.

Then he walked up to her, towering over her when he was close. The backs of his fingers grazed against her cheek, just the way they did when we were bound at the camp. "Goodbye, sweetheart." He pulled his fingers away...then walked off. As if he didn't want to watch her go, he moved to the other side of the house and disappeared.

For a second, I worried she wouldn't leave.

But then she turned to me, took my hand, and we left.

22

LIVE WELL. BE HAPPY.

WE ENTERED THE APARTMENT.

Melanie took a look around, examining every single surface, the laundry that had never been sorted on the couch, the open windows to reveal the brightness of the city lit up at night. "It's the same..."

I'd had the exact feeling when I walked in. "Yeah..."

She went into her bedroom, probably looking at her clothes and the things she'd left behind. Then she came back to me, sentimental toward the past, emotional because of the furniture. She stood there and looked at me. "I can't believe we're here."

"I know."

She came to me and hugged me again, the only person in the world that I had who knew exactly how it felt to be a prisoner in a labor camp. She was the only person who understood the trial that had tested us both. She pulled away, tears dripping from her eyes down her cheeks. "How did you get away?"

"Him."

Her eyes softened. "I can't believe what he did for you."

"Neither can I."

She pulled away and looked at the open doorway. "Where is he?"

I'd been so focused on her that I forgot about him. I turned around, expecting to see him standing there, but he was gone. "I'm not sure." I left the apartment and headed back to the street.

He stood on the sidewalk outside my apartment, indifferent to the raindrops that splashed on the bridge of his nose and dampened his hair. There was no one on the sidewalk because it was late at night. With his hands in his pockets, he stood there, looking up when he knew I was on the steps.

I knew why he didn't follow me inside, based on the look on his face.

I joined him in the rain, my clothes and hair slowly starting to dampen. I looked into his face, looking at a man I didn't understand. He was good, but he was bad. He was a hero...but he was also the villain.

He looked at me, his brown eyes staring into my face as if he knew this was the last time we would see each other.

"Thank you...so much." I shook my head because I didn't know what else to say, how to express my gratitude. My life had been returned to me, exactly as it had been before those men took us outside that bar— all because of him. "I...I don't even know how to thank you for what you've done for me."

With his hands in his pockets, he continued to stare at me, but he didn't have anything to say.

I moved closer to him and wrapped my arms around him, hugging him harder than I ever had, immune to the falling rain around us, soaking into our clothes.

He didn't hug me back right away. That took time. Then his arms wrapped around me, and he held me against his chest, his arms locked around me like they were the final cage that would ever contain me.

We stood there for a long time. My clothes were soaked. My makeup was ruined. My hair was flat like I'd stood under the falling water of the shower. But the cold and the rain weren't enough to make me turn around and walk back inside.

He was the one to pull away first, to release his hold on my body and step back slightly, his brown eyes softer than they'd ever been before. His heart was bright in the look, the goodness shining through his eyes.

There was no future for us. We were two people from two different worlds, our lives crossing unexpectedly and for a brief time. He would go back to his underworld, and I would walk to my coffee shop every morning on the way to class. The scars were permanent, so I would always have a piece of him, always remember the man who saved my life. His scars would carry my ghost as well.

We would just be ghosts to each other...to these memories.

But that was how it had to be, because we were too different.

He pulled his touch away and gave me a slight nod. "Live well. Be happy."

Tears welled up in my eyes, and my bottom lip quivered because those words hit me with unexpected pain. My hands were still on his arms because I wasn't ready to let go yet, to release the only person who had ever taken care of me.

He pulled his hands back and walked off.

I watched him go, standing in the rain, unable to leave until he left first.

He got into the car.

The door shut.

The engine roared.

If he looked at me, it was impossible to tell, because the windows were tinted.

Then he drove away, the tires splashing through the puddles.

When he was gone, I finally turned back to my apartment...as a free woman.

23

SURVIVOR'S GUILT

WE RETURNED TO OUR LIVES.

We finished the laundry, bought groceries, cleaned the apartment, all the things we used to dread. There was a lot of rain in Paris. It was the second week of February, so I figured I'd been gone for over six weeks. That wasn't long, but at the time, it had seemed like a lifetime.

My purse and wallet had been stolen, but thankfully, my passport was in the apartment, so I was able to get cash out of the bank to pay rent so I wouldn't be evicted, as well as get food on the table.

Melanie and I didn't talk much, as if we weren't ready to talk.

After a few days, we sat together at the kitchen island, drinking hot cups of coffee with a plate of pastries between us. We had access to all the food we could eat, but neither one of us was ever hungry, at least, not the way we used to be.

She sat with her chin down, her knuckles propped underneath. Her eyes were downcast, her fingers in the handle of the mug. It was gray and cloudy outside, and the rain never seemed to stop. It rained every single day, a constant sprinkle.

It was better than snow.

I cleared the lump in my throat. "You can talk to me...if you want to talk about it." Not once had we talked about what the boss did to her. It just happened...and went unacknowledged. Honestly, I didn't want to hear about it because it was just too painful to picture the person you loved most being subjugated to that, but I would be there for her, because that was my job.

She kept her eyes down. "I don't want to talk about it."

"Well, we can always find you a therapist...if you want to do that."

She shook her head then brought the mug to her lips for a drink. "Are you okay?"

I thought I would be blissfully happy to be free, but that high quickly wore off. Now guilt tied me down, made me think of the women who were still there, still working every single day, witnessing the death of a friend every week. "As okay as I'm going to be..."

"What about Magnus?"

I lifted my gaze and looked at her. "What about him?"

"Are you going to see him again?"

When he'd walked away, it hurt more than I thought it would. It was hard to say goodbye to someone who had experienced so much of your journey right at your side. He was the hero in my story, even if he was the villain in others. "No."

"I saw you two together outside...when he left."

I looked down at my coffee.

"It just seemed like...there was something there."

Because there was. "Some people are in your life for a reason. Once that reason is fulfilled, it's over. He saved me. He saved you. Transaction is over."

"Did you sleep with him?"

I almost didn't answer her because it was my business and not hers, but after everything we'd been through, there were no secrets at this point. "Yes. A couple times."

"Do you have feelings for him?"

I shrugged. "That's a complicated question."

"Not really. But I'm guessing it's a complicated answer."

I drank from my mug again. "What do we do now?"

She was quiet for a while. "I usually ask you that, not the other way around."

"The semester has already started, so I can't go back to school right now. I'll have to clear up everything with the immigration office. I'll have to get a full-time job, save up some money until I go back. Are you going to go back home?"

She shook her head. "I'm not leaving you."

I studied her face. "I'm not leaving Paris. This is my home now."

"That's fine. We stay together from now on."

I'd come here to get away from her, to have my own independence, but now I was happy she wanted to stay. Sharing an apartment and getting through this together sounded nice.

She stared at me for a while, like there was something she wanted to say.

I already knew what was coming. "I forgive you."

Her eyes immediately watered as she took a deep breath, like she needed to be cleansed of her sins, needed to remove the guilt from her shoulders. She'd been carrying it every single day since all this happened. "I know that I've been such a pain in the ass since Mom died, and I'm sorry for that..."

"Melanie—"

"But I'm a different person now. I'll get a job, my own apartment, and just be a better person, be more like you."

"I don't want you to be me. I want you to be you."

"But I know I've caused you so much grief..."

"It's okay, Melanie. It's in the past." I rested my hand on hers. "I want you to be a better version of you, not anyone else."

She gave a slight nod, tears glistening.

"Let it go. I have."

She inhaled a deep breath, the tears streaking down her cheeks. She quickly wiped them away with the napkin from her coffee.

"We've got lives to live. It's our chance to start again."

"Yeah...you're right."

I drank my coffee until the mug was empty and set it aside. "I'm gonna go down to the police precinct."

She stilled, snapping out of our emotional moment instantly. "What? You're going to the police?"

"We're reported as missing persons. I have to rectify that. And I'm going to tell them all about the camp."

She continued to give me that look, like she couldn't believe what I'd just said. "Seriously?"

"Why wouldn't I? There are still women stuck there. I'm bringing it down."

"I...I'm just surprised."

It would be more out of character for me to do nothing. "Why?"

"I mean...Magnus really put his ass on the line for you. Don't you think this is wrong? It's a betrayal."

I appreciated everything he'd done for me, and I didn't see him as anything like the others. It was unclear why he was involved in such a horrendous place when he still had a heart. Maybe it was a family obligation...or something else. "They're two separate things. I do appreciate what he did for me, but I'm loyal to those women who are stuck there, who weren't so lucky. I will tell the police everything, about the camp, the guards, the boss...but I won't mention Magnus. I can't just move on with my life knowing Bethany is still there, that Cindy is still there. Can you?"

All she did was stare.

"No, we can't." I rose out of the chair and left my mug aside.

"Raven?"

I turned back to her.

"I don't think going to the police is going to do anything..."

"Why?"

She was quiet, like she didn't want to say. "Fender is—"

"The boss?"

She nodded. "He's really powerful. I mean...you have no idea. I don't think reporting it will change anything. If anything, you're just bringing attention back to us."

That didn't change anything for me. "I have to do this, Melanie. Bethany risked her neck for me. I have to do the same for her."

I sat with a sergeant at his desk, and he took all my information, removing me from the missing persons file and helping me get a new ID, as well as some extra money to get me back on my feet again.

"You were trafficked?" He made the assumption, like that was the only possibility for my disappearance.

"No. I was kidnapped—and forced into a labor camp."

His pen was to the paper, finishing up my file, but he stopped and looked up at me.

"It's a camp in the south, near the Alps. There are camps everywhere, and the way to get there is on horseback. Planes drop crates of cocaine from the sky, they process it, and then distribute it. It's full of kidnapped women who are forced into servitude, and if they don't work hard enough, they're killed."

He stared at me blankly.

"What?"

"There's no shame in being the victim of trafficking. It happens to a lot of women, unfortunately. If you tell me the truth, it might help us catch these guys. No need to make up a story."

I stared at him for a few seconds, in disbelief. "Make up a story...?"

"Those drug operations are in South America. Not in France."

"Then how do you explain the drugs on the streets?"

"Tourism."

My eyebrows jumped up my face. "I'm telling you the truth."

"Then where is the camp?"

"I just told you—"

"I need more details than that. How do you expect me to send out men to investigate when I don't know where to send them?"

"I was a prisoner. You think they let me know that information? It was close to the Alps, so send a helicopter to scout the area—"

"Ma'am, this is a police station. We have crimes to solve. We don't have time for fantastical stories—"

"Don't you fucking ma'am me like I'm a Karen."

His expression turned blank. "What?"

It was an American thing. Probably had no idea what that term meant. "I'm telling you the truth. I'm giving you as much information as I can for you to discover and eliminate the biggest drug operation in France—"

"There is no drug operation." He stopped taking notes, like there was no further discussion.

My heart hit my chest with every beat.

Terror washed over me.

I knew exactly what had happened without needing any physical evidence. "You know exactly what I'm talking about..."

He stared at me, stone-faced.

"But he's paid you off..."

"Ma'am, I have no idea what—"

"Fuck off." I left the chair in front of his desk and stepped away. "There is a woman brutally executed every single week, just because she isn't as strong as everyone else. We work every single day as slaves. The only way out of that place is through death. If you choose to sit there with a fat wallet and look the other way, then you dishonor the badge. You dishonor everything you should stand for."

I SAT UP IN BED, the *Count of Monte Cristo* on my lap, the pages damp at the corners. The rain hit the window right next to me, and the hot coffee on my nightstand smelled like nutmeg and cinnamon. It was the middle of the day, but I had nowhere to go and nothing to do, so I never changed out of my pajamas.

My body had already started to return to its previous weakness since I didn't work all day anymore. My abs were slowly being covered with a layer of fat, and my breasts were getting bigger. I turned away from the book and looked out the window, seeing the rain-drops hit the glass and drip down in quick rivers, only to be replaced by another drop.

My entire adventure might have felt like just a dream, but this book was a piece of my story, and the memory of the man who'd slept by my side in that very bed told me it was all real...every single moment.

Melanie appeared in the open doorway, leaning against the frame with her arms crossed over her chest. "What happened to your book?"

I lifted it up, seeing the permanent stain on the corner of every page. "Dropped it." I wasn't sure why I didn't tell her the truth. It was between me and this story, between me and Magnus.

She looked out the window and stared at the rain.

I closed the book and stared at the cover, the title worn and faded, like it'd been in that camp for a long time, had belonged to another prisoner before they passed away. "I have to go back..."

Melanie turned back to me, her movements notice-able in my periphery.

I set the book on the nightstand and looked at her. "Bethany, Cindy...everyone else. I can't just leave them there."

"You went to the police, Raven. You did what you could."

I shook my head. "It's not enough..."

She sighed loudly. "You think you can go there alone and liberate the camp? By yourself."

"I won't be alone..." I continued my stare.

Her eyes fell when she understood.

"If we get caught, nothing will happen to you. The boss will protect you."

"He will not—"

"I saw the way he looked at you. You'll be safe."

"And what about you?"

I held the book in my arms and pulled it to my chest. "Doesn't matter. I can't live knowing they're there. I have to finish this, even if it costs my life."

"Raven—"

"I have to."

She turned quiet. "We don't even know where it is."

"We'll find it."

"How are we going to liberate an entire camp?"

"I'll come up with a plan."

"And what about Magnus?"

I squeezed the book tighter. "We won't hurt him."

"But you're coming back to destroy his camp, after everything he did for us."

I felt guilty when I shouldn't. His kindness didn't erase his cruelty. "I know, but it doesn't change anything. Every week that passes ends the life of someone innocent. Every week that passes results in new women taken from their homes and forced into servitude. Every week that we spend drinking coffee and eating cheese...is a week someone won't survive. Bethany could be next, or one of your friends. We owe it to those women, to women everywhere, to try. And my loyalty is to them...not him."

24

WITH KNIVES AND FIRE

I used my money to buy a horse.

I brought other supplies, stuff for our survival, but also gasoline, matches, knives, everything that we could use. It would be nice to have a gun, but that was something we couldn't buy.

Melanie sat behind me on the horse, pointing the flashlights up ahead so we could see where we were going. "Fuck, it's spooky out here."

I'd done this before, so I wasn't scared at all.

I used my phone to map out the landscape. On Google images, the camp wasn't there, which told me how deep this operation ran. But the chateau was there, so I was able to use that to figure out the possible locations of the camp.

We'd been out there for days, making campfires at night, eating dry food from the saddlebags. The vapor was in front of my face from my breathing, and the hooves of the horse crunched against the snow as we moved forward. "I know we're close." I could feel it.

I hoped Magnus wasn't there. He left for weeks at a time, so perhaps he hadn't returned.

Then I saw the distant light from one of the cabins. "I see it."

Melanie took a deep breath when she saw it. "Shit..."

We came closer then climbed off the horse. Her reins were tied to a branch of a tree.

Melanie breathed harder and harder, like she was hyperventilating.

"We're going to be fine."

"I just... I remember..."

My hand moved to her arm. "Think about why we're doing this. Think about the women we're saving." We lit torches along the path the wagons took to the main road, so the women would know where to go when they escaped.

She nodded, her breathing starting to slow.

"We can do this. I know we can." Even if I didn't survive, it was still worth it to me...just the possibility of success. Staying home and lying in bed all day was no way to live. I could never truly be free, not until everyone else was.

She nodded again.

We moved forward, stopping at the edge of the camp. I pulled out the tools from my bag, everything we could use to pick every lock. "You take the left. I'll take the right. Then we'll torch the cabins."

"Why not just take the girls and run?"

"Because we don't know where the snitches are." From what Magnus and Bethany described, there were quite a few of them. All they had to do was scream and the plan would be over. "Unlock every door, and we'll set everything on fire. The fire will wake up the girls, and they'll run. And hopefully... the guards will die in the fire."

"Should we block their doors?"

That would be smart. "No. Magnus might be here." I wanted to kill every single guard in that place, but I wouldn't sacrifice Magnus for it. There was no way to know if he was even there, so this was a gamble.

She nodded. "I'll meet you in the middle."

We went in our separate directions, quietly picking each lock so the doors would be unlocked. I'd taught her how to do it in Paris, and we'd practiced until we were both quick. I moved through the snow, knowing there were no guards outside because there was nothing to patrol since I was gone.

It was strange to be there again, to feel the cold burn my lungs with every breath. When I reached the clearing, I stopped and stared. There was a woman hanging from the noose, the snow red beneath her.

It made me angry—and fueled my determination.

We went to each cabin until we met in the middle.

"Now what?" she whispered.

I pulled down one of the torches they used for the Red Snow ceremony and handed it to her before I grabbed my own. I poured the gasoline on each one before I pulled out the lighter.

"Are you sure this is a good idea?" she whispered. "Setting everything on fire?"

"It'll get the girls out of their cabins. It'll cause confusion with the guards. If we had guns, I'd do this differently, but we don't."

She nodded.

"It's now or never, Melanie."

She took a breath to steel her nerves. "Okay."

I turned on the lighter then held it to the torch.

It immediately burst into flame.

Melanie held it away, held it high to shield herself from the heat. It lit up the center of the camp, a beacon of hope in this eternal darkness.

I stared for a moment...finding it beautiful.

It was the same torch that was lit for the Red Snow, but now it symbolized something completely new.

Freedom.

I lit mine, and it shone with hers, the flames bright, the crackling audible.

She stepped back so we weren't too close.

I stared at her and gave her a nod. "Let's do this."

We went our separate ways, running to light every single cabin on fire, moving quickly so we could torch everything at the same time. My breathing was loud in my ears because I heaved with the exertion of running with everything in my pack and the heavy torch. But my determination kept me going, lighting the rear of the cabins, moving from one to the next... and the next.

Then the screams started.

Doors burst open, and women sprinted into the snow.

"Follow the torches!"

I moved to the cabin Magnus had entered countless times and watched it turn into an inferno instantly.

When every building was on fire, I moved to the clearing and threw the torch at the wooden post that held the noose. The woman was still there, hanging, swaying left to right in the light breeze.

The post caught on fire instantly.

I pulled out my knife and cut her down, dragging her bloody corpse across the snow and away from the fire. She was already dead, so there was nothing I could do to save her...but she didn't deserve to become ash.

Her family would want her body.

The screams turned into a cacophony, an echo of horror. Women ran out in their undergarments, panicking as the camp burned in an inferno. Cabins crumbled as they were dissolved by the heat.

"Follow the torches!" I pointed to the line of torches outside the plains. "Follow the torches!"

Some of the women recognized me and halted to stare in disbelief. Others didn't care at all and just sprinted to safety. It was chaos, women trying to find their friends, looking over their shoulders for the guards.

Then the guards came.

"What the fuck is this?" One of the guards screamed, giving orders to his comrades. "Get the guns! Move! Whoever fucking did this is gonna die!"

I'd be lying if I said I wasn't scared.

I jogged over the snow, moving past the women who came my way. Shadows of men moved around the camp, trying to grab the women and stop them from escaping. I searched for Melanie, unsure if she'd run for it or if she was waiting for me. "Melanie!" I looked around, only catching glimpses of faces in the light of the fires.

The door to the guard cabin burst open, and a man ran out.

One with brown hair and brown eyes.

He was barefoot, in sweatpants and a t-shirt. He looked around at the camp, the flames reflecting in his dark eyes. He didn't round up the women like the others. He just stood there, like he knew it was futile to try anything at all.

I knew I should turn away, but I couldn't.

Then the cabin collapsed, the roof caving in, and it fell right on top of him. He collapsed underneath it, the wood and flames covering him completely.

"*Noooo!*" I sprinted at full speed to get to him as quickly as I could.

But my path was blocked.

By the executioner.

Shirtless, he stood in front of me, staring at me with eyes that showed the underworld in his soul.

I fell back, hitting the snow.

I should run at a dead sprint in the other direction and disappear into the crowd. It was dark outside the camp, and it would be hard to find me.

But my eyes moved to where Magnus lay.

"Look who it is!" He raised his voice so the other guards could hear. "That cunt couldn't get enough of us."

I stumbled back and got to my feet.

There was still time to run.

But I couldn't.

My eyes kept moving behind him, the fire growing over where Magnus was hidden.

Then he charged me.

I quickly dodged out of the way and reached for the blade in my pocket, the five-inch knife Magnus had given me. I fell into the snow and quickly got to my feet, knowing there was no chance I would win this fight—even if he was unarmed.

He faced me, grinning like this was amusing. "You think your little knife is going to stop me?"

I gripped it the way Magnus told me to.

He charged at me again.

I slammed my knife into his body.

But he steadied my wrist and stopped it from piercing his flesh. He slammed me down hard into the snow and gripped me by the throat, choking me so hard he was about to break my neck. His nostrils flared with rage as his eyes gleamed with revenge.

My life faded, but all I could think about was Magnus.

I didn't save him.

Then his body stiffened and his eyes widened. His hand slackened on my neck.

"Get." Melanie stabbed the knife into his back. "Off." She stabbed him again. "Her." She dug the knife all the way through, piercing him through the chest.

Before he collapsed on top of me, I rolled him off, getting free.

It wasn't just Melanie. Bethany was there too, stabbing him in the legs.

Angry tears streaked down Bethany's face. "Die, you fucking piece of shit!" She stabbed him again and again.

I stumbled to my feet again and headed to the cabin, which was burning more than before. "Magnus!" I ignored the burns on my hands from the flames and pulled the wood off his body. "Help!" I kept pulling everything off, screaming in pain every time I touched the white-hot wood. I pushed everything off until I got to the last piece.

I tried to lift it...and I couldn't.

I turned to the girls. "Help me!"

Melanie dropped her knife in the snow and ran to me with bloody hands.

Bethany did too.

"Pick up that side," I told Melanie.

Melanie got the corner and we tried, but we still couldn't do it.

Magnus's arm stuck out, and he didn't move.

"Bethany!" I pointed to the side. "Get that side."

She looked down at his arm and hesitated.

I knew exactly why. "Please, Bethany…please."

She still hesitated.

"Please." Tears burned my cheeks. "Not him."

She swallowed her anger and bent down to help.

We got the wood off him.

He lay there, passed out.

I gathered him in my arms and dragged him from the building and across the snow, away from all the buildings that continued to burn. When he was safe, I set him down then looked him over. Other than a few scratches and bruises, he was okay. His chest rose and fell as he continued to breathe. "Oh, thank god." I sat in the snow beside him and knew it was time for me to go.

I'd done what I had to do.

He would be fine there. The other guards would help him if he needed it.

Suddenly, his eyes opened, and he sat upright quickly, taking a deep breath like he had stopped breathing.

I fell back, jerking away at his sudden movement.

He breathed hard as he looked at his surroundings, seeing the fire that burned everything to ash. His nostrils were flared, and his eyes were panicked. His hand moved to his chest, like he needed to check that he was actually alive.

Then he looked at me.

And stopped breathing.

His brown eyes slowly narrowed in a look of pure rage. His nostrils flared once again, his skin turned beet red, and the vein emerged down his forehead, so angry that his body morphed into a whole different appearance. His jaw clenched, and he breathed deeper, like he wanted to kill me.

I scooted away, scared of him for the first time.

"I saved you..."

I kept moving.

"I fucking saved you."

I pushed myself to my feet.

He got to his quickly and rushed me.

I sprinted away and tripped, falling into the snow. I turned onto my back and pushed myself away, terrified.

He stood over me, his hands shaking, his body heaving, like he wanted to grab me by the neck with both hands until blood broke the skin and drowned my airway so I couldn't breathe. His entire body shook as he restrained himself from tearing me apart. He could barely get the words out of his mouth. "Run... before I kill you."

AFTERWORD

I realize this story is very different from what I've written lately. It's got so much suspense, so much anticipation, but we also have this incredible connection between Raven and Magnus. But will that connection be enough for everything that will happen next?

The next installment is really long, really intense, so make sure you're in the right place to dig into it.

The second installment is entirely from Magnus's point of view.

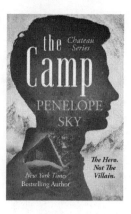

Also, this story is everything to me. I've never been so emotional when I've written something...while I was writing it. I love strong characters that never give up despite the odds, and I love the story of a woman who fights selflessly, who doesn't just save herself, but everyone she possibly can. I call that a hero...and she's one of the best heroes I've ever written. If it resonated with you too, it would mean the world if you left a review.

She betrayed me.

After everything I did for her.

Now I'll have to suffer the consequences of that mistake.

But then I'll get the revenge that I deserve.

Order Now

Made in the USA
Columbia, SC
06 August 2024